Even *Deadlier*

Even Deadlier

A SEQUEL TO

The 7 Deadly Sins
SAMPLER

Foreword by Al Gini

Selected and edited by Daniel Born,
Molly Benningfield, Judith McCue, Abigail Mitchell,
Lindsay Tigue, and Donald H. Whitfield

THE GREAT BOOKS FOUNDATION
A nonprofit educational organization

With generous support from Harrison Middleton University,
a Great Books distance-learning college

Published and distributed by

THE GREAT BOOKS FOUNDATION
A nonprofit educational organization

35 E. Wacker Drive, Suite 400
Chicago, IL 60601
www.greatbooks.org

With generous support from
Harrison Middleton University,
a Great Books distance-learning college
www.chumsci.edu

First printing
9 8 7 6 5 4 3 2 1

Library of Congress Cataloging-in-Publication Data
Even deadlier : a sequel to The 7 deadly sins sampler / foreword by Al Gini; selected and edited by Daniel Born . . . [et al.].
     p.cm.
   ISBN 978-1-933147-45-1 (alk. paper)
  1.   Deadly sins—Fiction. 2. Short stories, English. 3. Short stories, American. I. Born, Daniel. II. 7 deadly sins sampler.

PR1309.D36E84 2009
823'0108353—dc22   2009038632

Cover and interior illustration: Lisa Haney
Book design: Think Book Works

About the Great Books Foundation

The Great Books Foundation was established in 1947 by two University of Chicago educators, Robert Maynard Hutchins and Mortimer Adler. An independent, nonprofit educational organization whose mission is to help people learn how to think and share ideas, the Foundation promotes the reading and discussion of classic and contemporary texts across the disciplines, and publishes books and anthologies for readers of all ages. It also conducts hundreds of professional development courses each year in Shared Inquiry,™ a text-based Socratic method of learning that helps participants read actively, pose evocative questions, and listen and respond to others effectively in dialogue.

*Spelling and punctuation have been modernized
and slightly altered for clarity.*

Contents

Foreword

Even Deadlier: Further Reflections on the Seven Deadly Sins

Al Gini

It seems that our first volume on the nature of sin, *The Seven Deadly Sins Sampler*, struck a chord. We're not entirely surprised. Whether understood in John Portmann's words as a misuse of "the powers God gave us to do good," or as the Jewish historian Aviad Kleinberg puts it, a reflection of our "imperfect, fragile" being, sin has always proved fascinating. Even though postmodernity has defanged and detoxified the medieval concept of sin, reducing it to a formula more psychological than ecclesiastical, it remains entrenched in the popular mind.

In *A History of Sin: Its Evolution to Today and Beyond* (2007), Portmann observes that certain theologians and psychologists claim that we want to hold on to the concepts of sin and evil because they offer us a precise schematic on how to go about achieving redemption or damnation. In fact, it can be argued that many of us continue to grant iconic status to both the Ten Commandments and Pope Gregory the Great's seven deadly sins because these serve as a benchmark for attaining civilized, if not saintly, behavior. They also serve as a kind of "periodic chart," Portmann says, that helps us calculate and determine our personal moral worth.

Kleinberg provides another recent perspective on the subject in his *Seven Deadly Sins: A Very Partial List* (2008). There he argues that although Gregory's original deadly septet is open to reinterpretation, expansion, and contemporary exegesis, the original purpose of the list was to offer Christians (and, in a new ecumenical world, all believers) a remedy for sin. Christianity, says Kleinberg, is founded on sin. It is not that its founders were heavy sinners but rather that all of us, by virtue of being human beings, are susceptible. Christianity, says Kleinberg, above all, constitutes a remedy for the problem. In the view of standard Christian theology, there are no righteous people—we are all guilty of something. The bottom line here is clear, according to Kleinberg: Christianity offers redemption, and without sin, Christianity loses its entire raison d'être.

Furthermore, Kleinberg argues, there is no danger that Christianity or religion in general will go out of business soon. We are, after all, only human. Mistakes will always be made; transgressions and sins will inevitably occur. And there is a continuing human need for atonement and forgiveness, and hence only a slight chance that religion will fade away soon. But, says Kleinberg, because sin is cultural, contextual, and malleable, in the future the specific sins for which we seek forgiveness may well change. He contends that the original seven deadly sins are really a list of passions and desires, not an exact list of specific actions that are always and everywhere wrong.

These individual passions, when left unchecked or misapplied, can result in actions we deem sinful, but not always, says Kleinberg. What's wrong with a little sloth? Leisure is a necessary component of life. But inaction in the face of a recognized social evil is wrong. When you think about it, envy and greed are not so bad, either. They can breed competitive jealousy and desire for more. After all, in a capitalist economy, Kleinberg observes, isn't it actually good to want and desire what others have?

And what about obesity? When you think about it, a little gluttony is good for you. Without it, food would be just another quotidian task in life, joyless and without pleasure. Never mind haute cuisine, Kleinberg says, without a little gluttony, there would be no chocolate, cognac, or coffee to savor and enjoy. And it is also true that, while modesty and a balanced life require humility, without a little pride and self-confidence nothing would probably ever get done. Tasks and projects would not be initiated, let alone completed. Kleinberg pushes further. Certainly, everyone would agree that uncontrolled anger is a dangerous thing. But to lose one's temper when the occasion demands it, to demonstrate a little controlled anger with others, is sometimes necessary in life. And finally, yes, rape and sexual assault are clearly wrong. They represent pathological expressions of "carnal love," which, in Kleinberg's view, is in itself "neither vile nor ignoble." Where, Kleinberg asks, would any of us be without carnal love? What follows is a brief list of transgressions—one that shows just how culturally and historically contingent this matter of sin can be:

A Brief List of Old, No-Longer, and Debatable Sins
- Beating your workers
- Spouses as property
- Selling human beings
- Shopping on the Sabbath
- Lending money at interest
- Eating meat on Friday
- Gay marriage
- Masturbating
- Ordaining women as rabbis, ministers, or priests

Portmann maintains that although our notion of sin evolves over time, as of "September 11, 2001, when a new wave of religious fundamentalism was unleashed," sin "is making a powerful comeback." Christians, Jews, Muslims, and nonbelievers alike, he suggests, are once again very interested in the nature of virtue and moral imperfection. They care about matters that include assigning blame and understanding personal wrongdoing. They want to clarify how we initiate plans of moral self-improvement and how we recognize communal or collective responsibility.

Portmann argues that although the original seven deadly sins have retained their semi-sacred ontological status, it is perhaps time to expand the list. And so he takes up no fewer than thirteen additional topics that he believes call for serious ethical consideration. This eclectic batch of infractions includes harm to the environment, obesity, depression, failure to reach one's full potential, spousal abuse, harm to children, sexual harassment, homophobia, Holocaust denial, racism, drunk driving, disrespect for other religions, and even circumcision. (On the last item, perhaps an odd choice on this list overall, Portmann is emphatic about the crime of female genital mutilation, inflicted on millions of infant girls in numerous cultures, but he also points to the lively debate about the overlooked rights of infant males.)

However, when closely scrutinized, says Portmann, the naming of these additional matters for moral reflection is not all that new and radical. Mostly, the new thirteen conform to the spirit and purpose of Gregory's original deadly seven. Do not intentionally injure or hurt people. Do not intimidate or force yourself on others. Do not violate the physical and psychological autonomy of others. Do not irrationally discriminate against others. Avoid spiritual smugness. Do not lie or deny an obvious truth. Do not put others in unnecessary danger.

Most interesting about Portmann's list is that it leads off with our newfound concern about environmental issues. Until recently, matters such as global warming, pollution, soil erosion, deforestation, species extinction, overpopulation, and overconsumption were considered primarily economic rather than ethical concerns. Today, there is a growing awareness of our symbiotic relationship to the earth. More and more, we talk in terms of our ethical obligations to the living earth and future generations of all species of life.

The only other new emphasis in this list, according to Portmann, is the matter of taking care of the self. It becomes imperative to recognize that one can commit acts of "cruelty, negligence and unkindness" not only against others but also against oneself, and this new list explicitly recognizes that we have an ethical obligation for our own health and happiness: to eat properly, to be creative and industrious, to thrive and enjoy the gift of life. Portmann suggests that this new emphasis remains true to Gregory's initial intent in formulating his original list: to serve as a tool for contemplation and as an action guide in facing "the normal perils of the soul in the ordinary conditions of life."

In 2007, the magisterium of the Catholic Church decided to enter the growing dialogue on modern sin. Its initial contribution to the debate seemed practical and yet a little flippant. Papal representative Cardinal Renado Martino issued a document titled "Ten Guidelines for the Pastoral Care of the Road."

The guidelines aim to help keep drivers literally safe on the highway as well as spiritually safe on the road to salvation. According to Cardinal Martino, the Vatican believed that it was necessary to address the pastoral needs of motorists because driving has become such a big part of contemporary life. According to Reverend Keith Pecklers, a Jesuit professor at the Pontifical Gregorian University in Rome, the document both extols the benefits and laments the abuses and deaths associated with automobile driving.

YOU SHALL NOT KILL AND NINE OTHER RULES
The Vatican's Ten Commandments for Drivers

1. You shall not kill.

2. The road shall be for you a means of communion between people and not of mortal harm.

3. Courtesy, uprightness, and prudence will help you deal with unforeseen events.

4. Be charitable and help your neighbor in need, especially victims of accidents.

5. Cars shall not be for you an expression of power and domination, and occasion of sin.

6. Charitably convince the young and not so young not to drive when they are not in a fitting condition to do so.

7. Support the families of accident victims.

8. Bring guilty motorists and their victims together, at the appropriate time, so that they can undergo the liberating experience of forgiveness.

9. On the road, protect the more vulnerable party.

10. Feel responsible toward others.

"The point Cardinal Martino is making," said Reverend Pecklers, "is that driving is itself a moral issue. How we drive impacts . . . ourselves and others."

But outlining the rules for motorists was apparently not enough, and the authorities in Rome believed there was even more to say on the matter of deadly sins. In 2008, the Vatican formally added Pope Benedict XVI's "new seven deadly sins" to Gregory I's original list.

THE ORIGINAL DEADLY SEVEN	THE NEW SUGGESTED SEVEN
1. Pride	8. Genetic modification
2. Envy	9. Human experiments, such as cloning
3. Anger	10. Polluting the environment
4. Sloth	11. Causing social injustice
5. Greed	12. Causing poverty
6. Gluttony	13. Becoming obscenely wealthy
7. Lust	14. Taking drugs

In a press conference, Vatican spokesman Cardinal Gianfranco Girotti said that the church found it necessary to offer a broader range of sins that better reflect the challenges and temptation of the modern age. "Attention to sin is a more urgent task today," said Girotti, "precisely because its consequences are more abundant and destructive." The new reality is that "you offend God not only by stealing, blasphemy, or coveting your neighbor's wife, but also by polluting, cloning, taking drugs, promoting social injustice, or becoming obscenely rich. Where the standard sins are individual failings, in a global culture, sin is social."

Kleinberg argues that he would add only one more sin to the original list of seven: self-righteousness. Self-righteous individuals are those who believe that they, and a few select others like them, are spiritually advanced, are intellectually gifted, and therefore have a duty to be "shepherds of truth" for others. They believe, Kleinberg says, that they alone live in a state of full consciousness. They alone are the sacred interpreters, and they alone can negotiate the trials of an imperfect world.

Kleinberg dissects the principal dangers of self-righteousness in systematic fashion. The first problem with the self-righteous is their armor of absolute certitude. They are convinced beyond a shadow of doubt that they are the "critical elite," the bearers of "special gnosis." In theological terms, they are convinced that they have the wonderful power of "giving meaning to the word of God." They are adamant in their belief that they know "The Word," and "The Way," and "The Truth." Second, the self-righteous suffer from "moral myopia." Having seen the light, they claim to see the world with an absolutely clear moral eye—which allows them to denounce anyone who "speaks, thinks, or acts otherwise." Finally, perhaps the most pernicious danger of self-righteousness is its contagious nature. Kleinberg notes that once you have been told the truth by a self-assured true believer, you may feel obligated to pass the message on to others.

The Roman poet Ovid once said, "Beware the man of one book." Regarding the sin of self-righteousness, perhaps Ovid's famous warning should be rephrased to, "Beware of the man who is convinced that he knows the mind of God."

Although the ethical landscape has been redescribed in recent years, with different vocabularies used to identify our shortcomings, the bottom line remains the same. In regard to moral conduct and sin, it comes down to how we see our rights in relation to others and how we manage our obligations to others. We need one another. We are not herd animals, but we are communal creatures. We depend on one another to survive and thrive. Good choices or bad choices, our collective existence requires us to continually make choices about what we ought to do in regard to others.

For Muslims, Jews, Christians, and even agnostics, sin separates us from others. The query, What is in it for me? What do I get out of this? or How are my needs best served? is usually the saboteur of personal relations. The essential hubris of sin is that we become our own self-serving God in pursuit of our own hedonistic inclinations. When we sin, we deem ourselves sui generis. We deem our actions and desires as self-evident and self-justified. We become the sole arbitrators of truth. We make decisions and choose to act on the basis of our own parochial, narcissistic perspective.

Finally, whether you are intellectually and spiritually committed to Gregory's classic septet or a fan of Benedict's postmodern list of seven, or even if you are more attracted to the variation of sins produced by Professors Kleinberg or Portmann, the purpose of this meditation is not to come up with a definitive list of thou-shalts and thou-shalt-nots. Rather, it should stimulate both reflection and conduct.

Most important, we believe that working through stories about the choices humans make is a far more productive method of moral reflection than setting up mechanical lists, whether prescriptive or proscriptive. And so we offer here fourteen more stories, a follow-up to *The Seven Deadly Sins Sampler*, by a group of equally distinguished writers. The stories in *Even Deadlier* offer all kinds of perspectives on the amazing, fabulous, and sometimes grotesque range of possibilities for human behavior in this life. The stories offer a window to the human heart, clues about the moral life. Some of these stories can be affirmed unequivocally as masterpieces.

But to turn this into a merely verbal exercise is to miss the point. As Kleinberg so eloquently puts it, with the emphasis on behavior worthy of emulation, "The force of good resides in actions, not in words." Paradoxically, the act of reading itself constitutes a form of action. To sit in a pool of sunlight and read a text is not a form of idleness. Rather, reading is a good that can nourish the deepest sources of who we are and who we hope to become. It is vital to contemplating the question of how to live. And so we invite you, without hesitation, to the realm of *Even Deadlier*.

About Shared Inquiry

Shared Inquiry is the effort to achieve a more thorough understanding of a text by discussing questions, responses, and insights with others. For both the leader and the participants, careful listening is essential. The leader guides the discussion by asking questions about specific ideas and problems of meaning in the text, but does not seek to impose his or her own interpretation on the group.

During a Shared Inquiry discussion, group members consider a number of possible ideas and weigh the evidence for each. Ideas that are entertained and then refined or abandoned are not thought of as mistakes, but as valuable parts of the thinking process. Group members gain experience in communicating complex ideas and in supporting, testing, and expanding their thoughts. Everyone in the group contributes to the discussion, and while participants may disagree with one another, they treat one another's ideas respectfully.

This process helps develop an understanding of important texts and ideas rather than merely catalog knowledge about them. These guidelines keep conversation focused on the text and ensure all the participants a voice.

1. **Read the selection carefully before participating in the discussion.** This ensures that all participants are equally prepared to talk about the ideas in the work and helps prevent talk that would distract the group from its purpose.

2. **Support your ideas with evidence from the text.** This keeps the discussion focused on understanding the selection and enables the group to weigh textual support for different answers and to choose intelligently among them.

3. **Discuss the ideas in the selection, and try to understand them fully before exploring issues that go beyond the selection.** Reflecting on the ideas in the text and the evidence to support them makes the exploration of related issues more productive.

4. **Listen to other participants and respond to them directly.** Shared Inquiry is about the give-and-take of ideas, the willingness to listen to others and talk with them respectfully. Directing your comments and questions to other group members, not always to the leader, will make the discussion livelier and more dynamic.

5. **Expect the leader to only ask questions.** Effective leaders help participants develop their own ideas, with everyone gaining a new understanding in the process. When participants hang back and wait for the leader to suggest answers, discussion tends to falter.

How to Use This Book

The first set of questions following each story is *interpretive*—these questions call for the task of close reading. What is the specific language of the text meant to convey? Are there several interpretations, and can we justify our interpretation by appealing to the text itself? What key passages in the text help unlock its meaning? What passages are confusing and seem to defy understanding? In successful learning communities, close reading evolves into a rich give-and-take between participants who are able to summon specific passages in order to make a point. Thus the text does not get lost in the conversation between discussion participants but is viewed as the principal voice in the dialogue.

The second set of questions ("For Further Reflection") is *evaluative*. These questions invite participants to weigh the significance or validity of the work in a larger context, and they are best contemplated after a thoroughgoing interpretive discussion has taken place.

Be aware that the temptation to skip interpretive questions and jump straight into evaluative judgments can short-circuit meaningful conversation. Watch out for untethered, rambling testimonials and personal anecdotes or unrestrained academic monologues. These developments can distract a group from genuine textual encounter and interpretation.

When grounded in a prior discussion of the text, however, evaluative questions can push participants to a deeper level of engagement. These questions demand the resources of wider observation, experience, and reading. In the best discussions, evaluative questions can lead to extended dialogues or, for students in the classroom, written essays that help develop thoughtful articulation of ideas and beliefs.

Pride

HONORÉ DE BALZAC

Honoré de Balzac (1799–1850) is one of the most important innova-
tors of the modern, realist novel, in which detailed descriptions
of setting and incident contribute to psychologically discerning
portraits of men and women. Born in provincial France, Balzac later
made his home in Paris. In the early 1830s, he conceived the idea
of a vast literary project depicting all aspects of human society,
which he titled *The Human Comedy*. He eventually added dozens
of novels, short stories, and plays to this collection, many of them
concerned with conflicts arising from class and financial ambition.
Among Balzac's major works are the novels *Eugénie Grandet* (1833),
Père Goriot (1835), and *Lost Illusions* (3 vols., 1837–1843). Balzac
was an important influence on the writings of Henry James and
Marcel Proust.

La Grande Bretèche

About a hundred paces from Vendôme, on the banks of the Loire, stands an old brown house, topped by a very high roof, so completely isolated that neither evil-smelling tannery nor ill-favored tavern, so common on the outskirts of small towns, are found in its vicinity. In front of the house, sloping down to the river, is a garden where the box trees bordering the footpaths, all neatly trimmed in former days, now grow in wild freedom. Some willows, growing in the Loire, soon formed a hedge and nearly conceal the house. The plants we call weeds adorn the riverbanks with their luxuriant vegetation. The fruit trees, untended for ten years, have ceased to bear fruit, and their offshoots form a wealth of undergrowth. The espaliers have come to look like hedgerows. The paths, formerly strewn with sand, are now overrun with purslane; but indeed, there are no longer any traces of the paths. From the top of the mountain, where stand the ruins of the old castle of the dukes of Vendôme, the only place from which you can get a view of this enclosure, you have the impression that at some time past, which it is difficult to define, this little spot was the joy of some country gentleman, a lover of roses, tulips, horticulture in a word, but especially fond of good fruit. You can see an arbor, or rather the remains of one, under which there stands a table not entirely destroyed by time. The sight of this abandoned garden gives you an idea of the negative pleasures of a peaceful country life, just as the epitaph on his tombstone gives you some insight into the life of an honest merchant. As if to add a last touch to the melancholy, peaceful thoughts that fill your heart, one of the walls displays a sundial adorned with this respectable Christian inscription: ULTIMAM COGITA! The roofs of the house are terribly dilapidated, the shutters are always closed, the balconies are covered with swallows' nests, the doors remain shut night and day. Tall grasses trace green lines along the cracks in the steps, the ironwork is all rusty. The moon, the sun, winter, summer, and snowstorms, have worn away the woodwork, warped the boards, corroded the paint.

The gloomy silence which reigns there is only broken by the birds, martens, rats, and mice that scutter about, fight, and devour each other without fear of intrusion. Everywhere some invisible hand has written the word *mystery*. If curiosity induced you to go and look at the house from the street, you would see a great arched gate, in which the urchins of the neighborhood have made numerous holes. I learned later that this gate had not been opened for ten years. Through these irregular gaps, you could observe the perfect harmony existing between the front and back of the house, the garden and the courtyard. The same disorder reigns in both. Tufts of grass push up between the paving stones. Enormous cracks furrow the walls, and on their blackened tops the pellitory intertwines its thousand festoons. The steps up to the door are falling to pieces, the bell rope has rotted, the waterspouts are broken. "What fire has blasted the place? What court of justice has had salt scattered over this dwelling? Has God been flouted here? Has France been betrayed?" These are the questions you ask yourself. Reptiles crawl about without giving you an answer. This empty, deserted house is a formidable puzzle to which no one has the key. It was in former days a small fief, and bears the name of La Grande Bretèche. During my stay in Vendôme, where Desplein had left me in charge of a wealthy patient, one of my greatest pleasures was to gaze at this extraordinary dwelling. Was it not better than a mere ruin? Memories of unquestioned authenticity attach to a ruin; but this house, still standing in spite of its slow destruction by an avenging hand, concealed some secret, some unknown thought; at any rate it revealed a caprice. Several times of an evening, I landed by the hedge that shut in the enclosure. I risked getting badly scratched, I made my way into the abandoned garden, into these grounds that were neither public nor private; I spent long hours there, contemplating the desolation. I did not want to ask any gossiping inhabitant a single question for the sake of learning the story that would doubtless explain this curious sight. There, I invented delightful romances; I indulged in little fits of melancholy that charmed me. If I had known the reason, probably commonplace, of this neglect, I should have lost the novel poetry that enraptured me. To my eyes, this lonely spot was symbolic of the most varied images of human life, darkened by its miseries: Sometimes it reminded me of a cloister without monks, sometimes of a cemetery without the dead speaking their language of epitaphs; one day it seemed like the house of the leper, the next like that of the Atrides; but above all it represented the country, with its pensiveness, its existence dribbling away like sand in an hourglass. I often wept there; I never felt like laughing. More than once I was seized with an involuntary terror on hearing overhead the dull whir of a wood pigeon's wings as it flew swiftly on its way. The ground is damp there; you have to beware of the lizards, adders, frogs that move about in the wild abundance of nature; above all, you must not fear the cold, for in a few minutes you feel an icy mantle descending on your shoulders, like the hand of the commander on the neck of Don Juan. One evening I had a fright; the wind made an old rusty weathercock turn, and its screech sounded like a groan coming from the house, just as I was ending a fairly lugubrious drama, in which I explained the grief expressed in this building. I returned to my inn, a prey to gloomy thoughts. When I had finished supper, my landlady came into my room with an air of mystery and said:

"Monsieur Regnault to see you, sir."

"Who's Monsieur Regnault?"

"Why, sir, don't you know Monsieur Regnault? Oh, that is queer!" she exclaimed as she went away.

Suddenly I saw a tall, spare man, clad all in black, appear, holding his hat in his hand, and looking like a ram ready to charge its rival, with his receding brow, his small pointed head, and pale face rather like a glass of turbid water. He might have been taken for the gentleman usher of a minister. This stranger was wearing an old tailcoat nearly threadbare at the seams; but he had a diamond in his shirt frill and gold earrings in his ears.

"Whom have I the honor of addressing, sir?" I asked.

He sat down on a chair in front of the fire, put his hat on my table, and answered as he rubbed his hands together:

"Ah! It is very cold! My name is Regnault, sir."

I bowed, saying to myself: "*Il Bondo cani!* I'm none the wiser!"

"I am," he continued, "a notary practicing at Vendôme."

"Delighted, sir," I exclaimed, "but I don't want to make my will just now, for reasons known to myself."

"Just a moment!" he continued, raising his hand as if to impose silence. "Permit me, sir! Permit me! I have been informed that you sometimes go to walk in the garden of La Grande Bretèche."

"That is so, sir."

"Just a moment!" he said, making the same gesture. "You have been guilty of trespassing. Sir, I come on behalf of the late Countess of Merret, and as her executor to beg you to discontinue these visits. Just a minute, please! I am not unreasonable, and I don't want to accuse you of a crime. Besides, it is only natural that you should not be aware of the circumstances which oblige me to let the finest mansion in Vendôme go to ruin. Yet, sir, you appear well informed, and must know that the law forbids anyone to enter private grounds, under severe penalties. A hedge serves the same purpose as a wall. But the present condition of the house may excuse your curiosity. I would gladly give you permission to walk about the house and grounds; but as I have to execute the countess's will, I must ask you, sir, not to go into the garden again. I, myself, sir, since the reading of the will, have not set foot in the house, which, as I have had the honor of telling you, forms part of the estate of the late Madame de Merret. We have merely verified the number of doors and windows so as to assess the taxes I pay annually from a sum allotted for this purpose by the late Madame de Merret. Ah! my dear sir, her will caused a great deal of talk in Vendôme, I can tell you!"

At this point the worthy lawyer stopped to blow his nose. I respected his loquacity, understanding quite well that Madame de Merret's will was the most important event in his life—his reputation, his glory, his restoration. I must bid farewell to my dreams and romances; so I did not regret having to learn the truth from an official source.

"Sir," I said, "would it be impertinent to ask you the reasons for this strange state of things?"

At these words, an expression revealing all the satisfaction of a man used to riding his hobbyhorse passed over the lawyer's face. He arranged his shirt collar with a fatuous air; took out his snuffbox; opened it and offered me a pinch; and, on my refusing, helped himself copiously. He was happy! A man who has no hobbyhorse does not realize all that can be got out of life. Such a state is a happy medium between passion and monomania. At this moment I understood the full meaning of this pretty expression of Sterne's, and I had the lifelike picture of the joy with which Uncle Toby bestrode his charger, helped by Trim.

"Sir," said Monsieur Regnault, "I was head clerk in the office of Maître Roquin, in Paris. An excellent practice, of which you have heard perhaps? You haven't? Yet it was made famous by a regrettable bankruptcy. Not having a large-enough fortune to buy a practice at the price to which such offices soared in 1816, I came here and acquired the practice of my predecessor. I had relatives in Vendôme, among others, a very wealthy aunt, who gave me her daughter in marriage—Sir," he continued, after a short pause, "three months after I had been admitted by the Garde des Sceaux, I was sent for one evening, just as I was going to bed (I was not yet married), by the Countess of Merret at her Chateau of Merret. Her maid, a good girl who is now a servant at this inn, was at the door with the countess's barouche. Oh! just a moment, please!—I forgot to tell you, sir, that the count had gone to Paris and died there two months before I came here. He came to a sad end, indulging in all sorts of excesses. You understand, don't you? On the day of his departure, the countess left La Grande Bretèche, and had it dismantled. Some people even say that she had the furniture and tapestries burned, and in short all the various articles furnished the premises hereby let to the aforesaid tenant—(Oh! my goodness! What am I saying? Forgive me, I thought I was dictating a lease)—that she had them all burned in the meadow at Merret. Have you been there, sir? You have not?" he said, supplying my answer himself. "Well, it's a very beautiful spot! For about three months," he went on, after nodding his head, "the count and countess had been living a queer life; they stopped seeing any visitors, the countess lived on the ground floor, and her husband on the first floor. When the countess was left in solitude, she ceased going to church. Later on, in her chateau, she refused to see the friends who went to call on her. She had already greatly changed before she left La Grande Bretèche to go to Merret. Such a dear lady—I say 'dear' because she gave me this diamond; I only saw her once myself); so, this good lady was very ill; she had probably no hope of recovering, for she died without summoning a doctor; and indeed, many of the ladies about here thought she was queer in the head on that account. So my curiosity was greatly aroused, sir, when I learned that Madame de Merret required my services. I was not the only person who took an interest in the situation. That very evening, although it was late, the whole town knew I was going to Merret. The maid gave noncommittal answers to the questions I asked her on the way; nevertheless, she told me her mistress had received the last sacraments, administered by the curé of Merret that same day, and she would probably not live through the night. It was about eleven o'clock when I arrived at the chateau. I went up the great staircase. After passing through high, spacious rooms, dark, cold, horribly damp, I came to the state bedroom where the countess lay. Judging from the gossip one heard about this lady (I should never finish if I were to tell you all the rumors circulated about her), I fancied she must be a coquette. Well, you'll be surprised to learn that I could hardly distinguish her on the great bed where she lay. It is true she had only one of those ancient Argant lamps to light the enormous bedroom with its old-fashioned friezes, so dusty that the mere sight of them made you want to sneeze. But you haven't been to Merret! Well, sir, the bed is one of those old four-posters, with a high tester covered with flowered print. A small night commode stood near the bed, and, lying on it, I noticed the *Imitation of Christ*, which, by the way, I bought for my wife, together with the lamp. There was also a large armchair for the woman tending her, and two chairs. But no fire. That was all the furniture. It would not have filled ten lines in an inventory. Oh! my dear sir, if you had seen this enormous room, hung with brown tapestry, as I saw it then, you would have thought you had been wafted to the scene of a real romance. It was icy cold, and, what is more, deathlike," he added, raising his arm with a dramatic gesture, and pausing. "After gazing for a long time at the bed, I at last discovered Madame de Merret, thanks again to the glow from the lamp, whose light fell on the pillows. Her face was as yellow as wax, and looked like two clasped hands. The countess wore a lace cap, through which you could see her lovely hair, white as freshly spun yarn. She was sitting up, and appeared to do so with great difficulty. Her big black eyes, heavy and sunken with fever and already almost lifeless, hardly moved under the bones of the eyebrows. There," he said, touching his own brow. "Her forehead was damp. Her thin hands seemed like bones with skin stretched over them; her veins and muscles all stood out visibly. She must have been beautiful once; but at that moment an indefinable feeling came over me as I looked at her. Never, judging from what the persons who prepared her for burial said, had a human being reached such a stage of emaciation and remained alive. In short, it was a terrible sight. She had wasted away so completely during her illness that she was no more than a phantom. Her lips, pale violet in color, did not seem to move when she spoke to me. Although my profession has trained me to such sights, often taking me to the bedside of the dying to receive their last will and testament, I must admit that these stricken families and the death scenes I have witnessed were nothing compared to this lonely, silent woman in this spacious castle. I could hear no sound, I could not see the bedclothes rising and falling with the patient's breath, and I stood quite motionless, gazing at her intently in a sort of stupor. I feel as though I were still there. At last her great eyes moved, she tried to raise her right hand, which fell back on the bed, and these words came from her lips like a breath, for her voice was a voice no longer: 'I was waiting for you to come.' She flushed hotly. It was an effort for her to speak, sir. 'Madame—,' I said. She motioned me to be silent. At this moment the aged waiting woman rose and whispered in my ear: 'Do not speak, the countess cannot stand the slightest sound: and what you say might upset her.' I took a seat. A few minutes later, Madame de Merret summoned all her remaining strength to move her right arm, put it, not without great difficulty, under her bolster; she lay still a moment; then she made a last effort to withdraw her hand, and, when she had pulled out a sealed paper, drops of sweat rolled down her forehead. 'I leave my will in your hands—,' she said. 'Ah! my God! Ah!' That was all. She seized a crucifix that lay on her bed, put it quickly to her lips, and expired. The expression in her motionless eyes still makes me shudder when I think of it. She must have suffered cruelly! At the very last, there was a look of joy in her eyes, an expression which remained stamped there after she was dead. I took the will away with me; and when it was opened, I saw that Madame de Merret had appointed me her executor. She bequeathed her fortune, apart from a few private legacies, to the Vendôme Hospital. But there were stipulations with regard to La Grande Bretèche. She requested me to let the house stand untouched for a period of fifty years from the date of her death, forbidding any person whatsoever to enter the rooms, or any repairs to be done, even arranging for the payment of caretakers, if necessary, to make sure that her wishes were executed in every detail. At the expiration of this period, if the wishes of the testatrix are obeyed, the estate is to pass to my heirs, for you are aware, sir, that notaries are not allowed to accept legacies; otherwise La Grande Bretèche returns to the rightful heirs, but on condition they fulfill the terms stated in a codicil added to the will, and not to be opened before the expiration of the above-mentioned fifty years. The will has not been contested, so—"

With these words, and not troubling to finish his sentence, the lanky notary glanced at me with an air of triumph; I filled his cup of happiness by paying him a few compliments.

"Sir," I said, "your story has made so vivid an impression on me that I fancy I can see the dying countess, whiter than her sheets; her shining eyes fill me with terror; I shall surely dream of her tonight. But you must have formed some conjectures with regard to the provisions of the extraordinary will."

"Sir," he said, with comic reticence, "I never take the liberty of criticizing the doings of persons who have done me the honor of giving me a diamond."

I soon managed to loosen the tongue of the scrupulous lawyer, who told me, not without lengthy digressions, of the observations supplied by the shrewd wiseacres of both sexes whose word holds sway in Vendôme. But these observations were so contradictory, so diffuse, that I nearly fell asleep, in spite of the interest this authentic story roused in me. The dull tones and the monotonous speech of the lawyer, no doubt accustomed to listening to himself and making his fellows listen to him, got the better of my curiosity. Fortunately, he took leave of me.

"Let me tell you, sir," he said, as he went down the stairs, "there's a lot of people would like to live another forty-five years; but just a minute, please!"

And, with a knowing air, he laid the forefinger of his right hand against his nose, as if to say, "Yes, mark my words!"

"But to live as long as that," he said, "you must not have reached the age of sixty!"

I closed the door, after being roused from my state of apathy by this parting shot, which the lawyer thought very witty; then I sat down in my armchair with my feet on the two andirons in the fireplace. I was deep in a romance in the style of Mrs. Radcliffe built on the legal information supplied by Monsieur Regnault, when the door turned on its hinges, opened by the skillful hand of a woman. I saw my landlady come in, a stout, jolly, good-natured woman who had missed her vocation: she should have been a Flemish woman in one of Teniers's pictures.

"Well, sir," she said, "Monsieur Regnault has, no doubt, been telling you his favorite yarn about La Grande Bretèche?"

"Yes, he has, Madame Lepas."

"What did he tell you?"

I told her briefly the bleak, gloomy story of Madame de Merret. At every sentence the landlady strained her head forward, looking at me with an innkeeper's perspicacity, a sort of cross between the instinct of a gendarme, the cunning of a spy, and the craftiness of a tradesman.

"My dear Madame Lepas," I added when I had finished, "you seem to know more than I do, now don't you? Otherwise why should you have come up to see me?"

"Oh, on my honor, as true as my name is Lepas—"

"Now, don't be so positive; your eyes betray your secret. You knew Monsieur de Merret. What sort of a man was he?"

"Indeed, Monsieur de Merret was a fine, handsome gentleman, so tall you could hardly see the end of him! A worthy nobleman of Picard origin, who played the deuce, as we say, on small provocation. He always paid ready money to avoid having trouble with anyone. He was quick tempered, you see. The ladies were all very fond of him."

"Because he was quick tempered?" I asked her.

"Yes, perhaps," she said. "You'll quite understand, sir, that there must have been something about him, as the saying goes, for him to have married Madame de Merret, who, no offense to others of course, was the loveliest and richest lady in Vendôme. She had about twenty thousand francs' income. The whole town was at the wedding. The bride was charming and beautiful, a real treasure. Oh, they made a fine couple in those days!"

"Was it a happy marriage?"

"Well, yes and no, as far as one can guess, for you'll easily understand we were not on very familiar terms with them! Madame de Merret was a kind lady, very sweet tempered, who perhaps had to put up with her husband's bad temper at times; but we were fond of him, though he was rather standoffish. After all, it was only natural for him to be like that! When a man's of noble birth, you know—"

"Yet there must have been some catastrophe for them to have separated so violently?"

"I never said there had been any catastrophe, sir. I know nothing about it."

"All right. I'm sure now you know everything."

"Well, sir, I'll tell you everything. When I saw Monsieur Regnault going up to see you, I knew he'd talk about Madame de Merret, in connection with La Grande Bretèche. That made me think I'd consult you, sir, for you seem a man of good counsel, and incapable of betraying a poor woman like me who's never harmed anyone, and is now tortured by her conscience. Until now, I've never dared to confide in the people here, a lot of steel-tongued gossips. In short, sir, I've never yet had a gentleman stay as long as you at the inn, and a gentleman to whom I could tell the story of the fifteen thousand francs—"

"My dear Madame Lepas," I answered, stopping her flow of words, "if your disclosure is in any way likely to compromise me, I should not consent to hear it for anything in the world."

"Have no fear," she said, interrupting me. "You'll soon see."

Her eagerness made me certain that I was not the only person who has been entrusted with the good landlady's secret, of which I was to be the sole confidant, and I listened.

"Sir," she said, "when the emperor sent the Spanish or other prisoners of war here, I had a young Spaniard, sent to Vendôme on parole, billeted on me. Although he was on parole, he had to report every day at the subprefecture. He was a Spanish grandee! Just fancy! He had a name ending in -os and -dia, something like Bagos de Férédia. I've got it written on my registers; you can read it, if you like. Oh! he was a fine-looking fellow for a Spaniard, who are all said to be ugly. He was only some five foot two or three inches tall, but he was well built; he had small hands, and you should have seen how he looked after them! He had as many brushes for his hands as a woman has for the whole of her toilet! He had long, black hair, flashing eyes, a bronzed complexion, but I liked it all the same. He wore finer linen than I've ever seen on anyone, although I've had princesses stay here, and among others, General Bertrand, the Duke and Duchess of Abrantès, Monsieur Decazes, and the king of Spain. He ate very little; but he had such courteous, pleasant manners, that you couldn't bear him a grudge for that. I was very fond of him, I can tell you, although he didn't say four words a day, and it was impossible to have any conversation with him; if you spoke to him, he did not answer: It was a mania, a queer habit they all have, so I've been told. He read his breviary like a priest, he went regularly to Mass and all the church services. Where did he sit in church? We noticed that later: a few yards from Madame de Merret's chapel. As he took his place there the very first time he went to church, nobody thought he had any special reason for doing so. Besides, the poor young gentleman never raised his eyes from his prayer book. At that time, sir, he used to walk about the hillside of an evening, among the ruins of the castle. It was the poor gentleman's only distraction. There he was reminded of his own country. They say there's nothing but mountains in Spain! The very first day of his detention here, he stayed out very late. I was anxious at not seeing him come in till midnight; but we all grew used to his whims; he would take the door key, and we stopped sitting up for him. His room was in the house we have in the Rue des Casernes. Then, one of the stable boys told us that one evening, as he was going to water the horses, he thought he had seen the Spanish grandee swimming like a fish in the river some way off. When he returned, I told him to beware of the weeds; he seemed to be put out at having been seen in the water. At last, sir, one day or rather one morning, we found his room empty; he had not come back. After searching everywhere, I found a note in the drawer of his table where there were also fifty Spanish gold coins, which we call Portugueses, worth about five thousand francs, and diamonds to the value of about ten thousand francs in a small sealed box. The note said, that in case he should not return, he left us the money and the diamonds, on condition we had Masses said for the salvation of his soul, and to thank God for his escape. At that time my husband was alive, and he went to look for him. And—this is the queer part of the story!—he brought back the Spaniard's clothes, which he found beneath a big stone under some piles by the riverside, not far from the castle, almost opposite La Grande Bretèche. My husband had gone there so early that no one had seen him. He burned the clothes after he had read the letter, and we declared that the Count Férédia had escaped, as he asked us to. The subprefect sent all his gendarmes in pursuit of him; but it was all no use, they didn't catch him. Lepas thought the Spaniard has been drowned. I don't think so, sir; I am rather inclined to believe he played some part in the mystery of Madame de Merret, seeing Rosalie told me the crucifix her mistress was so attached to that it was buried with her was of ebony and silver; now, in the early days of his stay here, Monsieur Férédia had an ebony and silver one, which I did not see later on. Now, sir, is it not true that I need not let my conscious trouble me about the Spaniard's fifteen thousand francs, and that they are really mine?"

"Certainly. But haven't you tried to question Rosalie?" I said.

"Oh, yes, indeed I have, sir. But the girl's like a blank wall. She knows something, but it's impossible to get a word out of her."

After chatting a little longer with me, the landlady left me a prey to rambling, gloomy fancies, romantic curiosity, and a religious awe much like the deep emotion that comes over us when we go at night into a dark church, where a feeble light appears in the distance under the high arches, a dim form glides along, we can hear the rustling of a gown or cassock, and our flesh creeps. La Grande Bretèche, and its tall grass, its closed windows, its rusty ironwork, its shut doors, and empty rooms suddenly appeared fantastically before my eyes. I tried to penetrate into this mysterious dwelling by seeking the key to this gloomy tale, the drama that had caused the death of three people. Rosalie became in my eyes the most interesting person in Vendôme. As I looked at her, I fancied I could make out the traces of some secret knowledge, in spite of the robust health that shone on her plump face. There was in her some spring of remorse or hope; her bearing showed she had a secret to keep, as does that of pious women praying to excess, or of a girl who has killed her baby and hears its last cry unceasingly. Yet her behavior was simple and unrefined, there was nothing criminal in her silly smile, and you would have judged her innocent at the very sight of the big red-and-blue-checked kerchief that covered her ample bosom, tucked into a tightly fitting dress with white and purple stripes.

"No," I thought, "I will not leave Vendôme without getting to the bottom of the mystery of La Grande Bretèche. To gain my ends, I'll even become Rosalie's lover, if it's absolutely necessary."

"Rosalie?" I said to her one evening.

"Yes, sir."

"You're not married?"

She started slightly.

"Oh, I'll have plenty of men to choose from, when I've a fancy to make myself unhappy!" she said with a laugh.

She recovered quickly from her private emotion, for all women, from great ladies to maidservants in country inns, have a self-possession that is peculiar to them.

"You are young and attractive enough not to lack admirers! But, tell me, Rosalie, why you became a maid at this inn after you left Madame de Merret? Is it because she did not make any provision for you?"

"Oh, but she did indeed, sir. But I've the best place in Vendôme here."

This answer was what judges and attorneys would call noncommittal. Rosalie seemed to me to occupy in this romantic story a position like the middle square on the draught board; the interest and the truth centered around her; she seemed tied in the knot. She ceased to be an ordinary girl I was going to try to seduce; in her lay the last chapter of a romance; and so, from that time, Rosalie became the chief object of my attentions. Studying the girl, I discovered in her, as we do in all women that occupy the chief place in our thoughts, a crowd of good qualities: She was clean, neat, and tidy; needless to say, she was beautiful; she soon had all the attractions with which our desire endows women, whatever their rank. A fortnight after the notary's visit, I said to Rosalie one evening, or rather one morning, for it was in the early hours, "Now tell me all you know about Madame de Merret."

"Oh!" she answered in terror, "don't ask me that, Master Horace!"

Her beautiful face darkened, her vivid, glowing color grew pale, and her eyes lost their moist, innocent brightness. Nevertheless, I insisted.

"Well," she went on, "since you will have it so, I'll tell you: But you must be sure and keep the secret."

"I promise you, my poor girl, I'll keep your secret with a thief's honesty, the truest there is."

"I'd sooner you kept it with your own," she said, "if it's all the same to you."

Thereupon she smoothed her kerchief, and settled herself to tell her story; for, indeed, there is an attitude of confidence and ease necessary for the telling of a story. The best tales are told at a certain hour. Nobody can tell a good story standing, or on an empty stomach. But if I were to reproduce word for word the long-winded eloquence of Rosalie, a whole volume would hardly be enough. Now, as the event of which she gave me a confused account would stand halfway between the gossip of Madame Lepas and that of the notary, as precisely as the averages in an arithmetical proportion are between the two extremes, all I have to do is to relate it in a few words. This is it briefly:

The bedroom that Madame de Merret occupied at La Grande Bretèche was on the ground floor. A cupboard, some four feet in depth, built into the wall, served as her wardrobe. Three months before the evening I am going to tell you of, Madame de Merret was so unwell that her husband left her alone in her room, and took to sleeping in a bedroom on the first floor. By some unforeseen chance, on that evening, he returned two hours later than usual from the club where he went to read the newspapers and talk politics with the townspeople. His wife thought he was back, in bed, and asleep. But the invasion of France had been the subject of a very heated discussion; the game of billiards had become lively, he had lost forty francs, a large sum in Vendôme, where everyone is economical and a praiseworthy moderation is the rule, which perhaps becomes the source of real content, such as no Parisian cares for. For some time past, Monsieur de Merret had merely inquired of Rosalie if his wife had retired; as he invariably received an affirmative answer, he went to his own room immediately with the good humor born of habit and confidence. When he came back on that night, he took it into his head to go and see Madame de Merret, to tell her of his bad luck, and perhaps to get some consolation as well. During dinner he had thought Madame de Merret was very charmingly dressed; on his way back from the club he reflected that his wife no longer was ailing, that her con-valescence had increased her beauty, and, as is usually the case with husbands, he noticed it a little too late. Instead of calling Rosalie, who was in the kitchen at the time, busy watching the cook and coachman playing a difficult game of *brisque,* Monsieur de Merret turned his steps toward his wife's room, lighting himself with his lantern, which he had placed on the first step of the staircase. His footsteps, easily recognizable, echoed under the vaulted roof of the corridor. As he turned the key of his wife's room, he fan-cied he heard the door of the cupboard I told you of being closed; but when he entered, Madame de Merret was alone, standing in front of the fire. Her husband thought it was Rosalie in the closet; yet a suspicion, ringing in his ears like a bell, put him on his guard; he looked at his wife, and fancied he saw something mysteriously wild and anxious in her eyes.

"You're back very late," she said.

Her voice, usually so pure and musical, seemed to his ears to have lost some of its beauty. Monsieur de Merret did not answer, for Rosalie came in at that moment. He had had a terrible shock. He folded his arms and paced up and down the room, walking from window to window with absolute regularity.

"Have you had bad news, or are you not well?" his wife asked him timidly, while Rosalie undressed her.

He remained silent.

"You can leave me," said Madame de Merret to her maid. "I will put my curl papers in myself."

The very sight of her husband's face made her fear some misfortune, and she wished to be alone with him. When Rosalie had gone, or was thought to have gone, for she listened for a few moments in the corridor, Monsieur de Merret went and stood in from of his wife and said coldly: "Madam, there is someone in that cupboard!"

She looked calmly at her husband, and said simply: "There is not, sir."

This denial distressed Monsieur de Merret; he did not believe it: Yet never had his wife seemed to him purer and holier than at that moment. He rose to go and open the door; Madame de Merret seized his hand, stopped him, gazed at him sadly, and said in a strangely tremulous voice: "If you find no one, remember that all is over between us!"

The extraordinary dignity of his wife's attitude revived the nobleman's deep respect for her, and made him think of a course of action which only needed a more imposing setting to become immortal.

"No, Josephine," he said, "I will not go. In either case we should be separated forever. Now listen, I know how pure your heart is, and how good your life; you would not commit a deadly sin, even to save your life."

At these words, Madame de Merret glanced at her husband with haggard eyes.

"Come, take your crucifix," he added. "Swear before God that there is no one there, I will believe you, I will never open the door."

Madame de Merret took the crucifix and said: "I swear it."

"Louder," said her husband, "and repeat this: 'I swear before God that there is no one in that cupboard.'"

She repeated the sentence without embarrassment.

"Very good," said Monsieur de Merret coldly.

After a moment's silence, "This is a beautiful thing I have never seen before," he said, examining the ebony crucifix inlaid with silver and very artistically carved.

"I found it at Duvivier's; he bought it from a Spanish monk, when those troops of prisoners passed through Vendôme last year."

"Indeed!" said Monsieur de Merret, putting the crucifix back on its nail.

And he rang the bell. Rosalie was not long in coming. Monsieur de Merret hurried across the room to meet her, led her to the window overlooking the garden, and whispered: "I know that Gorenflot wants to marry you, and that you are only prevented from setting up house by your lack of money, and that you have told him that you won't be his wife until he becomes a master mason. . . . Well, go and bring him here; tell him to come with his trowel and his tools. See that you don't waken anyone but him in the house; his fortune will surpass your ambitions. Above all, don't chatter here before you go, or else—"

He frowned. Rosalie went off; he called her back.

"Here, take my key," he said.

"Jean!" shouted Monsieur de Merret down the corridor, in a voice of thunder.

Jean, who was his coachman as well as his valet, left his game of *brisque* and came.

"Go to bed, all of you," said his master, beckoning to him to approach.

And then the nobleman added in a whisper: "When they are all asleep, sound asleep, you understand, you are to come down and tell me."

Monsieur de Merret, who had not taken his eyes off his wife while he gave these orders, went calmly back to her by the fire, and began to tell her of the incidents of the game of billiards and the talk at the club. When Rosalie returned, she found Monsieur and Madame de Merret conversing in a friendly fashion. The nobleman had recently had all the ceilings of the reception rooms on the ground floor replastered. Plaster is very scarce at Vendôme, the transport increases its price considerably, so he had had a fairly large supply sent, knowing he would be able to sell it, if any were left over. This circumstance made him think of the plan he now put into action.

"Gorenflot has come, sir," said Rosalie in a whisper.

"Bring him in!" the gentleman answered aloud.

Madame de Merret turned a little pale on seeing the mason.

"Gorenflot," said her husband, "go and fetch the bricks from under the shed, and bring enough to wall up the door of this closet; you can coat it over with the rest of the plaster."

Then, drawing Rosalie and workman aside, he said in an undertone "Listen, Gorenflot, you must sleep here tonight. But tomorrow morning you shall have a passport to go abroad to a town I'll tell you of. I'll give you six thousand francs for your journey. You must stay in that town for ten years; if you don't like it, you can go elsewhere, as long as it is in the same country. You will travel via Paris, where you must wait for me. There I will give you an agreement whereby you will receive another sum of six thousand francs on your return, provided you have fulfilled the conditions of our contract. In return for this money, you must observe the most absolute silence about what you do here tonight. As for you, Rosalie, I will give you ten thousand francs which will only be paid to you on your wedding day, and on condition you marry Gorenflot; but you must both keep your counsel, if you want to marry. Otherwise you'll have no dowry."

"Rosalie," said Madame de Merret, "come and do my hair."

Her husband paced calmly up and down the room, keeping his eyes on the door, the mason, and his wife, but not betraying any offensive distrust. Gorenflot could not avoid making a noise. Madame de Merret took advantage of a moment when the workman was unloading some bricks and her husband was at the other end of the room, to say to Rosalie: "There's a thousand francs a year for you, dear girl, if you can tell Gorenflot to leave a crack at the bottom."

Then she said aloud with composure: "Now go and help him!"

Monsieur and Madame de Merret were silent all the time Gorenflot was walling in the door. This silence was strategic on the husband's part, for he did not want to give his wife an opportunity of saying words that might have a double meaning; and in the case of Madame de Merret it was prudence or pride. When the wall was halfway up, the cunning mason banged his pick through one of the glass panes of the door, taking advantage of a moment when the nobleman was at the other end of the room. This act proved to Madame de Merret that Rosalie had spoken to Gorenflot.

Then the three of them saw the dark, bronzed face of a man, with black hair, and flaming eyes. Before her husband had turned back again, the poor woman had time to nod to the stranger, to whom this signal meant: "Don't lose hope!" At four o'clock, when the day was beginning to dawn, for it was September, the wall was finished. The mason stayed on in the custody of Jean, and Monsieur de Merret slept in his wife's room. The next morning when he got up, he said carelessly: "Oh, by the way, I must go to Mairie to see about the passport!"

He put his hat on his head, took three steps toward the door, stopped as if something had just occurred to him, and took the crucifix. His wife's heart leaped with joy.

"He will go to Duvivier's," she thought.

As soon as the nobleman had gone, Madame de Merret rang for Rosalie; then she cried in a voice of anguish: "Quick, quick, bring me the pick. I saw how Gorenflot went to work yesterday; we shall have time to make a hole and block it up again!"

In less than no time Rosalie brought her mistress a sort of hatchet, and, with an indescribable energy, she began to demolish the wall. She had already displaced a few bricks, when, just as she was preparing to spring forward so as to strike a harder blow than before, she suddenly saw Monsieur de Merret behind her; she fainted.

"Put your mistress on her bed," said the nobleman coldly.

Foreseeing what was sure to happen in his absence, he had laid a trap for his wife; he had merely written to the mayor, and sent for Duvivier. The jeweler arrived just as the room had been put in order again.

"Duvivier," asked the nobleman, "have you not purchased crucifixes from the Spaniards who passed through the town?"

"No, sir."

"Very good, I thank you," he said, with a tigerish glance at his wife. "Jean," he added, turning to his valet, "you will serve my meals in Madame de Merret's room; she is unwell, and I shall not leave her until she is better."

The cruel count never left his wife for three weeks. At the beginning, when there was a sound in the walled cupboard, and Josephine made an attempt to beg him to have pity on the dying stranger, he answered, without allowing her to say a word: "You swore on the crucifix that there was no one there."

QUESTIONS

1. Why does the narrator derive so much pleasure from gazing at the dilapidated La Grande Bretèche? Why is he reluctant to ask the inhabitants of the town about the house?

2. Why does the notary Regnault disclose to the narrator so many details of his dealings with his client, the Countess of Merret, almost to the point of breaching professional confidentiality?

3. Does the landlady, Madame Lepas, have a clear conscience about the fifteen thousand francs that she acquired when the Spaniard disappeared?

4. Why does Rosalie tell the narrator the entire story of how the Spaniard was killed, even though she herself and her fiancé Gorenflot are implicated in the murder?

5. Why does the narrator make a point of comparing the ways of Vendôme, "where everyone is economical and a praiseworthy moderation is the rule," to the less restrained ways of the Parisians? (19)

6. Why doesn't the Countess of Merret recant her oath on the crucifix and admit to her husband that the Spaniard is concealed in the cupboard?

7. What explains the Countess of Merret's stipulation that La Grande Bretèche be untouched for fifty years after her death?

FOR FURTHER REFLECTION

1. Is there a difference between the professional pride of the notary and the pride of the Countess de Merret?

2. Why does Balzac tell his tale of events in a provincial town through the eyes of a sophisticated, urbane outsider?

3. How are greed and pride intermingled in the motivations and actions of the characters in the story?

FRANCES HWANG

Frances Hwang (1973–) grew up in Fairfax, Virginia, where her parents settled after moving from Taipei, Taiwan. She graduated from Brown University in 1994 and subsequently earned a master's degree in English at the University of Virginia and a master of fine arts in creative writing at the University of Montana. "The Old Gentleman," which appears in Hwang's debut short story collection, *Transparency* (2007), was originally published in *Tin House* magazine. For Hwang, the stories in *Transparency* are about "characters who don't belong to mainstream society, whose lives are inconspicuous and go unnoticed in our culture." Hwang was nominated for the Pushcart Prize for fiction in 2006, and she won the Sue Kaufman Prize for First Fiction from the American Academy of Arts and Letters in 2008. She has held fellowships at the Wisconsin Institute for Creative Writing and at Colgate University, and she has taught English at Saint Mary's College in Indiana.

The Old Gentleman

As a young girl, Agnes was often embarrassed by her father. Her family lived on the compound of a girls' high school in Taipei where her father worked as principal. On Monday mornings, after the flag had been raised and the national anthem sung, he liked to give speeches to the students assembled in the main courtyard. To get their attention, he stood with silent, aggrieved humility, his arms dangling at his sides, his limp suit already wrinkled from the humid weather, the front pockets stuffed with his reading glasses, a spiral notebook, a pack of cigarettes, and a well-used handkerchief. When he opened his mouth, he did not immediately speak, desiring that slight pause, that moment of breath in which everyone's attention was fixed on him alone. He quoted regularly from Mengzi, but his favorite writer was Cao Xueqin. " 'Girls are made of water and boys are made of mud,' " he declared. Or " 'The pure essence of humanity is concentrated in the female of the species. Males are its mere dregs and off-scourings.' " He clasped his hands behind his back, his eyes widening as he spoke. "Each of you is capable, but you must cultivate within yourself a sense of honesty and shame." He reminded the girls to rinse their mouths out with tea when they said a dirty word. He discussed matters of personal hygiene and reprimanded them for spitting on the streets. Agnes's father had a thick Jiangbei accent, and students often laughed when they heard him speak for the first time.

When Agnes was eleven, her mother was hospitalized after jumping off a two-story building and breaking her hand. The following Monday, her father opened his mouth in front of the student assembly, but no words came out, only a moaning sound. He covered his eyes with a fluttering hand. Immediately a collection was started among students and faculty, a generous sum of money raised to pay for her mother's hospital bill. A story was posted on the school's newspaper wall in the courtyard in which a student praised Agnes's father for his selfless devotion to "a walking ghost." Older girls came up to Agnes and pressed her hand. "Your poor mother!" they exclaimed in sad tones. They marveled at her father's goodness, assuring her that a kinder man could not be found.

Agnes intentionally flunked her entrance exams the next year so that she would not have to attend her father's school. She ended up going to a lesser school that was a half-hour commute by bus. Sometimes she rode her old bicycle in order to save bus fare.

Her family occupied a three-room house without running water in the school's outer courtyard. Because her mother was sick, a maid came every week to tidy up their rooms and wash their clothes. The school's kitchen was only twenty yards away, and Agnes washed her face in the same cement basin where the vegetables were rinsed. Her father paid the cook a small sum to prepare their meals, which were always delivered to them covered with an overturned plate. At night they used candles during scheduled blackouts, and, with the exception of her mother, who slept on a narrow bed surrounded by mosquito netting, everyone— her father, her brother, and Agnes—slept on tatami floors.

Sometimes when Agnes mentions her early life in Taiwan to her daughters, they look at her in astonishment, as if she had lived by herself on a deserted island. "That was the nineteen fifties, right?" one of them asks. The other says, "You were so poor!"

"It wasn't so bad," Agnes replies. "Everyone lived the same way, so you didn't notice."

What she remembers most from that time was following a boy in her choir whom she had a crush on. When she passed by him on her bicycle and the wind lifted her skirt, she was in no hurry to pull it down again. Some days, she picked up the cigarette butt that he tossed on the street and slipped the bittersweet end between her lips. She kept a diary, and it was a relief to write down her feelings, but she burned the pages a few years later when not even the handwriting seemed to be her own. She did not want a record to exist. No one in the world would know she had suffered. Agnes thinks now of that girl bicycling around the city, obsessed and burdened by love. It isn't surprising that she never once suspected her father of having a secret life of his own.

Her parents moved to the United States after her father's retirement, and for nine years they lived in their own house in Bloomington, Indiana, a few miles from her brother's farm. After her mother's death, Agnes thought her father would be lonely by himself in the suburbs and suggested that he move to Washington, D.C., to be closer to her and her daughters. She was a part-time real estate agent (she made most of her money selling life insurance), and she knew of a government-subsidized apartment building in Chinatown for senior citizens. At Evergreen House, he could socialize with people his age, and when he stepped out of his apartment, he had to walk only a couple of blocks to buy his groceries and a Chinese newspaper.

Her father eagerly agreed to this plan. Six months after her mother died, he moved into Evergreen House and quickly made friends with the other residents, playing mahjong twice a week, and even going to church, though he had never been religious before. For lunch, he usually waited in line at the nearby Washington Urban League Senior Center, where he could get a full hot meal for only a dollar.

At seventy-eight, her father looked much the same as he did in Taiwan when Agnes was growing up. For as long as she could remember, her father had been completely bald except for a sparse patch of hair that clung to the back of his head. By the time he was sixty, this shadowy tuft had disappeared, leaving nothing but shiny brown skin like fine, smooth leather. Her father had always been proud of his baldness. "We're more vigorous," he liked to say, "because of our hormones." He reassured Agnes that he would live to a hundred at least.

Every day, her father dressed impeccably in a suit and tie, the same attire that he wore as a principal, even though there was no longer any need for him to dress formally. "Such a gentleman!" Agnes's friends remarked when they saw him. He gazed at them with tranquillity, though Agnes suspected he knew they were saying flattering things about him. His eyes were good humored, clear, and benign, the irises circled with a pale ring of blue.

If anything, Agnes thought, her father's looks had improved with age. His hollow cheeks had filled out, and he had taken to wearing a fedora with a red feather stuck in the brim, which gave him a charming and dapper air. Maybe, too, it was because he now wore a set of false teeth, which corrected his overbite.

Every other weekend, he took the Metro from his place in Chinatown to Dunn Loring, where Agnes waited for him in her car. He would smile at Agnes as if he hadn't seen her for a year, or as if their meeting were purely a matter of chance and not something they had arranged by telephone. If her teenage daughters were in the car, he would greet them in English. "Hello! How are you?" he said, beaming.

Her daughters laughed. "Fine! And how are you?" they replied.

"Fine!" he exclaimed.

"Good!" they responded.

"Good!" he repeated.

Agnes supposed the three of them found it amusing, their lack of words, their inability to express anything more subtle or pressing to each other. Her daughters were always delighted to see him. They took him out shopping and invited him to the movies. They were good-natured, happy girls, if spoiled and a little careless. Every summer, they visited their father in Florida, and when they came back, their suitcases were stuffed with gifts—new clothes and pretty things for their hair, stuffed animals and cheap bits of jewelry, which they wore for a week and then grew tired of. Their short attention spans sometimes made Agnes feel sorry for her ex-husband, and she enjoyed this feeling of pity in herself very much.

In March, her father visited a former student of his in San Francisco. He came back two weeks later overflowing with health and good spirits. He gave silk purses to the girls and a bottle of Guerlain perfume to Agnes. It was unlike her father to give her perfume, much less one from Paris. She asked him how he had chosen it. "A kind lady helped me," he replied soberly. Agnes thought he meant a saleslady at the store. But later, as she was going through his suit pockets, emptying them of loose change and crumpled tissues and soft pads of lint—she planned on going to the dry cleaner that afternoon—she found a sliver of light blue paper folded into eighths. It was a rough draft of a letter, without a date or signature, addressed to a woman named Qiulian. Her father wrote in a quaint, tipsy hand. His characters were neat though cramped, etched on the page, as the ink from his pen was running out.

You cannot know how happy I was to receive your letter. I hope you are well in San Francisco, and that you have had restful days. I think of you often, perhaps more than I should. Like this morning, for instance, I wondered when exactly you had lived in Nanjing. Is it possible we lived in that city at the same time? I like to think that we passed each other on the street, I, a young man in his early thirties, and you, a schoolgirl in uniform with your hair cut just below the ear. We walked past each other, not knowing our paths would cross again—so many years later!

The cherry trees are in bloom here along the Potomac. I often find myself conversing with you in my head. Look at the falling blossoms, I say. Beautiful, yes? Some people, I know, don't have the courage for anything, but what is there to be afraid of? I thought I would spend the rest of my days alone. I can't help but think of the poet Meng Chiao. "Who says that all things flower in spring?"

A few characters had been blotted out, a phrase added between the vertical lines of script. Agnes couldn't help but laugh, even though there was a slight bitterness in it. How ridiculous that her father should be courting someone across the country. To be thinking of love when he should be thinking of the grave. She called up Hu Tingjun, her father's student in California. "So who is this Qiulian?" she demanded when he picked up the phone.

"Ah!" Tingjun said, his voice wavering. He had always been a little afraid of her since that time she had thrown a glass of water in his face. But he had a loose tongue, and Agnes knew he would not be able to resist the urge to gossip. "A real beauty from the mainland," he declared. "Your father has good taste."

Agnes allowed this remark to pass without comment. "And why is she so interested in my father? He doesn't have any money."

Tingjun laughed. "You underestimate your father's charms." He paused, and Agnes could hear him sucking his teeth. "I think she's had a sad life. You know what they say—every beauty has a tragic story."

Agnes frowned, switching the phone to her other ear.

"Her husband was an art history professor at Nanjing University," Tingjun said. "Struggled against, of course, and died in a reeducation camp. She married a second time, but this husband turned out to be a violent character—he beat her, I'm told, and she divorced him after a few years. She has two children from her first marriage, both of them in Guangzhou. She came here on a tourist's visa and is staying with an old friend from college."

"So she's been married twice already," Agnes said, "and wants to marry again. She doesn't have a very good track record."

"Have a heart, Shuling. What's so wrong with your father finding comfort in his last days? It's no good to be alone. No good at all."

"I never thought you were a sentimentalist," she said. "I wish I could hand you some tissues!"

Tingjun sighed. "You're always the same, Shuling."

When Agnes hung up the phone, she couldn't help but think of her mother, whom she had always loved more than she loved her father, just as you love something more because it is broken. Her mother had lived to the age of seventy-one, longer than anyone had believed possible, defying the prognostications of doctors, the resignation of her children, and even her own will. Her father had never murmured a word of complaint in all the years he cared for her. In the mornings, he prepared a breakfast for her of puréed apples or boiled carrots. At night he brought her three pills—one sleeping capsule, two that he had filled with sugar—and a tall glass of prune juice. Everything her mother ate had to go into a blender first. She chewed the same mouthful over and over again with slow awareness, sometimes falling asleep with the food still in her mouth.

She once told Agnes that every bite she swallowed was like swallowing a small stone. The only thing she enjoyed putting in her mouth were her sleeping pills, and these she swallowed all at once without a sip of water. Perhaps Agnes respected this sickness in her mother more than she did her father's health, his natural exuberance, and his penchant for histrionics.

The day before her mother's funeral, Agnes remembered, she and her brother had gone to a store to look for watches. They had selected a gold watch with a round face, and her brother had asked the salesclerk if there was a warranty, which struck Agnes as funny because the watch was going on her mother's wrist. "Who cares whether it runs beneath the ground or not?" she said. Nevertheless, her mother had always liked to wear a watch. They bought it for her because her old one was broken.

Then Agnes saw her mother lying in her coffin, the new gold watch ticking on her wrist. The sight of her mother lying in such a composed state, looking more content and peaceful than she did when she was alive, made Agnes desperate. She brushed her mother's cheeks and smoothed out her hair with increasing violence, clutching her hand and kissing her cold lips, all the while smelling her powder and the undertaker's handiwork beneath the cloying scent of lilies.

At the funeral reception, her father positioned himself on a stool at the front door of his house so that anyone who passed by had to confront him. At one point, he sprang off his stool and ran across the yard to speak to his neighbor, who had just come home from the store and was holding a bag of groceries. Agnes watched as her father waved his arms, his new suit a size too large for him, the cuffs dangling over his hands and flapping about his wrists. He squeezed his eyes and cried like a child, beating the side of his head with his palm. His neighbor set her bag down, took his hand between her own, and nodded in sympathy, even though she could not understand a word he was saying. Agnes's brother finally intervened, leading their father away so that the neighbor could go inside her house.

"Try to control yourself," Agnes told her father.

"You don't know what it's like to lose someone you saw every day of your life," he said, wiping his eyes.

When the reception was over, after the visitors had departed and her father had shut himself up in his bedroom, Agnes and her brother stood in the backyard, looking at their father's garden.

"The two of them lived in their own world together," her brother said.

Agnes looked at the glossy tomatoes that hung like ornaments from the vines. The winter melons sprawled on the grass like pale, overfed whales. Above them, the sunflowers rose, their faces somehow human, leaning from their stalks. For the first time, she wondered about her parents, the quiet life they had lived in that home.

Agnes never asked her father about the letter she found. In October, he informed her that Qiulian would be flying down in a month and that they would be married in a civil ceremony at the courthouse. He wondered if Agnes would be their witness. Also if there was a restaurant in the area suitable for a small wedding banquet. No more than three tables, he said.

In the marriage bureau, tiny pictures in pastel frames—a cheetah running, an eagle spreading its wings—decorated the walls of the waiting area. There was a sign in the room prohibiting photographs. Agnes sighed as she looked at her watch. Her daughters would be home from school in an hour and would be catching a ride to the banquet with Agnes's friend. Her brother wasn't coming. He had been depressed by their father's news and told Agnes it was too difficult for him to leave the farm. Agnes got up from her seat and inspected a picture of a sailboat skimming moonlit waters. The caption read: "You cannot discover new oceans unless you have the courage to lose sight of the shore." It made Agnes laugh out loud, and the receptionist glanced up at her from her desk.

Her father arrived a moment later with his bride. He was beaming, handsomely dressed in a dark gray suit and platinum tie, two red carnations fastened to his lapel. He introduced Agnes and Qiulian with mock solemnity, exaggerating the tones of their names, lifting himself in the air and falling back on his heels. Qiulian smiled and told Agnes that her American name was Lily. Everything Lily wore was white. There was her opaque white dress suit with its faintly puffed sleeves. Her pearl earrings and two strands of pearls wound closely around her neck. A corsage of white roses enmeshed in a swirl of white ribbon pinned to her chest. She had decided on white just as if she were a first-time American bride, even though white was no color at all, what you wore to another person's funeral. Perhaps it was a sign of Lily's true feelings.

Agnes grasped her father's arm and pulled him aside. "How old is she, by the way?" It infuriated her that this woman was closer to her age than she had expected.

"That's top secret," her father said, adjusting his carnations. "She's very nice, isn't she? Do I look all right? What do you think of my tie?" He glanced over at Lily, who stood serenely looking at her shoes. She held a small beaded purse between both hands, and it seemed from her empty expression that she was pretending not to hear their conversation. "Incredible!" he muttered. "I'm supposed to feel less as I grow old. But it's the opposite—I feel more and more!" His eyes widened, and he knocked his fist against his chest. "Can you believe it? A seventy-eight-year-old heart like mine!" He walked back to Lily, smiling and patting her hand.

Agnes felt her skin begin to itch. She wanted to lift her sweater, scratch herself luxuriously until she bled, but the receptionist told them it was time, and they were ushered into a narrow green-carpeted room where the justice of the peace stood waiting behind a podium. Behind him was a trellis on which a few straggling vines of artificial clematis drooped. It was a halfhearted attempt at illusion, and, for this reason, it gave Agnes some relief. It startled her to think that she had once cared about the color of roses matching her bridesmaids' dresses. That day had been a fantasy, with its exquisite bunches of flowers, so perfect they did not seem real. At one point, she had looked up at the sky and laughed. . . . She had felt so light and happy. She had worn a white ballroom dress and—of all things—a rhinestone tiara! If photographs still existed of her in that Cinderella outfit, they resided in other people's albums, for she had torn her own into bits.

Her father was listening to the justice with an impassive, dignified expression, his hands folded neatly in front of him. Agnes thought Lily's smile belonged on the face of a porcelain doll. Her hair was cut in short, fashionable waves and seemed ridiculously lustrous for someone her age. Dyed, no doubt. Neither of them understood what the justice was saying, and Agnes had to prompt them when it was time to exchange rings. When the justice pronounced them husband and wife, her father looked around the room, smiling good-naturedly. He thanked the justice with a bow of his head and took Lily gently by the elbow.

Her father visited less often after he was married. The few times he took the subway to Dunn Loring, he did not bring Lily with him. Agnes once asked him why, and he said Lily was quite popular at Evergreen House. "People are always inviting her out to restaurants," he said. "Or she goes over to other ladies' apartments, and they watch the latest Hong Kong melodramas. What sentimental drivel! But she enjoys it, she can't get enough of it . . ." He told Agnes that one day Lily wanted to eat *dan dan* noodles and nothing but *dan dan* noodles. "There is a restaurant we know, but the owners were away on vacation. Qiulian suggested another restaurant, but when we got there, it wasn't on the menu and she refused to go inside. She dragged me from one place to another, but none of them served *dan dan* noodles. I was so hungry by this time, I insisted we go into the next restaurant we saw. But she said she wouldn't eat at all if she couldn't have her *dan dan* noodles. So we ended up going home, and I had to eat leftovers." Her father shook his head, though he was clearly delighted by Lily's caprice.

From her father, Agnes learned that Lily had studied Chinese history at the prestigious Zhejiang University. She liked to take baths over showers, used Pond's cream on her face at night, and sipped chrysanthemum tea in bed. She rarely bought herself anything, and when she did, the things she chose were charming and fairly priced. Her father gave Lily a monthly allowance of five hundred dollars, which was half the income he received from Agnes and her brother as well as from the federal government. Lily, in turn, sent money to her son, a book vendor, and to her daughter, a truck driver in Guangzhou.

More than a year passed, and Agnes never saw her.

In December, she walked by Lily almost without recognizing her. She had stopped in Chinatown to buy duck for a New Year's Eve party, and a small group of older women approached her on the street. She would not have paid them any attention if the woman in the gray raincoat had not paused to stare in the middle of readjusting a silk scarf around her head. It took Agnes a moment to realize it was Lily. By that time, the women had passed, heading south in the direction of Evergreen House.

Agnes stood on the sidewalk, gazing absently at a faded brick building, its pink paint flaking off to reveal dark red patches. Even in the winter, the streets smelled of grease and the hot air blown out of ventilators. Behind a row of buildings, two looming cranes crisscrossed the sky. It was odd to think of someone like Lily living here. Agnes went inside the restaurant to get her duck, and by the time she stepped outside again, tiny flakes of snow were falling. She did not go back to her car but instead turned in the direction of her father's apartment.

Outside his door, she heard shrill voices and laughter, the noisy clacking of tiles being swirled along a table. The mahjong ladies, Agnes thought. Lily answered the door, her mild, empty eyes widening slightly. Her mass of glossy black hair was perfectly coiffed, and only her wrinkled neck betrayed her age.

"I saw you on the street," Agnes said. "Didn't you see me?"

"Yes," Lily said, pausing. "But I wasn't sure it was you until we had passed each other."

"The same with me." Agnes pulled off her coat and tossed it onto the sofa. "So, who are your friends here?"

"Oh yes, let me introduce you to my neighbors." The mahjong ladies half stood out of their seats, smiling at Agnes, but it was obvious they wanted to return to their game.

"Don't let me disturb you," Agnes told them. "Is my father here? "

"He's taking a nap," Lily said, seating herself at the table.

The living room was brightly lit compared with the dimness of the hallway. It seemed like its own island in space as the afternoon waned and the windows darkened. The mahjong ladies chattered, flinging their tiles to the middle of the table. They were older than Lily, in their seventies at least, their hands plowed with wrinkles, with bright green circles of jade hanging from their wrists. Their fingers, too, were weighed down by gaudy rings, the stones as shiny as candy, purple and turquoise and vermilion. "He ate oatmeal every day," a woman with badly drawn eyebrows was saying.

"I heard he took poison," another said, picking up a tile. She had thick, sour lips and wore red horn-rimmed glasses. "Didn't he lose everything?"

"No, it was a heart attack. His wife found him still sitting on the toilet! In the middle of reading a newspaper."

"He was too cheap to pay for his own funeral," the third one said. She had a sagging, magisterial face, her thick white hair pulled back into a bun. "In his will, he donated his body to science."

The one with the false eyebrows knocked down all of her tiles. "Hula!" she declared.

There were startled cries. "I wasn't even close!"

"Did anyone have three sticks?"

Agnes smiled as she poured herself a cup of tea from the counter. These ladies were real witches, talking about people's ends with such morbid assurance—how could Lily stand their company? Perhaps she liked the attention, for she seemed to be the silent center of the group, the one the ladies exclaimed over and petted. Lily glanced toward Agnes from time to time, smiling at her. She seemed impatient for Agnes to leave.

"Well," Agnes said, after she had finished her tea, "he won't mind too much if I wake him." She walked across the room and opened the bedroom door, even though she sensed this was precisely what Lily did not want her to do.

Her father sat at his desk reading a newspaper, his bifocals slipping down his nose. A single lamp illuminated his down-turned head, and it seemed from his silence that he had been exiled here. His manner changed the moment he saw her. His face broke into an exuberant smile as he stood up from his chair.

"So what are you doing here? Come to pay me a visit?"

Agnes closed the door behind her. "I've brought you a duck," she said. "And to wish you a happy new year."

"A duck? Did you go to the Golden Palace?"

"I did."

"That's the best place to go. They have better ducks than anywhere else. Number one ducks!" he said. "So plump! And with crispy skin."

Agnes looked at her father. "And how are you these days?"

"I'm fine!" he declared. "I'm good! Just look at me." He straightened his argyle sweater over his shirt and tie, then preened in front of the mirror, turning his head to one side and then the other.

"You don't play mahjong with the ladies," she said, looking around the room. The furniture was mismatched—things that she had given him which she no longer had any use for. A chair from an old dining room table set. A desk with buttercup yellow legs. A massive dresser with gothic iron handles. It bothered Agnes to see her daughter's stickers still on one of the drawers.

"You know me. I'm not good at these sorts of games. I'm a scholar, I read things . . . like this newspaper," he said, waving it in the air. "Besides, they want to talk freely without me hanging about."

"What's that doing in here?" Agnes asked. "Is that where she makes you sleep?" In the corner, between the bed and the closet, was a makeshift cot covered with a comforter folded in half like a sleeping bag.

"The bed is too soft on my poor back," her father said. He pressed his hand against his spine and winced. "This way is more comfortable."

Agnes sat down on the thin cot, which bounced lightly. "So this is how she treats you," she said. "She won't even let you into her bed."

"Her sleep isn't good." Her father cleared his throat, setting the newspaper down on his desk. "She often wakes up in the middle of the night." He didn't look at her as he fiddled with the pages, then folded the paper back together. Agnes felt an involuntary stirring in her chest. She had avoided him all this time, not wanting to know about his marriage because she had not wanted to know of his happiness. But she should have known Lily was the kind of person who took care only of herself.

"How else is she behaving?" she asked. "Is she mistreating you in any way?"

"No, no," her father said hurriedly, shaking his head.

"Is she a wife to you?" There was a pause as he looked at her. "You know what I mean," she said.

"She suffers a pain," he offered hesitantly. "In her ovaries."

Agnes laughed. She got up and strode across the room, flinging the door open.

"Don't say anything," her father said, following after her. "Don't let her know what I've told you."

In the living room, the mahjong ladies were laughing and knocking over their walls, and Agnes had to raise her voice above theirs.

"I'd like to talk to you," she said to Lily.

For a moment, Lily pretended not to hear, continuing her conversation with the white-haired lady beside her. Then she glanced over at Agnes, her face a mask of porcelain elegance except for one delicately lifted eyebrow. "What is it?"

"Why aren't you sleeping with my father?"

The ladies' voices fell to a murmur, their hands slowing down as they massaged the tiles along the tablecloth. They looked at Lily, who said nothing, though her smile seemed to be sewn on her lips.

Her father clutched Agnes's arm, but she refused to be silent. "You married him, didn't you? He pays for your clothes and your hairdo and this roof over your head. He deserves something in return!"

Her father laughed out loud and immediately put his hand over his mouth.

Lily stood up, but the mahjong ladies remained in their seats as if drunk, their eyes glazed with the thrill of the unexpected. "Perhaps we can resume our games later," Lily said. The one with the horn-rimmed glasses stood up slowly from the table, prompting the other two to rise. They looked as if they had been shaken out of a dream.

"Oh, my heavens!" the one with the eyebrows exclaimed as Agnes shut the door on them.

"Now," Agnes said, turning toward Lily and waiting for her to speak.

"I have an illness . . ." Lily began. "A gynecological disorder that prevents me . . ." Her gaze wandered to Agnes's father, who hovered near the bedroom door. "Well, in truth, he's an old man," she said, her expression hardening. "His breath stinks like an open sewer. I can't stand to smell his breath!" She snatched her scarf from the closet and wrapped it quickly around her head.

"If you don't sleep with him," Agnes said, "I'll send a letter to the immigration office. I'll tell them that you only married him to get a green card!"

Lily's hands trembled as she put on her coat. "Do as you like," she said, walking out the door.

Her father looked deeply pained.

"She won't refuse you now," Agnes told him.

"What has happened?" her father said, his voice shaking. "Who are you? You've become someone . . . someone completely without shame!"

"I should open up a brothel," Agnes declared. "That is exactly what I should do."

In February, her father called to tell her he wasn't sure whether or not his nose was broken. There had been a snowstorm two days before, whole cars sheathed in ice, the roads filled with irregular lumps, oddly smooth and plastic, where the snow had melted and then frozen again. In this weather, her father and Lily had gone out walking to buy groceries at Da Hua Market. Lily had walked ahead, and when she was almost half a block away, she turned around and asked Agnes's father to walk faster. He tried to keep up with her, but corns had formed along his toes and the soles of his feet. When he quickened his pace, he slipped on a deceptively bland patch of ice and hit his nose on the pavement.

When Agnes saw her father—a dark welt on the bridge of his nose, a purple stain beginning to form under his eyes—she couldn't help but feel a flood of anger and pity. "You could have lived your last years in peace," she wanted to say to him. Instead she glanced at the closed bedroom door. "Is that where she's hiding?"

He looked at her morosely. "She left earlier because she knew you were coming."

In the hospital, Agnes noticed that her father walked gingerly down the hall, stepping on the balls of his feet without touching his toes or heels to the ground. An X-ray revealed that his nose was not broken after all. Agnes told the resident he was having problems walking.

"That's not an emergency," the resident replied. Nevertheless, she left the room to call in a podiatrist.

Her father grew excited when he saw the podiatrist. He began speaking to him in Chinese.

"I'm sorry," the podiatrist said, shaking his head. "I'm Korean. Let's take these off, shall we?" He lightly pulled off her father's socks. There were red cone-shaped bumps along his toes and hard yellow mounds on the soles and heels of his feet. But what shocked Agnes most was the big toe on his left foot. The nail of this one toe looked a thousand years old to her, thick, encrusted, and wavy, black in the center and as impenetrable as a carapace.

"Older people's toenails are often like this," the podiatrist said, seeing Agnes's surprise.

Her father seemed oblivious to their comments. He was squeezing his eyes shut as the podiatrist worked on his foot, slicing the calluses off bit by bit with a small blade. Her father winced and jerked his feet up occasionally. "Oh, it hurts," he exclaimed to Agnes. "It's unbearable!"

"I know this isn't pleasant," the podiatrist said, looking at her father. He took a pumice stone out of his pocket and rubbed it gently against her father's foot.

When the podiatrist had finished paring away at his corns, her father covered his feet back up, slowly pulling on his socks and tying the laces of his shoes. He smiled at the podiatrist, yet because of his bruised nose, his face seemed pathetic and slightly grotesque. "It's better beyond words," he said.

In the parking lot, her father showed off by walking at a sprightly pace in front of her. "It's so much better now!" he kept exclaiming.

The doctor had told Agnes that the corns would eventually come back, but she didn't tell her father. She was thinking how well he had hidden the signs of old age from her. That big toe underneath his sock. Since the time she was a child, she and her father had lived their lives independent of each other. She had never demanded anything of him, and he had been too busy with his work at school, so that by the time she was six she had been as free as an adult. They left each other alone mostly because of her mother, whose sickness filled up the entire house and whose moods were inextricably bound with their own.

In the car, Agnes told her father that she thought he should divorce Lily.

"It's not as bad as that, Shuling."

"I hate how she humiliates you," she said.

Her father was silent, gazing out the window. "Love is humiliating," he finally replied.

When she dropped him off in front of his building, he did not immediately go inside but stood on the frozen sidewalk, waving at her. She knew he would stay there until her car was no longer in sight. It was his way of seeing her off, and he would do this no matter what the weather.

In June, her father called to see if Agnes had any photographs of his wedding banquet. He and Lily were going to be interviewed by an immigration officer next week in order to secure Lily's green card, and her father planned to present the photos as evidence. Agnes could find only one photograph. She had dumped it into a shoebox, to be lost in an ever growing stack of useless pictures. Years ago, she had stopped putting her family's photographs in an album. Now whenever their pictures were developed, after her daughters' initial enthusiasm of looking at themselves, Agnes put the photos back into their original envelopes and tossed them into a shoebox.

The photograph she found was of Lily, her father, and two old couples seated at their table. Lily was looking away from the camera, her mouth oddly pursed, as if she were in the middle of chewing her food while smiling at the same time. A pair of chopsticks rested between her fingers. It was an odd moment. Lily appeared sociable yet also removed. Her eyes were lively, though they looked at nothing in particular. It was as if two versions of her had been captured in the same photograph.

Actually, there were two photographs of Lily that Agnes found. Two copies of the same picture. Agnes wanted to find a difference, something very small—a gesture of the hand, the curve of an eyebrow—but the two pictures were exactly alike. Another photograph of Lily would reveal another world. But there she was—Lily could never break out of the picture, an elegant woman caught in the act of chewing. Beside her, her father looked radiant, a little too well satisfied, two red carnations and a wisp of baby's breath pinned right over his heart. He was the only person in the photograph looking at the camera.

"Do you want to come over on Saturday to pick it up?" she asked her father. "You can stay for the weekend, and I'll drive you to your interview on Monday."

Her father hesitated. "You don't have to come in with me. You can just drop me off at the immigration office."

"Fine," Agnes said.

The morning of his interview, her father ironed his own dress shirt and put on a suit that still smelled of the dry cleaner's fumes. He shaved the tiny white hairs that had begun to sprout on his chin, and even sprayed himself with an old bottle of cologne that he found in a bathroom drawer. An hour before his appointment, he began to fidget, looking at his watch and pacing around the room. "Shouldn't we be leaving?" he asked.

"Sit down. We have plenty of time."

"I don't want to be late," he said, picking up his bag. "Qiulian will be waiting."

Agnes sat down, tapping a pack of cigarettes in her hand. Smoking was one of the bad habits she blamed on her father, even though he had quit twenty years ago. "You realize, don't you," Agnes said, blowing smoke to the side away from him. "It's a certain fact. She'll leave you as soon as she gets her green card."

Her father cleared his throat and switched the bag to his other hand.

"You want her to stay, am I right?"

He sighed, heading toward the door. "Let's not talk about this anymore."

"I'm not taking you," she said. She flicked the ash off her cigarette onto a plate. "It's for your own good. I won't let her have it."

Her father shook his head. "Unbelievable," he said.

"I wrote a letter to the INS already. In the letter, I informed them that your marriage—your wife—is a fraud."

Her father closed his eyes, shaking his head. He began breathing heavily and grasped his collar.

"What would Mother say?" she said. "You were such an easy dupe!"

"You and her!" he said, looking at Agnes. "You make me want to die!" He hit his palm twice against his forehead. "I want to die!"

"You were so eager to jump into another woman's bed," Agnes said. "But you didn't know she wouldn't let you touch her. Not even if you married her!"

"A dirty old man," her father laughed. "Yes, I am a dirty old man! I sleep with whoever I want! I slept with our maids, you know that? It only cost a few dollars each time! Sometimes I did it when you were in the house, and you never knew. It was like you were knocked out, and I wondered if you took your mother's sleeping pills. Because you never knew! You never knew!" He was talking so fast that spittle was forming on his lips.

Agnes felt her throat burning and tried to swallow.

"I slept with all of them!" her father repeated.

"I don't believe you."

"Yes!"

"Those women? They were old and fat—"

"Who cares? Their bodies were warm."

"Disgusting."

"Yes, everything is disgusting to you." Her father walked to the front door.

"Where do you think you're going?" she screamed.

He left the door open, and she watched him walk down the driveway with a jaunty step. She wondered if he knew how to get out of the neighborhood. It was still morning, but the humidity was unbearable. She picked up the newspaper lying on the doorstep and went back inside. She would let him walk as much as he wanted. It would serve him right if he got heatstroke.

At eleven, the phone rang. It was Lily, waiting at the INS and wondering where her father was. "He won't be able to make it," Agnes said, and she hung up the phone. But she felt herself shaking. Wasn't it obvious, wasn't it to be expected—a healthy, vital man married to an invalid for over forty years? And yet, she had never suspected. She remembered the speeches he gave, how everyone had called him a gentleman . . . and it was not what he had done that disturbed her so much as her own sickening ignorance. She felt as if a hole had opened up inside her chest, all the things she had known and believed slipping through.

Another hour passed, and still her father had not returned. What if he should simply lie down and die like a dog in the street? The thought made Agnes leave her house. She drove around her neighborhood, turning down streets that ended in culs-de-sac. She felt something round and heavy inside her forehead, as if it were splitting open from the heat. She turned out of her neighborhood onto a narrow two-lane road that dipped and curved without warning, and she couldn't help but feel dread growing inside her, a darkness that she wanted to make small again, half expecting to see her father lying on the side of the road.

She spotted him three miles farther down. He was walking at a much slower pace with his jacket along his arm. He had loosened his tie, and his white shirt was semi-transparent with sweat. She slowed down and honked at him, but he kept trudging ahead, without turning to look at her. Agnes rolled down the passenger window. "Get in the car," she said, but he began to walk faster, with small, clumsy steps. He was panting and bobbing his head with each stride, intent on pressing forward, even though she knew his feet must be hurting him.

"It's useless to walk," she said, driving slowly beside him. "How far are you going to get, huh? Don't be foolish. Get in the car."

He shook his head, and she could see that he was crying.

"I'll take you back to your apartment. I promise, okay?"

He walked more slowly now, and she felt sorry for him, knowing there was nothing for him to do but give in. When she got out of the car, he was standing motionless, his arms hanging at his sides and his jacket on the ground. She touched his arm, and he blinked, looking around in bewilderment as she helped him into the car.

He began shivering as soon as he sat down in the passenger seat, and Agnes turned down the air conditioning. Neither of them spoke as Agnes drove to his apartment. At Evergreen House, he hurriedly got out of the car, searching his pockets for his keys. Agnes realized that they had forgotten to get his bag at her house. Nevertheless, the security guard recognized him and let him inside the building.

⌐⌐

When Agnes was twenty-two, she left Taiwan to study economics in Rochester, New York. She left her home and her parents with a feeling of relief. Her family life had become a source of embarrassment to her, and as her plane lifted into the air—it was the first time she had ever flown—she felt that she was abandoning an idea of herself. She looked outside her window, the things she knew shrinking steadily away until all she could see were clouds, and she welcomed the prospect of being unknown in another part of the world.

In Rochester, she received a blue rectangle of a letter every other week from her father in Taiwan. On the front, he would write out her address in English with a painstaking, scrupulous hand. He told her about the vegetables he was growing in the courtyard, the Siamese cat that Agnes had left in their care, the state of her mother's health and the various foods she could keep down, news of her brother in the army, and updates of their relatives and friends, some of whom were leaving for the States. She would write back, sometimes enclosing a money order for twenty dollars. She could not afford to call them on the phone, but the few times she did, she heard her own voice echoing along the line, a high, unfamiliar sound, and this distracted her, made her think of all the distance her voice had to cross to reach their ears. Her parents always asked the same questions—How are you? Are you eating well? Are you happy?—until the static took over and their voices ended abruptly. Listening to the silence, she imagined their voices being dropped from a high space into the ocean.

She sent her parents a hateful letter once. They had set a date for her brother's wedding without consulting her, and it enraged Agnes to find out that she would not be able to attend. The next letter she received came from her mother, who rarely wrote after her fall. Her handwriting resembled the large uncontrolled scrawl of a child or of someone who was right-handed trying to use her left. She had copied Agnes's address so poorly that it was a miracle the letter had arrived at all. "We received your letter in which you scolded us severely. Your father fainted after reading it, and it took him a long time before he could eat his dinner. He has heart trouble and cannot suffer any blows." At the time, Agnes had been amused by her mother's lies. Her father had no history of heart trouble, and as for his fainting, she knew what a good actor he was. But it was her mother's last phrase that had come to haunt her. "He . . . cannot suffer any blows."

Agnes did not hear from her father for over a month, and in that time she felt as removed from him as if he were living in another country. One day in August, she stopped by his apartment to give him a box of persimmons. Lily answered the door in gray slacks and a thin, watery blouse, a silk scarf wrapped around her head as if she were about to go out. "He's not here," she said coldly, and began to shut the door.

"Wait—" Agnes said, putting her hand out.

Lily held the door open only wide enough for her face to be visible. The powder she wore could not quite hide the fine lines etched beneath her eyes, or the age spots above her cheeks.

"Do you know when he'll be back?" Agnes asked.

"I have no idea."

"I'd like to wait for him if you don't mind."

"Wait for as long as you like," Lily said, turning away. She retreated to her bedroom and closed the door.

Agnes set the persimmons on the kitchen counter. Her father had hung red and gold New Year's greeting cards from the slats of the closet door. In the living room, he had decorated the walls with whimsical scrolled paintings of fruit and birds. She had always been somewhat relieved by his attempts to make the place more livable. Perhaps she was trying to console herself for the drab carpet and clumsy furniture, the sense of apology she always felt for things that were merely adequate. After two years, there was hardly any trace of Lily in the apartment, but this didn't surprise Agnes, as Lily had never intended to stay for long.

She paused outside the bedroom door before knocking. "I'd like to talk to you," she said.

"Come in, then," a voice evenly replied.

Agnes saw Lily sitting on the side of her bed, a ghostly smile on her lips as she studied the scarf in her hands. She seemed like another person to Agnes, ten or fifteen years older at least, and it took a moment for Agnes to realize that her beautiful, shiny black hair was gone. Instead, wisps of ash-colored hair were matted together in places like dead grass. The sparseness of her hair revealed mottled patches of scalp.

"What happened?" Agnes blurted. She couldn't help but stare at Lily's baldness.

"You didn't know?" Lily said. She touched her head lightly with a flat hand, her eyes vacant as she smiled to herself. "When I was struggled against, they pulled my hair out by the fistfuls, and it never grew back again. You would think it would grow back, but it doesn't always."

Agnes was silent for a moment. "Hu Tingjun told me about your first husband," she said.

"My first husband," Lily echoed, and it seemed to Agnes as if those words had lost their meaning to her. "Yes, my first husband was an avid collector of calligraphy. Did you know he had a work by Zhu Yunming that was more than four hundred years old? He said the characters flowed on the paper like a flight of birds. Like a wind was lifting them off the page."

Agnes shook her head. "I don't know much about calligraphy."

"This work was more than four hundred years old," Lily said. "Can you imagine? My husband begged them not to destroy it. 'I'll give it to the state!' he said. But they said, 'Why would the state want such an old thing?' And they burned it before his eyes. Sometimes I wish I could tell him, 'Is someone's handwriting worth more than your life?' I would have burned a hundred such pieces. You see, I'm not an idealistic person. There are things one must do out of necessity."

"My father is a foolish man," Agnes said.

Lily looked at her, twisting the scarf between her fingers. "Yet it's impossible to hate him. He doesn't have any cruelty in him."

"So you have your green card now."

"A few more months," Lily said.

"Where will you go after this?"

"California. My son is living there now."

"Does my father know?"

Lily nodded, dropping the scarf on the night table. "He's afraid, you see." She lay down on the bed, folding her hands over her stomach, her feet sheathed in brown pantyhose. "He knows his mind is fading, but he won't admit it. He shouldn't be allowed to live by himself for too long." Lily closed her eyes. "I once told myself that I'd be happy, I'd never complain, if only I was safe. But I'm so tired of living here. I can't tell you how bored I am!" She curled up on her side, placed both hands underneath her cheek. "Do you mind turning off the light as you go out? I'm going to take a little nap now. It seems all I can do is sleep." She murmured her thanks as Agnes left the room, closing the door behind her.

Her father never mentioned Lily's departure, nor did Agnes say anything, both of them lapsing into a silence that seemed to make Lily more present in the room, just as her mother was often there in the room between them, in the air they breathed and the words they did not say.

One night, while her father was visiting, Agnes woke to find the light still on in his bedroom. When she knocked on his door, she saw that he was dressed in his suit and tie, his bags already packed, even though it was only two in the morning. She told him to go back to sleep, that it was still too early, and he smiled at her, waving from behind his ear as he closed the door. She stood in the hallway, and after a moment he turned off his light, but she knew he was sitting in the dark, waiting.

In January, the manager of Evergreen House called Agnes to inform her that her father had stopped paying the rent. "He gets confused," the manager said. "Sometimes he doesn't recognize us."

Her father laughed when Agnes asked him about the rent. "Nobody pays rent here," he replied. Then he told her he suspected the manager of being a thief. "If anything happens to me, you should know that I have a hiding place for my cash. There's a brick in the wall which can be removed."

Agnes and her brother agreed that it was time for their father to live with one of them. Their father didn't offer a word of protest. An airplane ticket to Indiana was purchased, and one weekend in February Agnes went over to his apartment to help pack his things.

He answered the door in his slippers. The television was on, and he was watching a basketball game. His apartment smelled musty, like old newspapers. Perhaps it was the wood paneling or the brown carpet worn as soft as moss. The sick sweetness emanated from deep within the wood. The carpet had inhaled odors that had been pressed in for years by slippered feet.

She took a suitcase out of his closet and packed it hastily without too much folding. She did not like the intimacy of touching his clothes, as if he were already dead. He hung vaguely about her for a few minutes, then wandered out of the room. In a short while, he came back, looking around as if he were trying to find something.

"What are you looking for?" she asked him.

He shook his head, closing his eyes, then left the room.

She finished packing two of his suitcases and dragged them to the front door. She found him standing on his balcony, watching a plane as it flew over the building. "That's the ninth one today," he said when she looked at him.

"You tell me what else you want to bring, and I'll send it to you."

"What's the use?" he said. "I don't need anything here. I probably won't live to see another year."

"Don't be so self-pitying," she told him.

In the elevator, an old man stood in the corner, both hands leaning against his walking stick. "Mr. Cao," her father said, smiling suddenly. "How are you? Let me introduce you to my wife."

"I'm not your wife," Agnes said, irritated. "I'm your daughter."

Her father screwed up his eyes, his fingers digging into his temple. Then he let out a loud, embarrassed laugh. Yet he seemed delighted by his mistake. "My daughter," he said. "Please excuse me. Yes, of course, my daughter."

After she saw off her father at the airport, Agnes remembered the secret place he had told her about where he had hidden his money, and she decided to return to his apartment.

In the living room, she stared at the scrolled paintings on the wall. Melons with their curling vines, a powder-blue bird hanging on a branch too thin for its talons, a lopsided horse as fat as a cow scratching its neck against a tree. She took these scrolls off their hooks and rolled them up. Then she ran her hand along the wall, searching for a loose brick. She could not find one. She pressed her hands against the bricks until the skin on her palms tingled with rawness. Anyone who saw her groping this way would think she was mad.

She looked in his desk drawers and underneath his mattress. She crawled around trying to find a loose spot in the carpet, but there was no part that would come undone. She could almost swear the carpet smelled faintly carcinogenic.

Had he smoked a cigarette here? Maybe, after all, it was a habit he couldn't leave behind.

In his closet, she found a door to a crawl space that had been hidden by his clothes. She had to crouch through to get in. It was a place for storage and apparently had never been swept, the floor littered with sawdust. She couldn't see much of anything and went back for a lamp, which she left in the closet as far as the cord could reach. There was nothing in the space except an old crumpled shirt, which she knew was not her father's. But then in the dim recess where the light barely reached, she saw a yellow shape, which turned out to be a suitcase, and just looking at it she knew it was her father's, something her parents had used when they still lived in Taiwan. The suitcase lay on its side, and there were gashes in the fabric which he had covered up with duct tape.

Agnes sneezed twice when she unzipped the suitcase. She expected old clothes, maybe even the cash he had mentioned, but instead the suitcase was crammed full of letters. The envelopes were cold to the touch, permeated with the chill dankness of the room, as cold as a basement. Her father had thrown them in rather heedlessly, and the letters had conformed to the shape of each other. She could see this in the indentations of the envelopes, pressed and stuck together like so many leaves. Little rectangles of blue paper, with red and blue stripes along the borders. *Aérogramme. Par avion.* There were long, slender envelopes with torn sides, the corners cut out with scissors where the stamps had been. She recognized some of the names on the envelopes—Jia Wen, Wang Peisan, Zhou Meiping, Wu Yenchiu—various friends and colleagues of her father's, though she was unsure if any of them were still living.

In the pile, she spotted her own handwriting. A letter she had written to her father from Rochester. She had always been careless about her writing, and her characters now struck her as hasty and anonymous in their uniformity. She put the letter aside and searched through the pile for her mother's name. She felt a strange sensation similar to the hope she felt whenever she saw her mother in her dreams. The envelope she reached for was covered with tea-colored stains, fantastically bent, curling around the edges. Though her mother's name was on the front, the handwriting was unfamiliar to Agnes. She pulled out a tissue-thin sheet of rice paper, folded vertically in thirds. The letter was dated February 19, 1946. Her mother wrote with a strong, fluid hand.

> I have arrived safely in Yancheng. The doll you gave Shuling is quite beautiful and interesting. She is always playing with it, holding it in her hands, and I'm afraid she'll break it, so I put it in a glass jar so that she can look but not touch. Let her appreciate it more that way. Her appetite has improved lately. You would be amazed to see how quickly she moves about, how she turns left and right as she walks. She tries to talk, and I still don't understand her, but her hands point to different things, and I know what she wants.

Agnes couldn't finish the letter and slipped it back into its envelope. Better to forget, she told herself. Her fingers smelled of dust and old paper, and she stared vacantly at the suitcase full of letters. Had he left them behind for her? She wished she had never found them. On all the envelopes, his name. Hsu Weimin. Addresses she had forgotten and others she had never known. All the places he had ever lived. Yancheng and Hechuan and Nanjing and Taipei. Then the last places. Bloomington. Washington, D.C.

Agnes stood up, wiping the dust off her fingers. In the kitchen, she found an empty trash bag, and she returned to the crawl space, grabbing letters by the fistful and throwing them inside. How cold and brittle they were! She would never read them, she knew that, and their presence was a small stone in her heart. Nothing lasts, and she was not a sentimental person.

"You cannot blame me," she said out loud, as if her father were in the room, watching.

Somewhere in the sky, her father lives. Perhaps he is asleep, perhaps looking out of his window, the clouds washing past in a dizzying blur of motion. In the rush of the plane, does he too sense that there is nowhere for him to go?

QUESTIONS

1. Why doesn't Agnes want to attend her father's school?

2. Why, before her mother's funeral, had Agnes never "wondered about her parents, the quiet life they had lived in that home"? (35)

3. What does Agnes's father mean when he says, "I'm supposed to feel less as I grow old. But it's the opposite—I feel more and more!" (36)

4. What does it mean that Agnes "had not wanted to know of [her father's] happiness"? (42) Why does she say, "My father is a foolish man"? (53)

5. What accounts for Agnes's statement, "I should open up a brothel. . . . That is exactly what I should do"? (43)

6. Why does Agnes refuse to take her father to the immigration office?

7. Why do her mother's words, "He . . . cannot suffer any blows," haunt Agnes? (51)

FOR FURTHER REFLECTION

1. In what ways are Lily and Agnes similar?

2. What does it mean to be a gentleman? Is Agnes's father a gentleman?

3. Is it true that "you love something more because it is broken," just as Agnes admits to loving her sick mother more than her father?

Envy

JIM SHEPARD

Jim Shepard (1956–) has been an English professor at Williams College for more than twenty-five years, and his third collection of stories, *Like You'd Understand Anyway* (2007), won the 2007 Story Prize. Shepard was born in Bridgeport, Connecticut. He graduated from Trinity College in 1978 and earned a master's in fine arts from Brown University in 1980. Shepard's characters often come from disruptive families, and he repeatedly explores the inherent miseries of adolescence. "Krakatau" originally appeared in Shepard's first short story collection, *Batting Against Castro* (1996) and was reprinted in *Love and Hydrogen: New and Selected Stories* (2004). He has also written six novels. With William Holinger he has cowritten six young-adult novels under the joint pseudonym Scott Eller.

Krakatau

was twelve years old when I figured out that the look my brother would get around his eyes probably meant that there was a physiological basis for what was wrong with him. Six years later as a college freshman, I was flipping through Gardner's *Art Through the Ages*, fifth edition, and was shocked to come across that same look, Donnie's eyes, peering out at me from Géricault's *Madwoman*. The madwoman in question was elderly, wrapped in some kind of cloak. She wore a white bonnet. Her eyes looked away from the painter as if just piecing together the outlines of another conspiracy. She'd outsmarted the world, and was going to outsmart this painter. I recognized the hatred, the sheer animosity for *everything*, unconcealed. Red lines rimmed her eyelids in a way that did not resemble eyestrain or fatigue. It was as if the mind behind the eyes was soaking in anguish. The next morning my Intro to Art History professor flashed a slide of the painting, ten feet wide, on the screen in front of us. A gum-chewing class went silent. "How'd you like to wake up to that in the morning?" the professor joked.

That night I called my father. He and my mother and Donnie still lived in the house Donnie and I grew up in, two hours away. I was in the little public phone booth in the dorm. It was lined with cork and the cork was scribbled over with phone numbers and ballpoint drawings of dicks.

Donnie answered. "How ya doin'," he said.

"I'm all right," I said. "How about you?"

He snorted.

Some kid opened the door to the booth like I wasn't in there and poked his head in. "Who *you* talkin' to?" he said.

"No one," I said. "Get outta here."

The kid made a face and shut me back in.

"Who was that?" Donnie asked.

"Some asshole," I said. I didn't say anything else. Donnie sniffed in like he was doing a line of something.

"You wanna talk to Daddy?" he said. He was four years older but he still used words like that.

"Yeah, put him on," I said. You couldn't talk to him for five minutes? I thought to myself.

He put his hand over the receiver. Things went on on the other end, muffled. "Hey there," my father finally said.

"Hey," I said back. There was some dead air.

"What's up?" my father said.

"Not much," I said. I'd planned on my father being alone. I don't know why. My brother never went out. "Just callin'."

I was rubbing my knuckles hard over the cork next to the phone's coin box. Pieces were scrolling off as if from an eraser. "How's the money holding out?" my father said. Donnie made a comment behind him.

"Is he standing right next to you?" I asked.

"Yeah. Why?" my father said, instantly more alert. When I was little and I wanted his attention I just mentioned a problem with Donnie. By college it had gotten to the point that hashing over worries about my brother was pretty much it in terms of contact with my parents.

"I wanted to ask you something," I said.

"Is there something I should know about?" he said. Donnie was always doing things that we kept from him because he got so upset.

"Nothin' big. Maybe I should call back," I said.

"Awright. I'll see you," he said. It was a code we'd worked before.

"Short call," I heard Donnie say before my father hung up.

When my father called back, we went over the physiological thing again. I'd run this by him before. We thought drug therapy might be a possible way out.

I could see the blowups coming in Donnie's eyes. I could see the redness. And I usually didn't stop whatever I was doing to help them come on.

The problem was that Donnie had had drug therapy, back in the Dawn of Time, in 1969. Who knew anything? Various combinations of doctors tried various combinations of drugs. Most of the drugs had humiliating side effects. My brother became a master at lying to the doctors about what he'd taken and what he'd squirreled away, further confusing the issue. He came out eight months later as one of the Yale–New Haven Institute's complete failures—"We throw up our hands with him," the resident told my parents—and with a loathing even for Bufferin.

"In Géricault's paintings, suffering and death, battle frenzy, and madness amount to nature itself, for nature in the end is formless and destructive."

But really: How helpful are we going to find art history prose as an interpretive model?

We called the police six times on him. After high school I was home only a few weeks a year—the World Traveler, my father called me, caustically—yet I'd been home four of the six times we had to call the police. My father mentioned the coincidence.

While my brother was in a holding pen in New Orleans I received my B.S. from Swarthmore in geological engineering. While he was touring youth hostels on the East Coast on my father's dole, keeping to himself, a dour man in his late twenties surrounded by happy groups of much-younger Europeans, I was getting my Ph.D. in geology from Johns Hopkins. He had a scramble of fine black hair that he almost never combed. He wore pastel polyester tank tops long after even Kmart shoppers had abandoned them. He had a little gut, which he accentuated by tucking in his shirts and wearing too-tight pants without belts. While he was giving night school a shot in Florida I was mapping the geology of Mount Rainier. The fall he spent going through his old things at my parents' house and getting his baseball card collection sorted out, I spent crawling around ancient volcanoes in equatorial East Africa. The third time my parents had to call the police on him I was in a little boat in the Sunda Strait, getting my first look at Krakatau.

What were my parents supposed to do? They never went to college, and just wanted their sons comfortable and reasonably happy. A steady job in a stable business would have been nice. Instead one son disappeared into the academic ionosphere: I had to literally write down *postdoctoral fellow* so my mother could pull it out of her wallet and say it for people. She asked me to. They had a copy of *Volcanoes of the World* around the house, with my name listed among the fourteen junior authors contributing. My mother would say, "Here's his book." And their older son dropped out of high school because, as he put it, he was "being stared at." If I was hard to explain, my brother was impossible to explain.

For relatives the etiquette was to ask about the younger one and then move on to the older one. I was never around and always doing well. He was always around and never doing well. Yes, doctors had seen him, and yes, he was clearly disturbed, but no one had a diagnosis, and as far as their ability to present him as a coherent story went, he operated in that maddening middle ground: too disturbed to function and not disturbed enough to be put away.

The first time we called the police because he threw me down the stairs. I was twelve, and he'd dropped out of high school the month before. We'd been arguing about sports, matching feats of memory by reciting NFL championship scores ("1963, fourteen–ten; 1964, twenty-seven–zero; 1965, twenty-three–thirteen"), and he'd heard the contempt in my voice. He'd been livid and my father's mediation attempts had consisted of stepping between us and shouting for my brother to go upstairs. He had, finally, shouting abuse the whole time about my privileged and protected status, and for once I thought I wasn't going to back down and went up after him, as homicidal as he was. At the top of the stairs I jabbed a finger in his chest. Shouting was going on. I watched his face move into some new area of energy. He lifted me up. My feet kicked above the risers like a toddler's, and then he threw me. I caught the banister with my hands and landed on my elbow and side. The stairs were carpeted. I got up, unhurt. "Play with pain," he shouted down the stairs at me. "Play with pain."

"You're gonna kill them both," I screamed up at him, pulling out the ultimate weapon, his guilt. I said it so they could hear. "They're gonna kill *me*," he screamed back.

My mother, father, and I sat around the kitchen table after the police had taken him away. The policeman had been awkward and embarrassed and stood around Donnie's room while Donnie packed a little blue duffel in silence. We could hear the creaks in the floorboards above us as the policeman shifted his weight from foot to foot. The routine was that the police would drive him to the bus station and tell him he couldn't come back for a while. Then the police would come back and talk to us. While we waited for that, my mother would outline the fatal mistakes my father had made raising my brother.

We were three co-conspirators each operating with a different plan. My mother's theory was that special treatment was his undoing. My father's theory was that explosions could be avoided if everyone did their utmost to work around him. My theory was that something cyclical and inexorable was going on, and that one way or another, sooner or later, he had to go off.

That night my father had taken as much abuse as he was able to. He shouted at both of us, "You can't treat him like a normal human being; you can't keep baiting him." He said, "It's like having a dog on a chain. You don't keep sticking fingers in his mouth." Then he said to me, "And your situation doesn't help."

What my father meant was that just by being alive I made my brother's life harder. In Donnie's eyes I was proof that whatever had happened to him—genetically, environmentally, whatever—hadn't been inevitable. One of his consolations had always been that something in the alchemy of the parenting he'd gotten had been so lethal that he had had to turn out the way he did. But I was the problem with that theory, because if that was true, then why wasn't the kid (he called me the kid) affected?

Whatever I achieved threw the mess he'd made of his life into sharper relief. He went to Catholic school and it ruined him; I went to Catholic school and got good grades.

He was always shy and turned out to need hospitalization; I was always shy and turned out to be bookish.

At one point in Pompano Beach, he took a job as a dishwasher at a Bob's Big Boy. My mother's first response when she heard was to congratulate him. Her second was to remark that she thought they had machines for that now. That same day he went into work and the day manager was chatting him up. The day manager asked if he had any brothers or sisters. The day manager asked what his brother did. "He's a rocket scientist," Donnie said, up to his elbows in suds, thirty-eight years old.

My thesis adviser at Johns Hopkins always ate Fudgsicles while he looked over my work. All the charts and text he handled turned up with chocolate thumbprints. Slurping away, flipping through the data, he liked to ask, "What is it with you and Krakatoa, anyway?" He meant why was I so driven. He intentionally pronounced it the wrong way. He liked to think of himself as puckish.

The founder of the Smithsonian, James Smithson, explained his institute's interest in the subject this way: "A high interest attaches itself to volcanoes, and their ejections. They cease to be local phenomena; they become principal elements in the history of our globe; they connect its present with its former condition; and we have good grounds for supposing that in their flames are to be read its future destinies."

I quoted Smithson to my adviser as an answer. He shrugged and took out his Fudgsicle and said, "You can talk to someone like me now or talk to a shrink later."

Pictures came into my head periodically of what my brother must have gone through, on the road. He told me, occasionally, as well. When he traveled the country he stayed at youth hostels because they were so much cheaper, but he paid a price for it: he was pathological about his privacy, and there he had none. In Maine an older woman asked him about his hair. It was falling out. At Gettysburg some teenaged Germans took him out, got him drunk, and asked if he was attracted to one of the prettier girls in the group. Assuming that some sort of positive sexual fantasy was finally about to happen to him, he said yes, at which point they all laughed. He said he woke up the next morning near the site of Pickett's charge. A middle-aged couple with a video camera stood nearby, filming him alongside the stone wall.

The last time I was home he was on the road. We'd timed it that way. I spent one late night going through a family album that my mother was putting together in a spasm of masochism and love. Looking back over pictures of my brother developing year by year, his expressions progressively more closed off and miserable, brought back to me powerfully the first time I saw the sequence of photos tracking the birth of Paricutin, the Mexican volcano that grew from a tiny vent cone in a farmer's field.

The postdoctoral fellowship involved part-time work for SEAN, the Scientific Event Alert Network, which was designed to keep the geological and geophysical communities in touch about active volcanoes throughout the world. I compiled and cross-referenced known data about older eruptions so that it could be manipulated for studies of recent and expected volcanism. Which was where all my work on Krakatau came in.

My thesis adviser had been the first to point out that I'd developed what people in the field call a bias. I had a heightened appreciation for the value of eyewitness accounts. I always leaned toward the catastrophists' viewpoint that while the ordinary eruptions needed to be documented, the complete cataclysms had the real answers; they were the ones that had to be milked for all they could yield. "What do we have here?" my adviser would say wearily as he picked up another new batch of text. "More scream-ers?" *Screamer* was his term for Krakatau eyewitnesses. He called their rough calculations, made under what geolo-gists would laconically call stressful situations, "Fay Wray calculations."

And yet, often enough for me, working backward from a dispassionate scientific measurement—the tidal gauges at Jakarta, say—I'd be able to corroborate one more eyewit-ness account.

In my dumpy carrel at the grad library I had narrowed the actual subject of my thesis down to the precise causes of the Krakatau tsunamis that swamped Java and Sumatra. This was a reasonably controversial topic. There were all sorts of wave-forming mechanisms, all of which could have operated to some extent at Krakatau. The problem was to understand which mechanism was the dominant one. The expectation was not so much that I would find a solution to the problem as add something intelligent to the debate.

The first two years I worked eighteen-plus hours a day. I never got home, almost never talked to my family. Crises came and went; what did I care? I combed everything: the Library of Congress, the National Archives, the U.S. Geological Survey, the Smithsonian Library, the British Museum, the Royal Society of London, the Royal Institute for the Tropics, the Volcanological Survey of Indonesia, the *Bulletin Volcanologique*. I needed more help than any-one else on earth. And I turned out to possess the height of scientific naiveté. I believed everyone I read. Everyone sounded so reasonable. Everyone's figures looked so unassailable. I was a straw in the wind. I labored through

Verbeek's original monograph from 1885 as well as later papers by Wharton, Yokoyama, and Latter. At one point my adviser told me with exasperation, "Hey, know what? It's not likely that everyone's right." I incorporated this into my text. I wrote, "Nevertheless, it is safe to assume that all of these contradictory theories cannot be accurate."

I uncovered a few things. I turned up a few photographs of the devastation from as early as 1886. I tracked down some math errors in the computations of the air waves. Then, in 1983, the centennial year of the eruption, everything I'd done was surpassed, the dugout canoe swamped by the *Queen Mary*: the Smithsonian published *Krakatau 1883: The Volcanic Eruption and Its Effects*, providing me with 456 phone-book-sized pages to pore over. It would have been my fantasy book, if I hadn't already sunk two years into a thesis.

Everything had to be retooled. My new topic became this baggy, reactive thing that just got me through, something along the lines of "This Big New Book: Is It Almost Completely the Last Word?" The answer was yes.

I had a Career Crisis. My personal hygiene suffered. I stared openmouthed out windows. I sat around inert most mornings, working my way through tepid coffee and caramels for breakfast. I faced for the first time the stunning possibility that everything I touched was not going to turn to gold.

My mother called to see how I was doing. I put on a brave front. She called back the next day and said, "I told your brother you weren't doing so well."

"What'd he say?" I asked.

"Nothing," she said.

"I'm worried I'm gonna end up like him," I joked.

We heard a click on the line. "Uh-oh," my mother said.

A week later my brother sent me *Krakatoa, East of Java*. He'd taped it off a disaster film festival and mailed it in a box wrapped in all directions with duct tape. Maximilian Schell, Rossano Brazzi, Brian Keith: that kind of movie. What my brother remembered was that the second half of the film— the eruption itself, and the tidal waves that followed—was the really unendurable part, and always had been for me, ever since I sat through its sorry cheesiness with him when I was thirteen years old.

He didn't include a note with it, and he didn't have to: it was exactly his sense of humor, with the aggression directed everywhere at once.

Even my brother, in other words, had seen through the schematic of my private metaphor and knew the answer to my adviser's question: Why is he obsessed with volcanoes? Because they go off, regardless of what anyone can do. And because, when they do go off, it's no one's fault. Volcanology: the science of standing around and cataloging the devastation.

My father discouraged my brother from visiting me, wherever I was. He did it for my benefit, and my brother's. He was the peacemaker, he thought; if he wasn't around, anything could happen. My brother didn't particularly enjoy visiting me—anything new in my life seemed to cause him to take stock of his—but he had few places to go. Occasionally he'd call, with my father in the room, and drop a hint. My father would hear the hint and intervene in the background. The excuse he always came up with—I was too busy, I had all this work, this was a bad time for me to be receiving visitors— could not have helped my brother. But if he wanted to keep us apart, what else could he say? My brother was too busy?

"This isn't the greatest time anyway," I'd say. "What about around Thanksgiving? What're you doing around Thanksgiving?"

Knowing full well that the tiniest lack of enthusiasm would destroy whatever chance there was that he'd work up the courage to visit.

Donnie was sixteen when we went through family counseling. He'd been out of high school two months, and had had three jobs: landscaping, freight handling for UPS, and working construction. The construction work was for an uncle who owned a company. We'd had our first incident involving the police. That was how my father referred to it. I was twelve. I had relatively little to do during the sessions. I conceived of the time as an opportunity to prove to this psychiatrist that it wasn't all my parents' fault, what had happened. I acted normal.

Donnie called my father the Mediator. The shrink asked what he meant by that. Donnie said, "Mediator. You know. Zookeeper. What the fuck." It was the "What the fuck" that broke my heart.

Even then I had a mouth on me, as my mother would say. Christmas Eve we watched the Roddy McDowall–David Hartman version of *Miracle on 34th Street*, a version my brother hadn't seen but insisted was the best one. It was on for four minutes before it was clear to everyone in the room that it was terrible. Which made my brother all the more adamant in his position. The holidays were hard on him. We'd given up on the family counseling a few weeks before, as if to get ready for Christmas.

In the movie Sebastian Cabot did a lot of eye-twinkle stuff, whatever the situation. I made relentless fun of it. I mimicked Cabot's accent and asked if Santa came from England, stuff like that. I was rolling. Even my father was snickering. Roddy McDowall launched into something on the spirit of Christmas and I said it sounded like he was more interested in getting to know some of the elves. Donnie took the footstool in front of him and smashed the TV tube. That was the second time we had to call the police.

They took him to the Bridgeport bus station, 8:30 at night on Christmas Eve. The two cops who came to the house wanted to leave him with us, but he wouldn't calm down. One cop told him, "If you don't lighten up we're gonna have to get you out of here and *keep* you out of here," so Donnie started in on what he was going to do to each one of us as soon as the cop took off: "First I'm gonna break *his* fucking neck, and then *her* fucking neck, and then *his* fucking neck." Stuff like that. It was raining, and when they led him out, he had on a New York Jets windbreaker and no hat.

My father drove down to the bus station a half hour later to see if he was still there. The roads were frozen and it took him an hour to get back. My mother vacuumed up the glass from the picture tube. Then she sat in her bedroom with the little TV, flipping back and forth from *A Christmas Carol* to the Mass at St. Peter's.

When my father got back he made some tea and wandered the house. I remembered the nuns talking about the capacities of Christ's love and thought, What kind of reptile *are* you? I was filled with wonder at myself.

I finally went to midnight Mass, alone. My mother just waved me off when I asked if she wanted to go. I found myself once I got there running through a fractured Catechism, over and over: Who loves us? We love us. Who does this to us? We do this to ourselves. Whose victims are we? We are our own victims.

The next morning I was supposed to come downstairs and open presents.

Around noon we gathered in front of the tree with our coffee. I suppose we were hoping Donnie was going to come back. I opened the smallest present in my pile, a Minnesota Vikings coffee mug, and said, "That's great, thanks," and my parents' faces were so desolate that we quit right there.

He called from the bus station on the twenty-seventh. He opened one or two of his presents a week after that. The rest stayed where they were even after the tree came down. Some of them my mother gave the next year to our cousins. We never put tags on our presents; we just told each other who they belonged to.

The third time they had to call the police I was fourteen thousand miles away, fulfilling my dream, standing on what was left of Krakatau. I brought back pieces of pumice for everybody. Donnie had called my mother's sisters whores, and she'd slapped him, and he'd knocked her to the kitchen floor. When he was going full tilt he tried everything verbally until something clicked. He was thirty-four then and she was sixty. My father left his eggs frying at the stove and started wrestling with him. He was sixty-three. My brother let him wrestle.

From page 5 of my thesis: "Early theories explaining the size of the Krakatau explosion held that millions of tons of rock had unfortunately formed a kind of plug, so that pressure-relieving venting was not allowed, making the final detonations all the more cataclysmic. But in fact the opposite might also have been true: gas fluxing of the conduits and the release of pressure through massive cracks may have hastened the catastrophe, since once the vents were opened, the eruption might have grown, as deeper and hotter layers of magma were tapped, leading to the exhaustion of the reservoir, and following that, the collapse of its roof."

My adviser had written in the margin: "Anything new here?"

I had three reasons for my own passivity: selfishness, cowardice, and resentment.

As Donnie got older the anger inside him was not decreasing but increasing. His rage was driven by humiliation, and year by year he felt his situation—forty-one and living at home, unemployed, forty-two and living at home, unemployed—to be more and more humiliating. The friends-and-family question "So what are you up to?"—fraught when he was eighteen—was when he was forty suffused with subtextual insult. His violence was more serious. His threats were more pointed. He defined himself more and more as a misfit, and more and more he seemed to think that the gesture that was going to be necessary to redeem such a life, with each passing day, needed to be grander, more radical.

He was forty-two. I was thirty-eight, two hours away, mostly out of contact, and all of my failures with him were focused in one weekend that summer, when, despite everything, he visited. We spent two days circling each other, watching sports and old movies and making fun of what we saw. His last night there he told me about some of his fantasies. One of them ended with, "They'd *think* they knew what happened, but how could they *prove* it? How could they *prove* anything?" My stomach dropped out.

It was late. I'd turned off the TV. I could see his eyes in the dark.

"Listen," I said. "You've gotta see somebody."

"Don't you think I know that?" he said.

After two late movies he fell asleep face down on the sofa. I went to my office and called Psychological Services at the university. The guy on call gave me a referral number.

"I don't think you understand," I told him. "This isn't a kind of wait-and-see situation."

"Are you saying he should be picked up, for his own good?" the guy said. There was a buzzing on the line while he waited for my answer.

"No," I said.

The next morning my brother was leaving. I stood by my parents' car while he settled into the driver's seat. I told him I had the name of a guy he should talk to. "Thanks," he said.

"You want the name?" I said.

"Sure," he said. I could see his eyes, see a blowup coming on again. This was excruciating for him.

I fumbled around in my pockets. "I don't have a pencil," I said. "You gonna remember?"

"Sure," he said. I told him the name. He nodded, put the car in gear, said goodbye, and backed out of the driveway.

I warned my parents. Which, I thought to myself, would help my conscience later.

Why didn't I help? Why did I stand aside, peering down the rails toward the future site of the train wreck? Because even if he didn't know it, all along, he was the lucky one. Because he was the black sheep, he was the squeaky wheel, he was the engine that generated love from my parents.

I kept hoping that my worst feelings had been left behind in childhood, and that only analysis, diagnosis, remained.

Volcanoes, volcanoes, volcanoes. In a crucial way he didn't resemble volcanoes at all. Most volcanoes look like oceans. Because they're *under* oceans. Nothing happening for hundreds of years. Something destructive surfacing only very very rarely: Who did that *really* sound like?

The first record of explosions came months early, May 20 at 10:55 A.M., when the director of the observatory at Batavia, now Jakarta, noticed vibrations and the banging of loose windows in his house. Explosions brought lighter articles down from the shelves at Anjer. There was this homey little description from the captain of the German warship *Elisabeth*, in the Sunda Strait: "We saw from the island a white cumulus cloud rising fast. After half an hour, it reached a height of 11,000 m. and started to spread, like an umbrella." Or this, from the same ship's marine chaplain, now seventeen nautical miles away: "It was convoluted like a giant coral stock, resembling a club or cauliflower head, except that everything was in imposing gigantic internal motion, driven by enormous pressure from beneath. Slowly it became clear that the top of the entire continuously growing phenomenon was beginning to lean towards us."

Or this, from a telegraph master on the Java coast: "I remained at the office the whole morning and then went for a meal, intending to return at two. I met another man near the beach, and we remained there for a few minutes. Krakatau was already in eruption, and we plainly heard the rumbling in the distance. I observed an alternate rising and falling of the sea, and asked my companion whether the tide was ebbing or flowing. He remarked that it seemed to be getting unusually dark."

Or this, from the captain of the Irish steamer *Charles Bal*: "At 2:30 we noticed some agitation about the point of Krakatau, clouds or something being propelled from the NE point with great velocity. At 3:00 we heard all around and above us the sounds of a mighty artillery barrage, getting evermore furious and alarming; and the matter, whatever it was, was being propelled with even more velocity to the NE. It looked like a blinding rain, a furious moiling squall.

By 4:00 the explosions had joined to form a continuous roar, and darkness had spread across the sky."

And here's what I imagine, from the eyewitnesses who spent those last minutes standing around with their hands in their pockets on the Java coast and Sumatra, from Lampong Bay to Sebesi and all the other islands in the strait:

Some made out an enormous wave in the distance like a mountain rushing onwards, followed by others that seemed greater still.

Some made out a dark black object rising through the gloom, traveling towards the shore like a low range of hills, but they knew there were no hills in that part of the strait.

Some made out a dark line swelling the curve of the horizon, thickening as they watched.

Some heard the roar of the first wave, and the cry "A flood is coming."

Some heard the rushing wind driven before the immense dark wall.

Some heard a whipsawing noise and saw the great black thing a long way off, a cliff of water, trees and houses disappearing beneath it. They felt it through the earth as they ran for sloping ground. They made for the steepest ravines. There was a great crush. Those below climbed the backs of those above. The marks where this took place are still visible. Some of those who washed off must have dragged others down with them. Some must have felt those above giving way, and let go.

But this is the only account hand-copied and tacked to my bulletin board, the testimony of a Dutch pilot caught on shore near Anjer, a city now gone: "The moment of greatest anguish was not the actual destruction of the wave. The worst part by far was afterwards, when I knew I was saved, and the receding flood carried back past me the bodies of friends and neighbors and family. And I remembered clawing past other arms and legs as you might fight through a bramble. And I thought, 'The world is our relentless adversary, rarely outwitted, never tiring.' And I thought, 'I would give all these people's lives, once more, to see something so beautiful again.'"

QUESTIONS

1. Why is the narrator fascinated with Krakatau?

2. When Donnie and the narrator get into a fight before the first police call, why does Donnie yell and repeat, "Play with pain"? (67)

3. What does the narrator mean when he refers to Donnie's guilt as "the ultimate weapon"? (67)

4. Why is the narrator partial to eruption eyewitness, or "screamer," accounts? (71)

5. Why does Donnie send his brother the film *Krakatoa, East of Java*? Why does the narrator find the eruption and aftermath "the really unendurable part"? (73)

6. What does the narrator mean when he asks, "What kind of reptile *are* you?" (75)

7. What is the significance of the last line, quoted from a Krakatau witness: "I would give all these people's lives, once more, to see something so beautiful again"? (81)

FOR FURTHER REFLECTION

1. After the narrator's "Career Crisis," he says, "I faced for the first time the stunning possibility that everything I touched was not going to turn to gold." Is this a necessary and typical realization for most people? Does age make a difference?

2. Is the father right to discourage the brothers from seeing each other?

3. Do you have more sympathy for Donnie or for the narrator?

FAY WELDON

Fay Weldon (1931–) is one of Britain's most prolific and widely read contemporary authors. Since her first novel, *The Fat Woman's Joke* (1967), she has published more than fifty titles, across myriad literary genres. Weldon's writing frequently addresses women's issues and gender politics, and she contends that every woman must ask herself: "What is it that will give me fulfillment?" She sometimes holds women responsible for their own misery, but she also reveals the irreconcilable conflicts between the feminist ideal and the demands that are put on women as friends, lovers, wives, and mothers. Weldon's novel *Praxis* (1978) was shortlisted for the Man Booker Prize for Fiction, and *Wicked Women* (1995) won the PEN/ Macmillan Silver Pen Award.

Weekend

By seven-thirty they were ready to go. Martha had everything packed into the car and the three children appropriately dressed and in the back seat, complete with educational games and whole-wheat biscuits. When everything was ready in the car Martin would switch off the television, come downstairs, lock up the house, front and back, and take the wheel.

Weekend! Only two hours' drive down to the cottage on Friday evenings: three hours' drive back on Sunday nights. The pleasures of greenery and guests in between. They reckoned themselves fortunate, how fortunate!

On Fridays Martha would get home on the bus at six-twelve and prepare tea and sandwiches for the family: Then she would strip four beds and put the sheets and quilt covers in the washing machine for Monday; take the country bedding from the airing basket, plus the books and the games, plus the weekend food—acquired at intervals throughout the week, to lessen the load—plus her own folder of work from the office, plus Martin's drawing materials (she was a market researcher in an advertising agency, he a freelance designer) plus hairbrushes, jeans, spare T-shirts, Jolyon's antibiotics (he suffered from sore throats), Jenny's recorder, Jasper's cassette player and so on—ah, the so on!—and would pack them all, skilfully and quickly, into the boot. Very little could be left in the cottage during the week. ("An open invitation to burglars": Martin.) Then Martha would run round the house tidying and wiping, doing this and that, finding the cat at one neighbour's and delivering it to another, while the others ate their tea; and would usually, proudly, have everything finished by the time they had eaten their fill. Martin would just catch the BBC2 news, while Martha cleared away the tea table and the children tossed up for the best positions in the car. "Martha," said Martin, tonight, "you ought to get Mrs. Hodder to do more. She takes advantage of you."

Mrs. Hodder came in twice a week to clean. She was over seventy. She charged two pounds an hour. Martha paid her out of her own wages: Well, the running of the house was Martha's concern. If Martha chose to go out to work—as was her perfect right, Martin allowed, even though it wasn't the best thing for the children, but that must be Martha's moral responsibility—Martha must surely pay her domestic stand-in. An evident truth, heard loud and clear and frequent in Martin's mouth and Martha's heart.

"I expect you're right," said Martha. She did not want to argue. Martin had had a long, hard week, and now had to drive. Martha couldn't. Martha's license had been suspended four months back for drunken driving. Everyone agreed that the suspension was unfair: Martha seldom drank to excess; she was for one thing usually too busy pouring drinks for other people or washing other people's glasses to get much inside herself. But Martin had taken her out to dinner on her birthday, as was his custom, and exhaustion and excitement mixed had made her imprudent, and before she knew where she was, why, there she was, in the dock, with a distorted lamppost to pay for and a new bonnet for the car and six months' suspension.

So now Martin had to drive her car down to the cottage, and he was always tired on Fridays, and hot and sleepy on

Sundays, and every rattle and clank and bump in the engine she felt to be somehow her fault.

Martin had a little sports car for London and work: it could nip in and out of the traffic nicely; Martha's was an old estate car, with room for the children, picnic baskets, bedding, food, games, plants, drink, portable television and all the things required by the middle classes for weekends in the country. It lumbered rather than zipped and made Martin angry. He seldom spoke a harsh word, but Martha, after the fashion of wives, could detect his mood from what he did not say rather than what he did, and from the tilt of his head, and the way his crinkly, merry eyes seemed crinklier and merrier still—and of course from the way he addressed Martha's car.

"Come along, you old banger, you! Can't you do better than that? You're too old, that's your trouble. Stop complaining. Always complaining, it's only a hill. You're too wide about the hips. You'll never get through there."

Martha worried about her age, her tendency to complain, and the width of her hips. She took the remarks personally. Was she right to do so? The children noticed nothing: It was just funny, lively, laughing Daddy being witty about Mummy's car. Mummy, done for drunken driving. Mummy, with the roots of melancholy somewhere deep beneath the bustling, busy, everyday self. Busy: ah, so busy!

Martin would only laugh if she said anything about the way he spoke to her car and warn her against paranoia. "Don't get like your mother, darling." Martha's mother had, towards the end, thought that people were plotting against her. Martha's mother had led a secluded, suspicious life, and made Martha's childhood a chilly and a lonely time. Life now, by comparison, was wonderful for Martha. People, children, houses, conversations, food, drink, theatres—even, now, a career. Martin standing between her and the hostility of the world—popular, easy, funny Martin, beckoning the rest of the world into earshot.

Ah, she was grateful: little earnest Martha, with her shy ways and her penchant for passing boring exams—how her life had blossomed out! Three children too—Jasper, Jenny, and Jolyon—all with Martin's broad brow and open looks, and the confidence born of her love and care, and the work she had put into them since the dawning of their days.

Martin drives. Martha, for once, drowses.

The right food, the right words, the right play. Doctors for the tonsils: dentists for the molars. Confiscate guns, censor television, encourage creativity. Paints and paper to hand, books on the shelves, meetings with teachers. Music teachers. Dancing lessons. Parties. Friends to tea. School plays. Open days. Junior orchestra.

Martha is jolted awake. Traffic lights. Martin doesn't like Martha to sleep while he drives.

Clothes. Oh, clothes! Can't wear this: Must wear that. Dress shops. Piles of clothes in corners: duly washed, but waiting to be ironed, waiting to be put away.

Get the piles off the floor, into the laundry baskets. Martin doesn't like a mess.

Creativity arises out of order, not chaos. Five years off work while the children were small: back to work with seniority lost. What, did you think something was for nothing? If you have children, mother, that is your reward. It lies not in the world.

Have you taken enough food? Always hard to judge.

Food. Oh, food! Shop in the lunch hour. Lug it all home. Cook for the freezer on Wednesday evenings while Martin is at his car-maintenance evening class, and isn't there to notice you being unrestful. Martin likes you to sit down in the evenings. Fruit, meat, vegetables, flour for homemade bread. Well, shop bread is full of pollutants. Frozen food, even your own, loses flavour. Martin often remarks on it.

Condiments. Everyone loves mango chutney. But the expense!

London Airport to the left. Look, look, children! Concorde? No, idiot, of course it isn't Concorde.

Ah, to be all things to all people: children, husband, employer, friends! It can be done: yes, it can; superwoman.

Drink. Homemade wine. Why not? Elderberries grown thick and rich in London: And at least you know what's in it. Store it in high cupboards: lots of room, up and down the stepladder. Careful! Don't slip. Don't break anything.

No such thing as an accident. Accidents are Freudian slips: they are wilful, bad-tempered things.

Martin can't bear bad temper. Martin likes slim ladies. Diet. Martin rather likes his secretary. Diet. Martin admires slim legs and big bosoms. How to achieve them both? Impossible. But try, oh try, to be what you ought to be, not what you are. Inside and out.

Martin brings back flowers and chocolates: whisks Martha off for holiday weekends. Wonderful! The best husband in the world: look into his crinkly, merry, gentle eyes; see it there. So the mouth slopes away into something of a pout. Never mind. Gaze into the eyes. Love. It must be love. You married him. *You*. Surely *you* deserve true love?

Salisbury Plain. Stonehenge. Look, children, look! Mother, we've seen Stonehenge a hundred times. Go back to sleep.

Cook! Ah, cook. People love to come to Martin and Martha's dinners. Work it out in your head in the lunch hour. If you get in at six-twelve, you can seal the meat while you beat the egg white while you feed the cat while you lay the table while you string the beans while you set out the cheese, goat's cheese, Martin loves goat's cheese, Martha tries to like goat's cheese—oh, bed, sleep, peace, quiet.

Sex! Ah, sex. Orgasm please. Martin requires it. Well, so do you. And you don't want his secretary providing a passion you neglected to develop. Do you? Quick, quick, the cosmic bond. Love. Married love.

Secretary! Probably a vulgar suspicion: nothing more. Probably a fit of paranoics, à la mother, now dead and gone.

At peace.

R.I.P.

Chilly, lonely mother, following her suspicions where they led.

Nearly there, children. Nearly in paradise, nearly at the cottage. Have another biscuit.

Real roses round the door.

Roses. Prune, weed, spray, feed, pick. Avoid thorns. One of Martin's few harsh words.

"Martha, you can't not want roses! What kind of person am I married to? An anti-rose personality?"

Green grass. Oh, God, grass. Grass must be mown. Restful lawns, daisies, bobbing, buttercups glowing. Roses and grass and books. Books.

Please Martin do we have to have the two hundred books, mostly twenties' first editions, bought at Christie's book sale on one of your afternoons off? Books need dusting.

Roars of laughter from Martin, Jasper, Jenny, and Jolyon. Mummy says we shouldn't have the books: Books need dusting!

Roses, green grass, books, and peace.

Martha woke up with a start when they got to the cottage, and gave a little shriek which made them all laugh. Mummy's waking shriek, they called it.

Then there was the car to unpack and the beds to make up, and the electricity to connect, and the supper to make, and the cobwebs to remove, while Martin made the fire. Then supper—pork chops in sweet and sour sauce ("Pork is such a *dull* meat if you don't cook it properly": Martin), green salad from the garden, or such green salad as the rabbits had left ("Martha, did you really net them properly! Be honest now!": Martin), and sauté potatoes. Mash is so stodgy and ordinary, and instant mash unthinkable. The children studied the night sky with the aid of their star map. Wonderful, rewarding children!

Then clear up the supper; set the dough to prove for the bread; Martin already in bed, exhausted by the drive and lighting the fire. ("Martha, we really ought to get the logs stacked properly. Get the children to do it, will you?": Martin.) Sweep and tidy: Get the TV aerial right. Turn up Jasper's jeans where he has trodden the hem undone. ("He can't go around like *that*, Martha. Not even Jasper": Martin.)

Midnight. Good night. Weekend guests arriving in the morning. Seven for lunch and dinner on Saturday. Seven for Sunday breakfast, nine for Sunday lunch. ("Don't fuss, darling. You always make such a fuss": Martin.) Oh, God, forgotten the garlic squeezer. That means ten minutes with the back of a spoon and salt. Well, who wants *lumps* of garlic? No one. Not Martin's guests. Martin said so. Sleep.

Colin and Katie. Colin is Martin's oldest friend. Katie is his new young wife. Janet, Colin's other, earlier wife, was Martha's friend. Janet was rather like Martha, quieter and duller than her husband. A nag and a drag, Martin rather thought, and said, and of course she'd let herself go, everyone agreed. No one exactly excused Colin for walking out, but you could see the temptation.

Katie versus Janet.

Katie was languid, beautiful, and elegant. She drawled when she spoke. Her hands were expressive: Her feet were little and female. She had no children.

Janet plodded round on very flat, rather large feet. There was something wrong with them. They turned out slightly when she walked. She had two children. She was, frankly, boring. But Martha liked her: When Janet came down to the cottage she would wash up. Not in the way that most guests washed up—washing dutifully and setting everything out on the draining board, but actually drying and putting away too. And Janet would wash the bath and get the children all sat down, with chairs for everyone, even the littlest, and keep them quiet and satisfied so the grownups—well, the men—could get on with their conversation and their jokes and their love of country weekends, while Janet stared into space, as if grateful for the rest, quite happy.

Janet would garden, too. Weed the strawberries, while the men went for their walk; her great feet standing firm and square and sometimes crushing a plant or so, but never mind, oh, never mind. Lovely Janet, who understood.

Now Janet was gone and here was Katie.

Katie talked with the men and went for walks with the men, and moved her ashtray rather impatiently when Martha tried to clear the drinks round it.

Dishes were boring, Katie implied by her manner, and domesticity was boring, and anyone who bothered with that kind of thing was a fool. Like Martha. Ash should be allowed to stay where it was, even if it was in the butter, and conversations should never be interrupted.

Knock, knock. Katie and Colin arrived at one-fifteen on Saturday morning, just after Martha had gotten to bed. "You don't mind? It was the moonlight. We couldn't resist it. You should have seen Stonehenge! We didn't disturb you? Such early birds!"

Martha rustled up a quick meal of omelettes. Saturday nights' eggs. ("Martha makes a lovely omelette": Martin.) ("Honey, make one of your mushroom omelettes: Cook the mushrooms separately, remember, with lemon. Otherwise the water from the mushrooms gets into the egg, and spoils everything.") Sunday supper mushrooms. But ungracious to say anything.

Martin had revived wonderfully at the sight of Colin and Katie. He brought out the whisky bottle. Glasses. Ice. Jug for water. Wait. Wash up another sinkful, when they're finished. 2 A.M.

"Don't do it tonight, darling."

"It'll only take a sec." Bright smile, not a hint of self-pity. Self-pity can spoil everyone's weekend.

Martha knows that if breakfast for seven is to be manageable the sink must be cleared of dishes. A tricky meal, breakfast. Especially if bacon, eggs, and tomatoes must all be cooked in separate pans. ("Separate pans means separate flavours!": Martin.)

She is running around in her nightie. Now if that had been Katie—but there's something so *practical* about Martha. Reassuring, mind; but the skimpy nightie and the broad rump and the thirty-eight years are all rather embarrassing. Martha can see it in Colin and Katie's eyes. Martin's too. Martha wishes she did not see so much in other people's eyes. Her mother did, too. Dear, dead mother. Did I misjudge you?

This was the second weekend Katie had been down with Colin but without Janet. Colin was a photographer: Katie had been his accessoriser. First Colin and Janet; then Colin, Janet, and Katie; now Colin and Katie!

Katie weeded with rubber gloves on and pulled out pansies in mistake for weeds and laughed and laughed along with everyone when her mistake was pointed out to her, but the pansies died. Well, Colin had become with the years fairly rich and fairly famous, and what does a fairly rich and famous man want with a wife like Janet when Katie is at hand?

On the first of the Colin/Janet/Katie weekends Katie had appeared out of the bathroom. "I say," said Katie, holding out a damp towel with evident distaste, "I can only find this. No hope of a dry one?" And Martha had to run to fetch a dry towel and amazingly found one, and handed it to Katie who flashed her a brilliant smile and said, "I can't bear damp towels. Anything in the world but damp towels," as if speaking to a servant in a time of shortage of staff, and took all the water so there was none left for Martha to wash up.

The trouble, of course, was drying anything at all in the cottage. There were no facilities for doing so, and Martin had a horror of clotheslines which might spoil the view. He toiled and moiled all week in the city simply to get a country view at the weekend. Ridiculous to spoil it by draping it with wet towels! But now Martha had bought more towels, so perhaps everyone could be satisfied. She would take nine damp towels back on Sunday evenings in a plastic bag and see to them in London.

On this Saturday morning, straight after breakfast, Katie went out to the car—she and Colin had a new Lamborghini; hard to imagine Katie in anything duller—and came back waving a new Yves St Laurent towel. "See! I brought my own, darlings."

They'd brought nothing else. No fruit, no meat, no vegetables, not even bread, certainly not a box of chocolates. They'd gone off to bed with alacrity, the night before, and the spare room rocked and heaved: Well, who'd want to do washing up when you could do that, but what about the children? Would they get confused? First Colin and Janet, now Colin and Katie?

Martha murmured something of her thoughts to Martin, who looked quite shocked. "Colin's my best friend. I don't expect him to bring anything," and Martha felt mean. "And good heavens, you can't protect the kids from sex forever; don't be so prudish," so that Martha felt stupid as well. Mean, complaining, and stupid.

Janet had rung Martha during the week. The house had been sold over her head, and she and the children had been moved into a small flat. Katie was trying to persuade Colin to cut down on her allowance, Janet said.

"It does one no good to be materialistic," Katie confided. "I have nothing. No home, no family, no ties, no possessions. Look at me! Only me and a suitcase of clothes." But Katie seemed highly satisfied with the me, and the clothes were stupendous. Katie drank a great deal and became funny. Everyone laughed, including Martha. Katie had been married twice. Martha marvelled at how someone could arrive in their mid-thirties with nothing at all to their name, neither husband, nor children nor property and not mind.

Mind you, Martha could see the power of such helplessness. If Colin was all Katie had in the world, how could

Colin abandon her? And to what? Where would she go? How would she live? Oh, clever Katie.

"My teacup's dirty," said Katie, and Martha ran to clean it, apologising, and Martin raised his eyebrows, at Martha, not Katie.

"I wish *you'd* wear scent," said Martin to Martha, reproachfully. Katie wore lots. Martha never seemed to have time to put any on, though Martin brought her bottle after bottle. Martha leapt out of bed each morning to meet some emergency—meowing cat, coughing child, faulty alarm clock, postman's knock—when was Martha to put on scent? It annoyed Martin all the same. She ought to do more to charm him.

Colin looked handsome and harrowed and younger than Martin, though they were much the same age. "Youth's catching," said Martin in bed that night. "It's since he found Katie." Found, like some treasure. Discovered; something exciting and wonderful, in the dreary world of established spouses.

On Saturday morning Jasper trod on a piece of wood ("Martha, why isn't he wearing shoes? It's too bad": Martin) and Martha took him into the hospital to have a nasty splinter removed. She left the cottage at ten and arrived back at one, and they were still sitting in the sun, drinking, empty bottles glinting in the long grass. The grass hadn't been cut. Don't forget the bottles. Broken glass means more mornings at the hospital. Oh, don't fuss. Enjoy yourself. Like other people. Try.

But no potatoes peeled, no breakfast cleared, nothing. Cigarette ends still amongst old toast, bacon rind, and marmalade. "You could have done the potatoes," Martha burst out. Oh, bad temper! Prime sin. They looked at her in amazement and dislike. Martin too.

"Goodness," said Katie. "Are we doing the whole Sunday lunch bit on Saturday? Potatoes? Ages since I've eaten potatoes. Wonderful!"

"The children expect it," said Martha.

So they did. Saturday and Sunday lunch shone like reassuring beacons in their lives. Saturday lunch, family lunch, fish and chips. ("So much better cooked at home than bought": Martin.) Sunday. Usually roast beef, potatoes, peas, apple pie. Oh, of course. Yorkshire pudding. Always a problem with oven temperatures. When the beef's going slowly, the Yorkshire should be going fast. How to achieve that? Like big bosom and little hips.

"Just relax," said Martin. "I'll cook dinner, all in good time. Splinters always work their own way out: no need to have taken him to hospital. Let life drift over you, my love. Flow with the waves, that's the way."

And Martin flashed Martha a distant, spiritual smile. His hand lay on Katie's slim brown arm, with its many gold bands.

"Anyway, you do too much for the children," said Martin. "It isn't good for them. Have a drink."

So Martha perched uneasily on the step and had a glass of cider, and wondered how, if lunch was going to be late, she would get cleared up and the meat out of the marinade for the rather formal dinner that would be expected that evening. The marinaded lamb ought to cook for at least four hours in a low oven; and the cottage oven was very small, and you couldn't use that and the grill at the same time and Martin liked his fish grilled, not fried. Less cholesterol.

She didn't say as much. Domestic details like this were very boring, and any mild complaint was registered by Martin as a scene. And to make a scene was so ungrateful.

This was the life. Well, wasn't it? Smart friends in large cars and country living and drinks before lunch and roses and bird song—"Don't drink *too* much," said Martin, and told them about Martha's suspended driving license.

The children were hungry so Martha opened them a can of beans and sausages and heated that up. ("Martha, do they have to eat that crap? Can't they wait?" Martin.)

Katie was hungry: She said so, to keep the children in face. She was lovely with children—most children. She did not particularly like Colin and Janet's children. She said so, and he accepted it. He only saw them once a month now, not once a week.

"Let me make lunch," Katie said to Martha. "You do so much, poor thing!"

And she pulled out of the fridge all the things Martha had put away for the next day's picnic lunch part—Camembert cheese and salad and salami—and made a wonderful tomato salad in two minutes and opened the white wine—"Not very cold, darling. Shouldn't it be chilling?"—and had it all on the table in five amazing competent minutes. "That's all we need, darling," said Martin. "You are funny with your fish-and-chip Saturdays! What could be nicer than this? Or simpler?"

Nothing, except there was Sunday's buffet lunch for nine gone, in place of Saturday's fish for six, and would the fish stretch? No. Katie had had quite a lot to drink. She pecked Martha on the forehead. "Funny little Martha," she said. "She reminds me of Janet. I really do like Janet." Colin did not want to be reminded of Janet, and said so. "Darling, Janet's a fact of life," said Katie. "If you'd only think about her more, you might manage to pay her less." And she yawned and stretched her lean, childless body and smiled at Colin with her inviting, naughty little girl eyes, and Martin watched her in admiration.

Martha got up and left them and took a paint pot and put a coat of white gloss on the bathroom wall. The white surface pleased her. She was good at painting. She produced a smooth, even surface. Her legs throbbed. She feared she might be getting varicose veins.

Outside in the garden the children played badminton. They were bad tempered, but relieved to be able to look up and see their mother working, as usual; making their lives for ever better and nicer; organising, planning, thinking ahead, sidestepping disaster, making preparations, like a mother hen, fussing and irritating; part of the natural boring scenery of the world.

On Saturday night Katie went to bed early: She rose from her chair and stretched and yawned and poked her head into the kitchen where Martha was washing saucepans. Colin had cleared the table and Katie had folded the napkins into pretty creases, while Martin blew at the fire, to make it bright. "Good night," said Katie.

Katie appeared three minutes later, reproachfully holding out her Yves St. Laurent towel, sopping wet. "Oh, dear," cried Martha. "Jenny must have washed her hair!" And Martha was obliged to rout Jenny out of bed to rebuke her, publicly, if only to demonstrate that she knew what was right and proper. That meant Jenny would sulk all weekend, and that meant a treat or an outing midweek, or else by the following week she'd be having an asthma attack. "You fuss the children too much," said Martin. "That's why Jenny has asthma." Jenny was pleasant enough to look at, but not stunning. Perhaps she was a disappointment to her father? Martin would never say so, but Martha feared he thought so.

An egg and an orange each child, each day. Then nothing too bad would go wrong. And it hadn't. The asthma was very mild. A calm, tranquil environment, the doctor said. Ah, smile, Martha smile. Domestic happiness depends on you. 21 × 52 oranges a year. Each one to be purchased, carried, peeled and washed up after. And what about potatoes. 12 × 52 pounds a year? Martin liked his potatoes carefully peeled. He couldn't bear to find little cores of black in the mouthful. ("Well, it isn't very nice, is it?": Martin.)

Martha dreamt she was eating coal, by handfuls, and liking it.

Saturday night. Martin made love to Martha three times. Three times? How virile he was, and clearly turned on by the sounds from the spare room. Martin said he loved her. Martin always did. He was a courteous lover; he knew the importance of foreplay. So did Martha. Three times.

Ah, sleep. Jolyon had a nightmare. Jenny was woken by a moth. Martin slept through everything. Martha pottered about the house in the night. There was a moon. She sat at the window and stared out into the summer night for five minutes, and was at peace, and then went back to bed because she ought to be fresh for the morning.

But she wasn't. She slept late. The others went out for a walk. They'd left a note, a considerate note: "Didn't wake you. You looked tired. Had a cold breakfast so as not to make too much mess. Leave everything 'til we get back." But it was ten o'clock, and guests were coming at noon, so she cleared away the bread, the butter, the crumbs, the smears, the jam, the spoons, the spilt sugar, the cereal, the milk (sour by now), and the dirty plates, and swept the floors, and tidied up quickly, and grabbed a cup of coffee, and prepared to make a rice and fish dish, and a chocolate mousse, and sat down in the middle to eat a lot of bread and jam herself. Broad hips. She remembered the office work in her file and knew she wouldn't be able to do it. Martin anyway thought it was ridiculous for her to bring work back at the weekends. "It's your holiday," he'd say. "Why should they impose?" Martha loved her work. She didn't have to smile at it. She just did it.

Katie came back upset and crying. She sat in the kitchen while Martha worked and drank glass after glass of gin and bitter lemon. Katie liked ice and lemon in gin. Martha paid for all the drink out of her wages. It was part of the deal between her and Martin—the contract by which she went out to work. All things to cheer the spirit, otherwise depressed by a working wife and mother, were to be paid for by Martha. Drink, holidays, petrol, outings, puddings, electricity, heating: It was quite a joke between them. It didn't really make any difference: It was their joint money, after all. Amazing how Martha's wages were creeping up, almost to the level of Martin's. One day they would overtake. Then what?

Work, honestly, was a piece of cake.

Anyway, poor Katie was crying. Colin, she'd discovered, kept a photograph of Janet and the children in his wallet. "He's not free of her. He pretends he is, but he isn't. She has him by a stranglehold. It's the kids. His bloody kids. Moaning Mary and that little creep Joanna. It's all he thinks about. I'm nobody."

But Katie didn't believe it. She knew she was somebody, all right. Colin came in, in a fury. He took out the photograph and set fire to it, bitterly, with a match. Up in smoke they went. Mary and Joanna and Janet. The ashes fell on the floor. (Martha swept them up when Colin and Katie had gone. It hardly seemed polite to do so when they were still there.) "Go back to her," Katie said. "Go back to her. I don't care. Honestly, I'd rather be on my own. You're a nice old-fashioned thing. Run along then. Do your thing, I'll do mine. Who cares?"

"Christ, Katie, the fuss! She only just happens to be in the photograph. She's not there on purpose to annoy. And I do feel bad about her. She's been having a hard time."

"And haven't you, Colin? She twists a pretty knife, I can tell you. Don't you have rights too? Not to mention me. Is a little loyalty too much to expect?"

They were reconciled before lunch, up in the spare room. Harry and Beryl Elder arrived at twelve-thirty. Harry didn't like to hurry on Sundays; Beryl was flustered with apologies for their lateness. They'd brought artichokes from their garden. "Wonderful," cried Martin. "Fruits of the earth? Let's have a wonderful soup! Don't fret, Martha. I'll do it."

"Don't fret." Martha clearly hadn't been smiling enough. She was in danger, Martin implied, of ruining everyone's weekend. There was an emergency in the garden very shortly—an elm tree which had probably got Dutch elm disease—and Martha finished the artichokes. The lid flew off the blender and there was artichoke puree everywhere. "Let's have lunch outside," said Colin. "Less work for Martha."

Martin frowned at Martha: He thought the appearance of martyrdom in the face of guests to be an unforgivable offence.

Everyone happily joined in taking the furniture out, but it was Martha's experience that nobody ever helped to bring it in again. Jolyon was stung by a wasp. Jasper sneezed and sneezed from hay fever and couldn't find the tissues and he wouldn't use loo paper. ("Surely you remembered the tissues, darling?": Martin.)

Beryl Elder was nice. "Wonderful to eat out," she said, fetching the cream for her pudding, while Martha fished a fly from the liquefying Brie—("You shouldn't have bought it so ripe, Martha": Martin)—"except it's just some other woman has to do it. But at least it isn't *me*." Beryl worked too, as a secretary, to send the boys to boarding school, where she'd rather they weren't. But her husband was from a rather grand family, and she'd been only a typist when he married her, so her life was a mass of amends, one way or another. Harry had lately opted out of the stockbroking rat race and become an artist, choosing integrity rather than money, but that choice was his alone and couldn't of course be inflicted on the boys.

Katie found the fish and rice dish rather strange, toyed at it with her fork, and talked about Italian restaurants she knew. Martin lay back soaking in the sun: crying, "Oh, this is the life." He made coffee, nobly, and the lid flew off the grinder and there were coffee beans all over the kitchen, expecially in amongst the row of cookery books which Martin gave Martha Christmas by Christmas. At least they didn't have to be brought back every weekend. ("The burglars won't have the sense to steal those": Martin.)

Beryl fell asleep and Katie watched her, quizzically. Beryl's mouth was open and she had a lot of fillings, and her ankles were thick and her waist was going, and she didn't look after herself. "I love women," sighed Katie.

"They look so wonderful asleep. I wish I could be an earth mother."

Beryl woke with a start and nagged her husband into going home, which he clearly didn't want to do, so didn't. Beryl thought she had to get back because his mother was coming round later. Nonsense! Then Beryl tried to stop Harry drinking more homemade wine and was laughed at by everyone. He was driving, Beryl couldn't, and he did have a nasty scar on his temple from a previous road accident. Never mind.

"She does come on strong, poor soul," laughed Katie when they'd finally gone. "I'm never going to get married"—and Colin looked at her yearningly because he wanted to marry her more than anything in the world, and Martha cleared the coffee cups.

"Oh don't *do* that," said Katie, "do just sit *down*, Martha, you make us all feel bad," and Martin glared at Martha who sat down and Jenny called out for her and Martha went upstairs and Jenny had started her first period and Martha cried and cried and knew she must stop because this must be a joyous occasion for Jenny or her whole future would be blighted, but for once, Martha couldn't.

Her daughter Jenny: wife, mother, friend.

QUESTIONS

1. Are we meant to admire Martha or feel sorry for her? Does Katie envy her or pity her?

2. According to the story, is Martha to blame for her own domestic drudgery?

3. Why does Martin invite Colin and Katie to come for the weekend?

4. Would Martin like Martha to be more like Katie?

5. Why does Martha put up with Martin? Why does she cry when Jenny's first period starts?

6. Why does Katie peck Martha on the forehead and say, "Funny little Martha. . . . She reminds me of Janet. I really do like Janet"? (97)

7. Why is it "quite a joke" between Martha and Martin that they have a "contract by which she went out to work," so that Martha must pay for specific comforts and necessities? (99) If Martha has to pay for certain things, why doesn't Martin do his share around the house?

8. Why does Katie tell Colin that she's never going to get married?

FOR FURTHER REFLECTION

1. Is it possible for a woman to combine a successful career with a fulfilling family life?

2. Why do some women stay in unequal or abusive relationships even if they are financially independent?

3. Who determines more the relationships in marriage—men or women?

Anger

JOHN CHEEVER

Born in Quincy, Massachusetts, John Cheever (1912–1982) sold his first short story to the *New Republic* at the age of seventeen. During his career he published most of his fiction in the *New Yorker*, and his collection *The Stories of John Cheever* (1978) earned the Pulitzer Prize for fiction. He also wrote five novels, including *The Wapshot Chronicle* (1957), which won the National Book Award. In his stories, Cheever explores the human tendencies toward both self-loathing and self-deception, all the while imbuing his characters—generally successful, suburban, white commuters—with the desire for aesthetic and spiritual wholeness. Nearly destroyed by alcoholism, Cheever stopped drinking in 1975. Toward the end of his life, he summed up what his writing was about: "Literature is the only continuous and coherent account of our struggle to be illustrious, a monument of aspiration, a vast pilgrimage."

Torch Song

After Jack Lorey had known Joan Harris in New York for a few years, he began to think of her as the Widow. She always wore black, and he was always given the feeling, by a curious disorder in her apartment, that the undertakers had just left. This impression did not stem from malice on his part, for he was fond of Joan. They came from the same city in Ohio and had reached New York at about the same time in the middle thirties. They were the same age, and during their first summer in the city they used to meet after work and drink martinis in places like the Brevoort and Charles', and have dinner and play checkers at the Lafayette.

Joan went to a school for models when she settled in the city, but it turned out that she photographed badly, so after spending six weeks learning how to walk with a book on her head, she got a job as a hostess in a Longchamps. For the rest of the summer she stood by the hat rack, bathed in an intense pink light and the string music of heartbreak, swinging her mane of dark hair and her black skirt as she moved forward to greet the customers. She was then a big, handsome girl with a wonderful voice, and her face, her whole presence, always seemed infused with a gentle and healthy pleasure at her surroundings, whatever they were.

She was innocently and incorrigibly convivial, and would get out of bed and dress at three in the morning if someone called her and asked her to come out for a drink, as Jack often did. In the fall, she got some kind of freshman executive job in a department store. They saw less and less of each other and then for quite a while stopped seeing each other altogether. Jack was living with a girl he had met at a party, and it never occurred to him to wonder what had become of Joan.

Jack's girl had some friends in Pennsylvania, and in the spring and summer of his second year in town he often went there with her for weekends. All of this—the shared apartment in the Village, the illicit relationship, the Friday-night train to a country house—was what he had imagined life in New York to be, and he was intensely happy. He was returning to New York with his girl one Sunday night on the Lehigh line. It was one of those trains that move slowly across the face of New Jersey, bringing back to the city hundreds of people, like the victims of an immense and strenuous picnic, whose faces are blazing and whose muscles are lame. Jack and his girl, like most of the other passengers, were overburdened with vegetables and flowers. When the train stopped in Pennsylvania Station, they moved with the crowd along the platform, toward the escalator. As they were passing the wide, lighted windows of the diner, Jack turned his head and saw Joan. It was the first time he had seen her since Thanksgiving, or since Christmas. He couldn't remember.

Joan was with a man who had obviously passed out. His head was in his arms on the table, and an overturned highball glass was near one of his elbows. Joan was shaking his shoulders gently and speaking to him. She seemed to be vaguely troubled, vaguely amused. The waiters had cleared off all the other tables and were standing around Joan, waiting for her to resurrect her escort. It troubled Jack to see in these straits a girl who reminded him of the trees and the lawns of his home town, but there was nothing he could do to help. Joan continued to shake the man's shoulders, and the crowd pressed Jack past one after another of the diner's windows, past the malodorous kitchen, and up the escalator.

He saw Joan again, later that summer, when he was having dinner in a Village restaurant. He was with a new girl, a Southerner. There were many Southern girls in the city that year. Jack and his belle had wandered into the restaurant because it was convenient, but the food was terrible and the place was lighted with candles. Halfway through dinner, Jack noticed Joan on the other side of the room, and when he had finished eating, he crossed the room and spoke to her. She was with a tall man who was wearing a monocle. He stood, bowed stiffly from the waist, and said to Jack, "We are very pleased to meet you." Then he excused himself and headed for the toilet. "He's a count, he's a Swedish count," Joan said. "He's on the radio, Friday afternoons at four-fifteen. Isn't it exciting?" She seemed to be delighted with the count and the terrible restaurant.

Sometime the next winter, Jack moved from the Village to an apartment in the East Thirties. He was crossing Park Avenue one cold morning on his way to the office when he noticed, in the crowd, a woman he had met a few times at Joan's apartment. He spoke to her and asked about his friend. "Haven't you heard?" she said. She pulled a long face. "Perhaps I'd better tell you. Perhaps you can help." She and Jack had breakfast in a drugstore on Madison Avenue and she unburdened herself of the story.

The count had a program called *The Song of the Fiords*, or something like that, and he sang Swedish folk songs. Everyone suspected him of being a fake, but that didn't bother Joan. He had met her at a party and, sensing a soft touch, had moved in with her the following night. About a week later, he complained of pains in his back and said he must have some morphine. Then he needed morphine all the time. If he didn't get morphine, he was abusive and violent. Joan began to deal with those doctors and druggists who peddle dope, and when they wouldn't supply her, she went down to the bottom of the city. Her friends were afraid she would be found some morning stuffed in a drain. She got pregnant. She had an abortion. The count left her and moved to a fleabag near Times Square, but she was so impressed by then with his helplessness, so afraid that he would die without her, that she followed him there and shared his room and continued to buy his narcotics. He abandoned her again, and Joan waited a week for him to return before she went back to her place and her friends in the Village.

It shocked Jack to think of the innocent girl from Ohio having lived with a brutal dope addict and traded with criminals, and when he got to his office that morning, he telephoned her and made a date for dinner that night. He met her at Charles'. When she came into the bar, she seemed as wholesome and calm as ever. Her voice was sweet, and reminded him of elms, of lawns, of those glass arrangements that used to be hung from porch ceilings to tinkle in the summer wind. She told him about the count. She spoke of him charitably and with no trace of bitterness, as if her voice, her disposition, were incapable of registering anything beyond simple affection and pleasure. Her walk, when she moved ahead of him toward their table, was light and graceful. She ate a large dinner and talked enthusiastically about her job. They went to a movie and said goodbye in front of her apartment house.

That winter, Jack met a girl he decided to marry. Their engagement was announced in January and they planned to marry in July. In the spring, he received, in his office mail, an invitation to cocktails at Joan's. It was for a Saturday when his fiancée was going to Massachusetts to visit her parents, and when the time came and he had nothing better to do, he took a bus to the Village. Joan had the same apartment. It was a walkup. You rang the bell above the mailbox in the vestibule and were answered with a death rattle in the lock. Joan lived on the third floor. Her calling card was in a slot in the mailbox, and above her name was written the name Hugh Bascomb.

Jack climbed the two flights of carpeted stairs, and when he reached Joan's apartment, she was standing by the open door in a black dress. After she greeted Jack, she took his arm and guided him across the room. "I want you to meet Hugh, Jack," she said.

Hugh was a big man with a red face and pale-blue eyes. His manner was courtly and his eyes were inflamed with drink. Jack talked with him for a little while and then went over to speak to someone he knew, who was standing by the mantelpiece. He noticed then, for the first time, the indescribable disorder of Joan's apartment. The books were in their shelves and the furniture was reasonably good, but the place was all wrong, somehow. It was as if things had been put in place without thought or real interest, and for the first time, too, he had the impression that there had been a death there recently.

As Jack moved around the room, he felt that he had met the ten or twelve guests at other parties. There was a woman executive with a fancy hat, a man who could imitate Roosevelt, a grim couple whose play was in rehearsal, and a newspaperman who kept turning on the radio for news of the Spanish Civil War. Jack drank martinis and talked with the woman in the fancy hat. He looked out of the window at the backyards and the ailanthus trees and heard, in the distance, thunder exploding off the cliffs of the Hudson.

Hugh Bascomb got very drunk. He began to spill liquor, as if drinking, for him, were a kind of jolly slaughter and he enjoyed the bloodshed and the mess. He spilled whiskey from a bottle. He spilled a drink on his shirt and then tipped over someone else's drink. The party was not quiet, but Hugh's hoarse voice began to dominate the others. He attacked a photographer who was sitting in a corner explaining camera techniques to a homely woman. "What did you come to the party for if all you wanted to do was to sit there and stare at your shoes?" Hugh shouted. "What did you come for? Why don't you stay at home?"

The photographer didn't know what to say. He was not staring at his shoes. Joan moved lightly to Hugh's side. "Please don't get into a fight now, darling," she said. "Not this afternoon."

"Shut up," he said. "Let me alone. Mind your own business." He lost his balance, and in struggling to steady himself, he tipped over a lamp.

"Oh, your lovely lamp, Joan," a woman sighed.

"Lamps!" Hugh roared. He threw his arms into the air and worked them around his head as if he were bludgeoning himself. "Lamps. Glasses. Cigarette boxes. Dishes. They're killing me. They're killing me, for Christ's sake. Let's all go up to the mountains and hunt and fish and live like men, for Christ's sake."

People were scattering as if a rain had begun to fall in the room. It had, as a matter of fact, begun to rain outside. Someone offered Jack a ride uptown, and he jumped at the chance. Joan stood at the door, saying goodbye to her routed friends. Her voice remained soft, and her manner, unlike that of those Christian women who the face of disaster can summon new and formidable sources of composure, seemed genuinely simple. She appeared to be oblivious of the raging drunk at her back, who was pacing up and down, grinding glass into the rug, and haranguing one of the survivors of the party with a story of how he, Hugh, had once gone without food for three weeks.

In July, Jack was married in an orchard in Duxbury, and he and his wife went to West Chop for a few weeks. When they returned to town, their apartment was cluttered with presents, including a dozen after-dinner coffee cups from Joan. His wife sent her the required note, but they did nothing else.

Late in the summer, Joan telephoned Jack at his office and asked if he wouldn't bring his wife to see her; she named an evening the following week. He felt guilty about not having called her, and accepted the invitation. This made his wife angry. She was an ambitious girl who liked a social life that offered rewards, and she went unwillingly to Joan's Village apartment with him.

Written above Joan's name on the mailbox was the name Franz Denzel. Jack and his wife climbed the stairs and were met by Joan at the open door. They went into her apartment and found themselves among a group of people for whom Jack, at least, was unable to find any bearings.

Franz Denzel was a middle-aged German. His face was pinched with bitterness or illness. He greeted Jack and his wife with that elaborate and clever politeness that is intended to make guests feel that they have come too early or too late. He insisted sharply upon Jack's sitting in the chair in which he himself had been sitting, and then went and sat on a radiator. There were five other Germans sitting around the room, drinking coffee. In a corner was another American couple, who looked uncomfortable. Joan passed Jack and his wife small cups of coffee with whipped cream. "These cups belonged to Franz's mother," she said. "Aren't they lovely? They were the only things he took from Germany when he escaped from the Nazis."

Franz turned to Jack and said, "Perhaps you will give us your opinion on the American educational system. That is what we were discussing when you arrived."

Before Jack could speak, one of the German guests opened an attack on the American educational system. The other Germans joined in, and went on from there to describe every vulgarity that had impressed them in American life and to contrast German and American culture generally. Where, they asked one another passionately, could you find in America anything like the Mitropa dining cars, the Black Forest, the pictures in Munich, the music in Bayreuth? Franz and his friends began speaking in German. Neither

Jack nor his wife nor Joan could understand German, and the other American couple had not opened their mouths since they were introduced. Joan went happily around the room, filling everyone's cup with coffee, as if the music of a foreign language were enough to make an evening for her.

Jack drank five cups of coffee. He was desperately uncomfortable. Joan went into the kitchen while the Germans were laughing at their German jokes, and he hoped she would return with some drinks, but when she came back, it was with a tray of ice cream and mulberries.

"Isn't this pleasant?" Franz asked, speaking in English again.

Joan collected the coffee cups, and as she was about to take them back to the kitchen, Franz stopped her.

"Isn't one of those cups chipped?"

"No, darling," Joan said. "I never let the maid touch them. I wash them myself."

"What's that?" he asked, pointing at the rim of one of the cups.

"That's the cup that's always been chipped, darling. It was chipped when you unpacked it. You noticed it then."

"These things were perfect when they arrived in this country," he said.

Joan went into the kitchen and he followed her.

Jack tried to make conversation with the Germans. From the kitchen there was the sound of a blow and a cry. Franz returned and began to eat his mulberries greedily. Joan came back with her dish of ice cream. Her voice was gentle. Her tears, if she had been crying, had dried as quickly as the tears of a child. Jack and his wife finished their ice cream and made their escape. The wasted and unnerving evening enraged Jack's wife, and he supposed that he would never see Joan again.

Jack's wife got pregnant early in the fall, and she seized on all the prerogatives of an expectant mother. She took long naps, ate canned peaches in the middle of the night, and talked about the rudimentary kidney. She chose to see only other couples who were expecting children, and the parties that she and Jack gave were temperate. The baby, a boy, was born in May, and Jack was very proud and happy. The first party he and his wife went to after her convalescence was the wedding of a girl whose family Jack had known in Ohio.

The wedding was at St. James's, and afterward there was a big reception at the River Club. There was an orchestra dressed like Hungarians, and a lot of champagne and Scotch. Toward the end of the afternoon, Jack was walking down a dim corridor when he heard Joan's voice: "Please don't, darling," she was saying. "You'll break my arm. *Please* don't, darling." She was being pressed against the wall by a man who seemed to be twisting her arm. As soon as they saw Jack, the struggle stopped. All three of them were intensely embarrassed. Joan's face was wet and she made an effort to smile through her tears at Jack. He said hello and went on without stopping. When he returned, she and the man had disappeared.

When Jack's son was less than two years old, his wife flew with the baby to Nevada to get a divorce. Jack gave her the apartment and all its furnishings and took a room in a hotel near Grand Central. His wife got her decree in due course, and the story was in the newspapers. Jack had a telephone call from Joan a few days later.

"I'm awfully sorry to hear about your divorce, Jack," she said. "She seemed like *such* a nice girl. But that wasn't what I called you about. I want your help, and I wondered if you could come down to my place tonight around six. It's something I don't want to talk about over the phone."

He went obediently to the Village that night and climbed the stairs. Her apartment was a mess. The pictures and the curtains were down and the books were in boxes. "You moving, Joan?" he asked.

"That's what I wanted to see you about, Jack. First, I'll give you a drink." She made two old-fashioneds. "I'm being evicted, Jack," she said. "I'm being evicted because I'm an immoral woman. The couple who have the apartment downstairs—they're charming people, I've always thought—have told the real estate agent that I'm a drunk and a prostitute and all kinds of things. Isn't that fantastic? This real estate agent has always been so nice to me that I didn't think he'd believe them, but he's canceled my lease, and if I make any trouble, he's threatened to take the matter up with the store, and I don't want to lose my job. This nice real estate agent won't even talk with me anymore. When I go over to the office, the receptionist leers at me as if I were some kind of dreadful woman. Of course, there have been a lot of men here and we sometimes are noisy, but I can't be expected to go to bed at ten every night. Can I? Well, the agent who manages this building has apparently told all the other agents in the neighborhood that I'm an immoral and drunken woman, and none of them will give me an apartment. I went to talk with one man—he seemed to be such a nice old gentleman—and he made me an indecent proposal. Isn't it fantastic? I have to be out of here on Thursday and I'm literally being turned out into the street."

Joan seemed as serene and innocent as ever while she described this scourge of agents and neighbors. Jack listened carefully for some sign of indignation or bitterness or even urgency in her recital, but there was none. He was reminded of a torch song, of one of those forlorn and touching ballads that had been sung neither for him nor for her but for their older brothers and sisters by Marion Harris. Joan seemed to be singing her wrongs.

"They've made my life miserable," she went on quietly. "If I keep the radio on after ten o'clock, they telephone the agent in the morning and tell him I had some kind of orgy here. One night when Philip—I don't think you've met Philip; he's in the Royal Air Force; he's gone back to

England—one night when Philip and some other people were here, they called the police. The police came bursting in the door and talked to me as if I were I don't know what and then looked in the bedroom. If they think there's a man up here after midnight, they call me on the telephone and say all kinds of disgusting things. Of course, I can put my furniture into storage and go to a hotel, I guess. I guess a hotel will take a woman with my kind of reputation, but I thought perhaps you might know of an apartment. I thought—"

It angered Jack to think of this big, splendid girl's being persecuted by her neighbors, and he said he would do what he could. He asked her to have dinner with him, but she said she was busy.

Having nothing better to do, Jack decided to walk uptown to his hotel. It was a hot night. The sky was overcast. On his way, he saw a parade in a dark side street off Broadway near Madison Square. All the buildings in the neighborhood were dark. It was so dark that he could not see the placards the marchers carried until he came to a streetlight. Their signs urged the entry of the United States into the war, and each platoon represented a nation that had been subjugated by the Axis Powers. They marched up Broadway, as he watched, to no music, to no sound but their own steps on the rough cobbles. It was for the most part an army of elderly men and women—Poles, Norwegians, Danes, Jews, Chinese. A few idle people like himself lined the sidewalks, and the marchers passed between them with all the self-consciousness of enemy prisoners. There were children among them dressed in the costumes in which they had, for the newsreels, presented the mayor with a package of tea, a petition, a protest, a constitution, a check, or a pair of tickets. They hobbled through the darkness of the loft neighborhood like a mortified and destroyed people, toward Greeley Square.

In the morning, Jack put the problem of finding an apartment for Joan up to his secretary. She started phoning real estate agents, and by afternoon she had found a couple of available apartments in the West Twenties. Joan called Jack the next day to say that she had taken one of the apartments and to thank him.

Jack didn't see Joan again until the following summer. It was a Sunday evening; he had left a cocktail party in a Washington Square apartment and had decided to walk a few blocks up Fifth Avenue before he took a bus. As he was passing the Brevoort, Joan called to him. She was with a man at one of the tables on the sidewalk. She looked cool and fresh, and the man appeared to be respectable. His name, it turned out, was Pete Bristol. He invited Jack to sit down and join in a celebration. Germany had invaded Russia that weekend, and Joan and Pete were drinking champagne to celebrate Russia's changed position in the war. The three of them drank champagne until it got dark. They had dinner and drank champagne with their dinner. They drank more champagne afterward and then went over to the Lafayette and then to two or three other places. Joan had always been tireless in her gentle way. She hated to see the night end, and it was after three o'clock when Jack stumbled into his apartment. The following morning he woke up haggard and sick, and with no recollection of the last hour or so of the previous evening. His suit was soiled and he had lost his hat. He didn't get to his office until eleven. Joan had already called him twice, and she called him again soon after he got in. There was no hoarseness at all in her voice. She said that she had to see him, and he agreed to meet her for lunch in a seafood restaurant in the Fifties.

He was standing at the bar when she breezed in, looking as though she had taken no part in that calamitous night. The advice she wanted concerned selling her jewelry. Her grandmother had left her some jewelry, and she wanted to raise money on it but didn't know where to go. She took some rings and bracelets out of her purse and showed them to Jack. He said that he didn't know anything about jewelry but that he could lend her some money. "Oh, I couldn't borrow money from you, Jack," she said. "You see, I want to get the money for Pete. I want to help him. He wants to open an advertising agency, and he needs quite a lot to begin with." Jack didn't press her to accept his offer of a loan after that, and the project wasn't mentioned again during lunch.

He next heard about Joan from a young doctor who was a friend of theirs. "Have you seen Joan recently?" the doctor asked Jack one evening when they were having dinner together. He said no. "I gave her a checkup last week," the doctor said, "and while she's been through enough to kill the average mortal—and you'll never know what she's been through—she still has the constitution of a virtuous and healthy woman. Did you hear about the last one? She sold her jewelry to put him into some kind of business, and as soon as he got the money, he left her for another girl, who had a car—a convertible."

Jack was drafted into the army in the spring of 1942. He was kept at Fort Dix for nearly a month, and during this time he came to New York in the evening whenever he could get permission. Those nights had for him the intense keenness of a reprieve, a sensation that was heightened by the fact that on the train in from Trenton women would often press upon him dog-eared copies of *Life* and half-eaten boxes of candy, as though the brown clothes he wore were surely cerements. He telephoned Joan from Pennsylvania Station one night. "Come right over, Jack," she said. "Come right over. I want you to meet Ralph."

She was living in that place in the West Twenties that Jack had found for her. The neighborhood was a slum. Ashcans stood in front of her house, and an old woman was there picking out bits of refuse and garbage and stuffing them into a perambulator. The house in which Joan's apartment was located was shabby, but the apartment itself seemed familiar. The furniture was the same. Joan was the same big, easygoing girl. "I'm so glad you called me," she said. "It's so good to see you. I'll make you a drink. I was having one myself. Ralph ought to be here by now. He promised to take me to dinner." Jack offered to take her to Cavanagh's, but she said that Ralph might come while she was out. "If he doesn't come by nine, I'm going to make myself a sandwich. I'm not really hungry."

Jack talked about the army. She talked about the store. She had been working in the same place for—how long was it? He didn't know. He had never seen her at her desk and he couldn't imagine what she did. "I'm terribly sorry Ralph isn't here," she said. "I'm sure you'd like him. He's not a young man. He's a heart specialist who loves to play the viola." She turned on some lights, for the summer sky had got dark. "He has this dreadful wife on Riverside Drive and four ungrateful children. He—"

The noise of an air-raid siren, lugubrious and seeming to spring from pain, as if all the misery and indecision in the city had been given a voice, cut her off. Other sirens, in distant neighborhoods, sounded, until the dark air was full of their noise. "Let me fix you another drink before I have to turn out the lights," Joan said, and took his glass. She brought the drink back to him and snapped off the lights. They went to the windows, and, as children watch a thunderstorm, they watched the city darken. All the lights nearby went out but one. Air-raid wardens had begun to sound their whistles in the street. From a distant yard came a hoarse shriek of anger. "Put out your lights, you Fascists!" a woman screamed. "Put out your lights, you Nazi Fascist Germans. Turn out your lights. Turn out your lights." The last light went off. They went away from the window and sat in the lightless room.

In the darkness, Joan began to talk about her departed lovers, and from what she said Jack gathered that they had all had a hard time. Nils, the suspect count, was dead. Hugh Bascomb, the drunk, had joined the merchant marine and was missing in the North Atlantic. Franz, the German, had taken poison the night the Nazis bombed Warsaw. "We listened to the news on the radio," Joan said, "and then he went back to his hotel and took poison. The maid found him dead in the bathroom the next morning." When Jack asked her about the one who was going to open an advertising agency, she seemed at first to have forgotten him. "Oh, Pete," she said after a pause. "Well, he was always very sick, you know. He was supposed to go to Saranac, but he kept putting it off and putting it off and—" She stopped talking when she heard steps on the stairs, hoping, he supposed, that it was Ralph, but whoever it was turned at the landing and continued to the top of the house. "I wish Ralph would come," she said, with a sigh. "I want you to meet him." Jack asked her again to go out, but she refused, and when the all clear sounded, he said goodbye.

Jack was shipped from Dix to an infantry training camp in the Carolinas and from there to an infantry division stationed in Georgia. He had been in Georgia three months when he married a girl from the Augusta boarding-house aristocracy. A year or so later, he crossed the continent in a day coach and thought sententiously that the last he might see of the country he loved was the desert towns like Barstow, that the last he might hear of it was the ringing of the trolleys on the Bay Bridge. He was sent into the Pacific and returned to the United States twenty months later, uninjured and apparently unchanged. As soon as he received his furlough, he went to Augusta. He presented his wife with the souvenirs he had brought from the islands, quarreled violently with her and all her family, and, after making arrangements for her to get an Arkansas divorce, left for New York.

Jack was discharged from the army at a camp in the East a few months later. He took a vacation and then went back to the job he had left in 1942. He seemed to have picked up his life at approximately the moment when it had been interrupted by the war. In time, everything came to look and feel the same. He saw most of his old friends. Only two of the men he knew had been killed in the war. He didn't call Joan, but he met her one winter afternoon on a cross-town bus.

Her fresh face, her black clothes, and her soft voice instantly destroyed the sense—if he had ever had such a sense—that anything had changed or intervened since their last meeting, three or four years ago. She asked him up for cocktails and he went to her apartment the next Saturday afternoon. Her room and her guests reminded him of the parties she had given when she had first come to New York. There was woman with a fancy hat, an elderly doctor, and a man who stayed close to the radio, listening for news from the Balkans. Jack wondered which of the men belonged to Joan and decided on an Englishman who kept coughing into a handkerchief that he pulled out of his sleeve. Jack was right. "Isn't Stephen brilliant?" Joan asked him a little later, when they were alone in a corner. "He knows more about the Polynesians than anyone else in the world."

Jack had returned not only to his old job but to his old salary. Since living costs had doubled and since he was paying alimony to two wives, he had to draw on his savings. He took another job, which promised more money, but it didn't last long and he found himself out of work. This didn't bother him at all. He still had money in the bank, and anyhow it was easy to borrow from friends. His indifference was the consequence not of lassitude or despair but rather of an excess of hope. He had the feeling that he had only recently come to New York from Ohio. The sense that he was very young and that the best years of his life still lay before him was an illusion that he could not seem to escape. There was all the time in the world. He was living in hotels then, moving from one to another every five days.

In the spring, Jack moved to a furnished room in the badlands west of Central Park. He was running out of money. Then, when he began to feel that a job was a desperate necessity, he got sick. At first, he seemed to have only a bad cold, but he was unable to shake it and he began to run a fever and to cough blood. The fever kept him drowsy most of the time, but he roused himself occasionally and went out to a cafeteria for a meal. He felt sure that none of his friends knew where he was, and he was glad of this. He hadn't counted on Joan.

Late one morning, he heard her speaking in the hall with his landlady. A few moments later, she knocked on his door. He was lying on the bed in a pair of pants and a soiled pajama top, and he didn't answer. She knocked again and walked in. "I've been looking everywhere for you, Jack," she said. She spoke softly. "When I found out that you were in a place like this I thought you must be broke or sick. I stopped at the bank and got some money, in case you're broke. I've brought you some Scotch. I thought a little drink wouldn't do you any harm. Want a little drink?"

Joan's dress was black. Her voice was low and serene. She sat in a chair beside his bed as if she had been coming there every day to nurse him. Her features had coarsened, he thought, but there were still very few lines in her face. She was heavier. She was nearly fat. She was wearing black cotton gloves. She got two glasses and poured Scotch into them. He drank his whiskey greedily. "I didn't get to bed until three last night," she said. Her voice had once before reminded him of a gentle and despairing song, but now, perhaps because he was sick, her mildness, the mourning she wore, her stealthy grace, made him uneasy. "It was one of those nights," she said. "We went to the theater. Afterward, someone asked us up to his place. I don't know who he was. It was one of those places. They're so strange. There were some meat-eating plants and a collection of Chinese snuff bottles. Why do people collect Chinese snuff bottles? We all autographed a lampshade, as I remember, but I can't remember much."

Jack tried to sit up in bed, as if there were some need to defend himself, and then fell back again, against the pillows. "How did you find me, Joan?" he asked.

"It was simple," she said. "I called that hotel. The one you were staying in. They gave me this address. My secretary got the telephone number. Have another little drink."

"You know, you've never come to a place of mine before—never," he said. "Why did you come now?"

"Why did I come, darling?" she asked. "What a question! I've known you for thirty years. You're the oldest friend I have in New York. Remember that night in the Village when it snowed and we stayed up until morning and drank whiskey sours for breakfast? That doesn't seem like twelve years ago. And that night—"

"I don't like to have you see me in a place like this," he said earnestly. He touched his face and felt his beard.

"And all the people who used to imitate Roosevelt," she said, as if she had not heard him, as if she were deaf. "And that place on Staten Island where we all used to go for dinner when Henry had a car. Poor Henry. He bought a place in Connecticut and went out there by himself one weekend. He fell asleep with a lighted cigarette and the house, the barn, everything burned. Ethel took the children out to California." She poured more Scotch into his glass and handed it to him. She lighted a cigarette and put it between his lips. The intimacy of this gesture, which made it seem not only as if he were deathly ill but as if he were her lover, troubled him.

"As soon as I'm better," he said, "I'll take a room at a good hotel. I'll call you then. It was nice of you to come."

"Oh, don't be ashamed of this room, Jack," she said. "Rooms never bother me. It doesn't seem to matter to me where I am. Stanley had a filthy room in Chelsea. At least, other people told me it was filthy. I never noticed it. Rats used to eat the food I brought him. He used to have to hang the food from the ceiling, from the light chain."

"I'll call you as soon as I'm better," Jack said. "I think I can sleep now if I'm left alone. I seem to need a lot of sleep."

"You really *are* sick, darling," she said. "You must have a fever." She sat on the edge of his bed and put a hand on his forehead.

"How is that Englishman, Joan?" he asked. "Do you still see him?"

"What Englishman?" she said.

"You know. I met him at your house. He kept a handkerchief up his sleeve. He coughed all the time. You know the one I mean."

"You must be thinking of someone else," she said. "I haven't had an Englishman at my place since the war. Of course, I can't remember everyone." She turned and, taking one of his hands, linked her fingers in his.

"He's dead, isn't he?" Jack said. "That Englishman's dead." He pushed her off the bed, and got up himself. "Get out," he said.

"You're sick, darling," she said. "I can't leave you alone here."

"Get out," he said again, and when she didn't move, he shouted, "What kind of an obscenity are you that you can smell sickness and death the way you do?"

"You poor darling."

"Does it make you feel young to watch the dying?" he shouted. "Is that the lewdness that keeps you young? Is that why you dress like a crow? Oh, I know there's nothing I can say that will hurt you. I know there's nothing filthy or corrupt or depraved or brutish or base that the others haven't tried, but this time you're wrong. I'm not ready. My life isn't ending. My life's beginning. There are wonderful years ahead of me. There are, there are wonderful, wonderful, wonderful years ahead of me, and when they're over, when it's time, then I'll call you. Then, as an old friend, I'll call you and give you whatever dirty pleasure you take in watching the dying, but until then, you and your ugly and misshapen forms will leave me alone."

She finished her drink and looked at her watch. "I guess I'd better show up at the office," she said. "I'll see you later. I'll come back tonight. You'll feel better then, you poor darling." She closed the door after her, and he heard her light step on the stairs.

Jack emptied the whiskey bottle into the sink. He began to dress. He stuffed his dirty clothes into a bag. He was trembling and crying with sickness and fear. He could see the blue sky from his window, and in his fear it seemed miraculous that the sky should be blue, that the white clouds should remind him of snow, that from the sidewalk he could hear the shrill voices of children shrieking, "I'm the king of the mountain, I'm the king of the mountain, I'm the king of the mountain." He emptied the ashtray containing his nail parings and cigarette butts into the toilet, and swept the floor with a shirt, so that there would be no trace of his life, of his body, when that lewd and searching shape of death came there to find him in the evening.

QUESTIONS

1. Why does Joan seem able to accept abuse from the men in her life?

2. Why does Joan remind Jack of a torch song?

3. Why is Joan the only friend to come to Jack when he is sick? Why does she call him "darling"?

4. Why does Joan behave as if she hasn't heard Jack when he tells her to get out at the end of the story?

5. If Jack has helped Joan in the past, then why won't he accept her help when he is sick?

6. What explains Jack's accusation that Joan gets "dirty pleasure" from watching the dying? (125) Why doesn't she take offense?

7. Why does Jack make his only phone call to Joan when he is on leave from the army?

FOR FURTHER REFLECTION

1. Is Joan a good friend? Is Jack?

2. Why do some people seem to derive pleasure from the misfortunes of others?

3. What does Jack learn from his experiences with (and observations of) Joan over the years?

NADINE GORDIMER

Born in the small South African mining town of Springs, near Johannesburg, Nadine Gordimer (1923–) began writing as a child and published her first short story when she was fifteen. She recalls that reading the stories of the New Zealand writer Katherine Mansfield helped her understand that "it was possible to be a writer even if you didn't live in England." Gordimer published her first book, *Face to Face,* a collection of short stories, in 1949. Among her most highly regarded novels are *The Conservationist* (1974), winner of the Booker Prize; *Burger's Daughter* (1979); *July's People* (1981); and *A Sport of Nature* (1987). Her collections of essays include *Writing and Being* (1995) and *Living in Hope and History: Notes from Our Century* (1999). She was awarded the 1991 Nobel Prize in Literature. Her books can stand as a kind of history of South Africa's apartheid nightmare during the latter half of the twentieth century, with the intersection of public and private life as a recurring theme.

My First Two Women

I have been trying to remember when and where I saw my father's second wife for the first time. I must have seen her frequently, without singling her out or being aware of her, at many of those houses, full of friends, where my father and I were guests in the summer of 1928. My father had many friends, and it seems to me (I was not more than four years old at the time) that, at weekends at least, we were made much of at a whole roster of houses, from tiny shacks, which young couples had "fixed up" for themselves, to semi-mansions, where we had two guest rooms and a bathroom all to ourselves. Whether we sat under a peach tree on painted homemade chairs at a shack, or around the swimming pool on cane chaises longues at a mansion, the atmosphere of those Saturdays and Sundays was the same: the glasses of warm beer, full of sun, into which I sometimes stuck a finger; the light and color of a Johannesburg summer, with thousands of midges, grasshoppers, and other weightless leaping atoms exploding softly over your face as you lay down on the grass; the laughter and voices of the men and women, as comforting and pleasant as the drunken buzz of the great bluebottles that fell sated from rotting fruit, or bees that hung a moment over your head, on their way to and fro between elaborate flowering rockeries. She must have been there often—one of the women who would help me into the spotted rubber Loch Ness monster that kept me afloat, or bring me a lemonade with a colored straw to drink it through—so often that I ceased to see her.

During the months of that summer, I lived at one or another of those friends' houses, along with the children of the house; sometimes my father stayed there with me, and sometimes he did not. But even if he was not actually living in the same place with me, he was in and out every day, and the whole period has in my mind the blurring change and excitement of a prolonged holiday—children to play with, a series of affectionate women who arranged treats, settled fights, and gave me presents. The whereabouts of my mother were vague to me and not particularly troubling. It seems to me that I believed her not to be back yet from her visit to my grandmother in Kenya, and yet I have the recollection of once speaking to her on the telephone, as if she were in Johannesburg after all. I remember saying, "When are you coming back?" and then not waiting for her to answer but going on, "Guess what I've got in my hand?" (It was a frog, which had just been discovered to have completed its metamorphosis from a tadpole in a tin basin full of stones and water.)

The previous winter, when my mother had gone to Kenya, my father and I had lived in our house, my parents' own house, alone. This was not unusual; I am aware that I had been alone with him, in the care of servants, time and again before that. In fact, any conception I have in my mind of my mother and father and me living together as a family includes her rather as a presence—rooms that were hers, books and trinkets belonging to her, the mute testimony of her grand piano—rather than a flesh-and-blood actuality. Even if she *was* there she did little or nothing of an intimate nature for me; I do not connect her with meal or bath times. So it came about, I suppose, that I scarcely understood, that summer, that there was a real upheaval and change over my head. My father and I were never to go back to that house together. In fact, we both had left it for good; even though I, before the decision was to be made final for me, was to return for a few weeks, it was not to the *same house*, in any but the brick-and-mortar sense, and my position in it and the regrouping of its attention in relation to me were so overwhelmingly changed that they wiped out, in a blaze of self-importance and glory, the dim near babyhood that had gone before.

For, suddenly, in a beautiful autumn month (it must have been March), I found myself back in our house with my mother. The willows around the lawn were fountains spouting pale-yellow leaves on the grass that was kept green all year round. I slept with my mother, in her bed. Surely I had not done so before. When I said to her, "Mummy, didn't I used to sleep in the nursery before you went to Kenya?" she pushed up my pajama jacket and blew in my navel and said, "Darling, I really have no idea where your Daddy put you to sleep while I was away."

She had short, shiny black hair cut across her forehead in a fringe. She took me to the barber and had my hair, my black hair, cut in a fringe. (Daddy used to brush my hair back, first dipping the brush in water. "Water dries out the hair," she said.) We would get out of her car together, at the houses of friends, and she would walk with me slowly up the path toward them, hand in hand. We looked exactly alike, they all said, exactly alike; it was incredible that a small boy could look so much the image of his mother.

My mother would put me up on the long stool beside her while she played the piano; I had never been so close to a piano while it was being played, and sometimes the loud parts of the music swelled through my head frighteningly, like the feeling once when I slipped through my Loch Ness monster and went under in a swimming pool. Then I got used to the sensation and found it exciting, and I would say to her, "Play loudly, Mummy. Make it boom." Sometimes she would stop playing suddenly and whirl around and hold me tight, looking out over my head at the guests who had been listening. I would hear the last reverberation die away in the great rosewood shape behind us while silence held in the room.

My mother walked up and down a room when she talked, and she talked a great deal, to people who seemed to have no chance to answer her, but were there to listen. Once, in the bathroom, I threw a wet toy and it hit my African nanny on the mouth, and when she smacked my behind and I yelled, my mother rushed in and raged at her, yelling as loudly as I did. My mother was beautiful when she was angry, for she was one of those women who cry with anger, and her eyes glistened and her natural pallor was stained bright with rising blood.

She took me to a circus. She took me to a native mine-workers' "war" dance. She came home from town with a pile of educational toys and sat over me, watching, while I hesitated, caught her long, black, urging eye, brilliant as the eye of an animal that can see in the dark, and then, with a kind of hypnotized instinct born of the desire to please, fitted the right shape on the right peg.

There were still a few leaves, like droplets not yet shaken off, on the twigs of the willows when my clothes and toys were packed up again and my father came to fetch me away.

This time I went to the sea, with the family of three little boys and their mother, with whom I had stayed before. I had a wonderful time, and when I came back, it was to a new house that I had never seen. In it were my father and his second wife.

I was not surprised to see this woman, and, as I have said, she was not a stranger to me. I liked her, and, made gregarious by the life of the past year, asked, "How much days can Deb stay with us?"

"For always," said my father.

"Doesn't she ever have to go home?"

"This is her home, and yours, and Daddy's."

"Why?"

"Because she is married to me now, Nick. She is my wife, and husbands and wives love each other and live together in the same house."

There was a pause, and when I spoke again, what I said must have been very different from what they expected. They did not know that while I was on holiday at the sea I had been taken, one rainy afternoon, along with the older children, to the cinema. There I had seen, in all the rose and crystalline blur of Technicolor, a man and woman dance out beneath the chandeliers of a ballroom. When I had asked what they were doing, I was told that this was a wedding—the man and the woman had just been married.

"Do you mean like this?" I asked my father and my stepmother, taking my father's hand, bending my knees, and shaping out my arms in a jiglike posture. I hopped around solemnly, dragging him with me.

"Dancing?" guessed my father, mystified and affectionate, appealing to his wife.

"Oh, that's wonderful!" she cried in sudden delight. "Bless his formal heart! A real wedding!"

There followed a confusion of hugging, all around. I was aware only that in some way I had pleased them.

I was now nearly five years old and due to begin going to school. My stepmother took me to town with her, and together we bought the supplies for my birthday party, and my school uniform, and a satchel with a fancy lock—soon to be stained as greasy as an old fish-and-chip wrapping with the print of successive school lunches—and the elaborate equipment of pencil sharpeners, erasers, and rulers indispensable to the child who has not yet learned to write. Deb understood what a birthday party for a five-year-old boy should be like. She had ideas of her own, and could sway a wavering torment of indecision between candleholders in the guise of soldiers or elephants, imparting to the waverer a comforting sense of the rightness of the final choice, but she also knew when to efface her own preferences entirely and let me enjoy my own choice for my own unexplained reasons. In fact, she was so good at the calm management of the practical details of my small life that I suppose I quickly assumed this stability as my right, and took it altogether for granted, as children, in their fierce unconscious instinct for personal salvation, take all those rights which, if withheld from them, they cannot consciously remark, but whose lack they exhibit and revenge with equal unconscious ferocity. Of course Deb bought neat and comfortable clothes for me, found the books I would best like to hear her read from, took me with her on visits that would be interesting to me, but left me at home to play when she was going where there would be nothing to amuse me; she always had, hadn't she, right from the first day?

The children at school wanted to know why I called my mother "Deb." When I said that she was not my mother, they insisted that she must be. "Are you my mother now, Deb?" I asked her.

"No," she said. "You know that you have your own mother."

"They say you must be, because you live with Daddy and me."

"I'm your second mother," she said, looking to see if that would do.

"Like my godmother?"

"That's right." I dashed off to play; it was perfectly satisfactory.

There came a stage when school, the preparation for which had been so enjoyable, palled. I suppose there must have been some incident there, some small failure which embarrassed or shamed me. I do not remember. But I know that, suddenly, I didn't want to go to school. Deb was gentle but insistent. I remember my own long, sullen silence one day, after a wrangle of "Whys?" from me and firm explanations from her. At last I said, "When I'm at my mother's I stay home all the time."

My stepmother was squatting on her heels in front of a low cupboard, and her eyes opened up toward me like the eyes of those sleeping dolls which girl children alternately lower and raise by inclining the doll's body, but her voice was the same as usual. "If you lived with your mother now, you would go to school just as you do here," she said.

I stood right in front of her. She looked up at me again, and I said, "No I wouldn't." I waited. Then I said, "She lets me do what I like." I waited again. "I can even play her piano. She's got a big piano. As big as this room."

My stepmother went on slowly putting back into the cupboard the gramophone records she had been sorting and cleaning. Standing over her, I could see the top of her head, an unfamiliar aspect of a grownup. It was then, I think, that I began to see her for the first time, not as one of the succession of pretty ladies who petted and cared for me, but as Deb, as someone connected in wordless depths with my father and me, as my father and I and, yes, my mother were connected. Someone who had entered, irrevocably, the atavistic tension of that cunning battle for love and supremacy that exists between children and parents sometimes even beyond the grave, when one protagonist is dead and mourned, and lives on in the fierce dissatisfaction of the other's memory.

She was a fair woman, this Deb, this woman beloved of my father; on all faces there is some feature, some plane, that catches the light in characteristic prominence of that face, and on her face, at that moment and always, it was her long golden eyebrows, shining. They were bleached from much swimming, but her dull, curly hair, always protected from sun and water by a cap, hung colorless and nowhere smooth enough to shine. The face was broad and brown across strong cheekbones, and she had a big, orange-painted mouth, the beautiful underlip of which supported the upper as calmly as a carved pediment. Her eyes, moving from record to cupboard, lowered under my presence, were green or blue, depending upon what color she wore. As she squatted, her knees, with thighs and calves showing under the short skirt, closed back against each other like the blades of a knife, were particularly pretty—smooth and pink skinned, with a close speckling of dainty freckles, like the round tops of her arms and her long calves. She was the sort of fair woman who would never be called a blonde.

Deb. I knew what it smelled like in that pink freckled neck. I knew the stiff and ugly ears that she kept hidden under that hair, and that sometimes, when she was hot and lifted her hair off her neck a moment for coolness, were suddenly discovered.

I shall never forget the feeling I had as I stood there over her. If I search my adult experience as a man to approximate it, I can only say that now it seems to me that physically it was rather like the effect of the first drink you take after a long wet day of some strenuous exercise—rowing or hunting. It was a feeling of power that came like an inflow of physical strength. I was only five years old, but power is something of which I am convinced there is no innocence this side of the womb, and I knew what it was, all right; I understood, without a name for it, what I had. And with it came all the weapons—that bright, clinical set that I didn't need to have explained to me, as my father had had to explain to me the uses of the set of carpenter's tools I had been given for my birthday. My hand would go out unfalteringly for these drills and probes, and the unremembered pain of where they had been used on me would guide me to their application.

"Deb," I said, "why didn't Daddy marry my mother?"

"He did," she said. "Once he was married to her. But they were not happy with each other. Not like Daddy and me—and you. Not happy together like us." She did not ask me if I remembered this, but her voice suggested the question, in spite of her.

Daddy. My mother. *My mother* was simply a word I was using at that moment. I could not see her in my head. She was a mouth moving, singing; for a second she sat at the piano, smiled at me, one of her swift, startling smiles that was like someone jumping out of concealment and saying "Boo!" Inside me, it gave me a fright. If my dog had been there, I would have pulled back his ears, hard, to hear him yelp. There was Deb, squatting in front of me. I said, "My mother's got a piano as big as this house. I want to go and stay with her."

Deb got up from the floor and rubbed down her thighs. "Soon," she said. "You'll go on a visit soon, I'm sure. Let's see if tea's ready." We did not take each other's hand, but walked out onto the porch side by side, with a space between us.

It was after that day that I began to be conscious of the relationship between my father and Deb. This was not the way he and those others—the pretty, helpful friends who were the mothers of my friends—had behaved toward each other. I watched with unbiased interest, as I would have watched a bird bringing his mate tidbits where she balanced on our paling fence, when my father ate an apple bite-and-bite-about with this woman, or, passing her chair at breakfast, after he had kissed me goodbye in the morning, paused to press his cheek silently, and with closed eyes, against hers. In the car, I noticed that she rested her hand on his knee as he drove. Sometimes, in the evenings, both she and I sat on his lap at once.

There were no images in my memory to which to match these. They were married, Deb and my father. This behavior was marriage. Deb herself had told me that marriage once had existed between my father and my mother. One day I came home from a visit to my mother and remarked, conversationally, in the bedroom Deb and my father shared, "My mother's got a bed just like yours, Deb, and that's where Daddy and she used to sleep when he lived there, didn't you, Daddy?"

It was Sunday, and my father still lay in bed, reading the paper, though Deb's place was empty and she was gathering her clothes together before she went off to the bathroom. He said, "No, son. Don't you remember? Mine was the room with the little balcony."

"Oh, yes," I said. "Of course, I know." All at once I remembered the smell of that rather dark, high room, a smell of shirts fresh from the iron, of the two leather golf bags in the corner, and some chemical with which the carpet had been cleaned. All this—the smell of my father—had disappeared under the warmer, relaxing, and polleny scents of the room he now shared with a woman, where peach-colored dust from her powder settled along his hairbrushes, and the stockings she peeled off retained the limp, collapsed semblance of her legs, like the newly shed skin of a snake I had come upon in the bush when I was on holiday at the sea.

I think that there must have been something strongly attractive to me in the ease of this feminine intimacy to which my father and I found ourselves admitted with such naturalness. Yet because it was unfamiliar, the very seductiveness of its comfort seemed, against the confusion of my short life, a kind of disloyalty, to which I was party and of which I was guilty. Disloyalty—to what? Guilty—of what?

I was too young for motives; I could only let them bubble up, manifest in queer little words and actions. I know that that Sunday morning I said stoutly, as if I were explaining some special system of living, "There we each had our *own* rooms. Everybody slept in their own room."

Before the end of the first year of the marriage that power that had come to me like a set of magical weapons, the day when my stepmother knelt before me at the record cupboard, became absolute. It crushed upon my little-boy's head the vainglory and triumph of the tyrant, crown or thorn. I was to wear it as my own for the rest of my childhood.

I was cuddling Deb, secure in her arms one day, when I said, out of some gentle honey of warmth that I felt peacefully within me, "I'm going to call you Mummy because I love you best." I am sure that she knew that the statement was not quite so stunning and meaningful as it sounds now, out of the context of childhood. Quite often, she had heard me say of an animal or a new friend, "You know whom I love. I love only Eddie." (Or "Sam," or "Chris.") Sometimes the vehement preference was expressed not out of real feeling for the friend or animal in question, but out of pique toward some other child or animal. At other times it was merely an unreasonable welling up of well-being that had to find an object. But I had never before said this particular thing to her. I felt her thighs tighten suddenly beneath me; all four fingers and the thumb of her hand seized round my arm. She shook back her hair fumblingly and held her face away from mine to look at me; she was awkward with joy. I looked up into the stare of her eyes—grown-up eyes that fell before mine—and in me, like milk soured by a flash of lightning, the sweet secretion of affection became insipid in the fearful, amazed thrill of victim turned victor.

That was our story, really, for many years. My father and Deb were deeply in love and theirs was a serene marriage. The three of us lived together in amity; it was a place of warmth for a child to grow in. I visited my mother at regular, if widely spaced, intervals. I went to her for short periods at Christmas, birthdays, and during holidays. Thus, along with her, with that elegant black head and those hard wrists volatile with all the wonderful bracelets she had picked up all over the world, went excitement and occasion, treats and parties, people who exclaimed over me, and the abolishment of that guillotine of joys, bedtime. Sometimes the tide of grown-up activities would pass on over my head and leave me stranded and abandoned on a corner of somebody's sofa, rubbing my eyes against the glare of forgotten lights. It did not matter; the next day, or the day after that, I was sure to be delivered back to Deb and my father and the comfort of my child's pace.

Thus it was, too, that along with home and Deb and my father went everyday life, the greater part of life, with time for boredom, for transgressions and punishments. When I visited my mother for a weekend or a day I was on my best behavior, befitting a treat or an occasion; I was never with her long enough to need chastisement. So when, at home, I was naughty and my father or Deb had to punish me, I would inflame myself against them with the firm belief that my mother would never punish me. At these times of resentment and injury, I would see her clearly and positively, flaming in the light of a Christmas tree or the fiery ring of candles on a birthday cake, my champion against a world that would not bend entirely to my own will. In the same way, for the first few days after my return from a visit to her, everything about the way she lived and the things about her were lit up by the occasion with which my visit had coincided; her flat (when I was seven or eight, she moved into a luxurious penthouse in a block overlooking a country club) was like the glowing cardboard interior of the king's castle, carried away in my mind from a panto-mime matinee. "There's a swimming pool right on top of the building, on the roof garden," I would tell Deb. "I swim there every morning. Once I swam at night. My mother lets me. The lift doesn't go up to the top—you have to walk the last flight of stairs from the twelfth floor." "My mother's got a car with an overhead drive. Do you know what that is, Deb? It means you don't have to change the gears with your hands." "I wish we had a swimming pool here. I don't like this old house without even a swimming pool."

Deb always answered me quietly and evenly. Never, even when I was very young, did she try to point out rival attractions at home. But in time, when I grew older and was perhaps eleven or twelve, I struggled against something that went more than quiet—went dead—in her during these one-sided conversations. I felt not that she was not listen-ing, but that she was listless, without interest in what I said. And then I did not know at whom the resentment I sud-denly felt was directed, whether at my mother—that glossy-haired kingfisher flashing in and out of my life—for having a roof-garden swimming pool and a car without gears, or at Deb, for her lack of attention and negative reaction to my relation of these wonders. This reaction of hers was all the more irking, and in some vague, apprehensive way dismaying, when one remembered the way she watched and listened to me sometimes, with that look in her eyes that wanted something from me, wondered, hesitated, hopeful—that look I had known how to conjure up ever since the first day when I suggested I would call her my mother, and that, in perverse, irresistible use of the same power, I had also known how never to allow to come to articulacy, to emotional fulfillment, between us. The business of my calling her mother, for instance; it had come up several times again, while I was small. But she, in the silence that followed, had never managed anything more than, once, an almost unintelligibly murmured "If you like." And I, once the impulsive, casually pronounced sentence had exploded and left its peculiar after-silence, had dropped my avowal as I left a toy, here or there, for someone else to pick up in house or garden. I never did call her mother; in time, I think I should have been surprised to hear that there had ever been any question that she should be anything else but "Deb."

I was strongly attached to her, and when, at twelve or thirteen, I entered adolescence and boarding school at the same time, there was in fact a calm friendship between us unusual between a woman, and a boy walking the knife edge dividing small-boy scorn of the feminine from awakening sex interest. I suppose if she had been truly in the position of a mother, this relationship would not have been possible. Her position must have been curiously like that of the woman who, failing to secure as a lover the man with whom she has fallen in love, is offered instead his respect and his confidences.

I was fifteen when I asked the question that had taken a thousand different forms—doubts, anxieties, and revenges—

all through my life but had never formulated itself directly. The truth was, I had never known what that question *was*— only felt it, in all my blood and bones, fumbled toward it under the kisses of people who loved me, asked it with my seeking of my father's hands, the warmth of Deb's lap, the approval of my form master's eye, the smiles of my friends. Now it came to me matter-of-factly, in words.

I was home from school for the weekend, and there had been guests at lunch. They had discussed the divorce of a common friend and the wrangle over the custody of the children of the marriage. One of the guests was a lawyer, and he had gone into the legal niceties in some detail. After the guests had gone, my father went off for his nap and Deb and I dragged our favorite canvas chairs out onto the lawn. As I settled mine at a comfortable angle, I asked her, curiously, "Deb, how was it that my mother didn't get me? The custody of me, I mean."

She thought for a moment, and I thought she must be trying how best to present some legal technicality in a way that both she and I would understand.

"I mean, their divorce was an arranged thing, wasn't it—one of those things arranged to look like desertion that Derrick spoke about? Why didn't my mother get me?" The lawyer had explained that where parents contested the custody, unless there was some strong factor to suggest that the mother was unsuitable to rear a child, a young child was usually awarded to her care.

Then quite suddenly Deb spoke. Her face was red and she looked strange, and she spoke so fast that what she said was almost blurted. "She gave you up."

Her face and tone so astonished me that the impact of what she had said missed its mark. I stared at her, questioning.

She met my gaze stiffly, with a kind of jerky bravado, intense, looking through me.

"How do you mean?"

"Voluntarily. She gave you over to your father."

The pressure in her face died slowly down; her hands moved, as if released, on the chair arms. "I should never have told you," she said flatly. "I'd promised myself I never should."

"You mean she didn't want me?"

"We don't know what her reasons were, Nick. We can't know them."

"Didn't try to get me?"

There was a long silence. "We made up our minds. We decided it was best. We decided we would try and make your relationship with her as normal as possible. Never say anything against her. I promised myself I wouldn't try—for myself. I often wanted to tell you—oh, lots of things. I wanted to punish you for what I withheld for your sake. I wanted to hurt you; I suppose I forgot you were a child. . . . Well, what does it matter anyway? It's all worked itself out, long ago. Only I shouldn't have told you now. It's pointless." She smiled at me, as at a friend who can be counted on to understand a confession. "It didn't even give me any pleasure."

My stepmother talked about this whole situation in which we had all lived as if it were something remembered from the past, instead of a living situation out of the continuity of which I was then, at that moment, beginning my life as a man. All worked itself out, long ago. Perhaps it had. Yes, she was right. All worked itself out, without me. Above and about me, over my head, saving me the risk and the opportunity of my own volition.

My mother? That black-haired, handsome woman become rather fleshy, who, I discovered while I sat, an awkward visitor among her admiring friends (I had inherited her love of music), sang off-key.

But it was not toward her that I felt anger, regret, and a terrible, mournful anguish of loss, which brought up from somewhere in my tall, coarse, half man's, half child's body what I was alarmed to recognize as the raking turmoil that precedes tears.

"We're really good friends, aren't we?" said my step-mother lovingly, with quiet conviction.

It was true: that was what we were—all we were.

I have never forgiven her for it.

QUESTIONS

1. What is the power the narrator refers to as coming "like an inflow of physical strength" as Deb kneels before him at the record cupboard? Why does he associate this feeling with "all the weapons"? (136)

2. Instead of questioning his father, why does the narrator ask Deb, "Why didn't Daddy marry my mother"? (136)

3. What are the disloyalty and guilt that the narrator experiences on finding his father and himself in the ease of Deb's "feminine intimacy"? (138)

4. Why does the narrator's statement to Deb that he is going to call her Mummy because he loves her best bring about in him a "fearful, amazed thrill of victim turned victor"? (139)

5. After telling Deb that he would call her Mummy, why does he never do so?

6. When the narrator asks Deb why his mother didn't get him after the divorce, why does Deb tell him, "She gave you up"? (142) What does she mean when she explains that telling him is "pointless"? (143)

7. Why has the narrator never forgiven Deb for their being "really good friends"? (144)

FOR FURTHER REFLECTION

1. Why are women judged more harshly than men for giving up their children?

2. Should parents stay together for the sake of the children?

3. Why is the narrator's anger directed at Deb but not at his mother or father? Is anger toward a stepparent inevitable?

Sloth

F. SCOTT FITZGERALD

F. Scott Fitzgerald (1896–1940) was born in St. Paul, Minnesota. He enrolled at Princeton University in 1913 and, despite less-than-promising academic work, began to develop a reputation as a talented writer. He enlisted in the army in 1917 to avoid flunking out of college, and he started writing a novel, titled *The Romantic Egotist*, during officer training at Fort Leavenworth, Kansas. Maxwell Perkins, an editor at Scribner's publishing company, asked Fitzgerald to revise and resubmit it, which he did. Published as *This Side of Paradise* in 1920, the work became an immediate bestseller. But Fitzgerald's major achievements were still ahead: *The Great Gatsby* (1925), one of the great American novels ever written, and *Tender Is the Night* (1934), as well as several volumes of short stories. The experiences of Fitzgerald and his wife, Zelda, in New York and then in Paris as part of the expatriate "lost generation" of writers provided the material for much of Fitzgerald's fiction and have been amply documented by biographers since. In 1937, following Zelda's hospitalization for mental illness, Fitzgerald went to Hollywood to be a screenwriter. Already suffering from alcoholism, he died there of a heart attack, leaving behind an unfinished manuscript, *The Last Tycoon*.

Babylon Revisited

A nd where's Mr. Campbell?" Charlie asked.

"Gone to Switzerland. Mr. Campbell's a pretty sick man, Mr. Wales."

"I'm sorry to hear that. And George Hardt?" Charlie inquired.

"Back in America, gone to work."

"And where is the Snow Bird?"

"He was in here last week. Anyway, his friend, Mr. Schaeffer, is in Paris."

Two familiar names from the long list of a year and a half ago. Charlie scribbled an address in his notebook and tore out the page.

"If you see Mr. Schaeffer, give him this," he said. "It's my brother-in-law's address. I haven't settled on a hotel yet."

He was not really disappointed to find Paris was so empty. But the stillness in the Ritz bar was strange and portentous. It was not an American bar any more—he felt polite in it, and not as if he owned it. It had gone back into France. He felt the stillness from the moment he got out of the taxi and saw the doorman, usually in a frenzy of activity at this hour, gossiping with a chasseur by the servants' entrance.

Passing through the corridor, he heard only a single, bored voice in the once-clamorous women's room. When he turned into the bar he traveled the twenty feet of green carpet with his eyes fixed straight ahead by old habit; and then, with his foot firmly on the rail, he turned and surveyed the room, encountering only a single pair of eyes that fluttered up from a newspaper in the corner. Charlie asked for the head barman, Paul, who in the latter days of the bull market had come to work in his own custom-built car—disembarking, however, with due nicety at the nearest corner. But Paul was at his country house today and Alix giving him information.

"No, no more," Charlie said, "I'm going slow these days."

Alix congratulated him: "You were going pretty strong a couple of years ago."

"I'll stick to it all right," Charlie assured him. "I've stuck to it for over a year and a half now."

"How do you find conditions in America?"

"I haven't been to America for months. I'm in business in Prague, representing a couple of concerns there. They don't know about me down there."

Alix smiled.

"Remember the night of George Hardt's bachelor dinner here?" said Charlie. "By the way, what's become of Claude Fessenden?"

Alix lowered his voice confidentially: "He's in Paris, but he doesn't come here any more. Paul doesn't allow it. He ran up a bill of thirty thousand francs, charging all his drinks and his lunches, and usually his dinner, for more than a year. And when Paul finally told him he had to pay, he gave him a bad check."

Alix shook his head sadly.

"I don't understand it, such a dandy fellow. Now he's all bloated up—" He made a plump apple of his hands.

Charlie watched a group of strident queens installing themselves in a corner.

"Nothing affects them," he thought. "Stocks rise and fall, people loaf or work, but they go on forever." The place oppressed him. He called for the dice and shook with Alix for the drink.

"Here for long, Mr. Wales?"

"I'm here for four or five days to see my little girl."

"Oh-h! You have a little girl?"

Outside, the fire-red, gas-blue, ghost-green signs shone smokily through the tranquil rain. It was late afternoon and the streets were in movement; the bistros gleamed. At the corner of the Boulevard des Capucines he took a taxi. The Place de la Concorde moved by in pink majesty; they crossed the logical Seine, and Charlie felt the sudden provincial quality of the Left Bank.

Charlie directed his taxi to the Avenue de l'Opéra, which was out of his way. But he wanted to see the blue hour spread over the magnificent façade, and imagine that the cab horns, playing endlessly the first few bars of *Le Plus que Lent*, were the trumpets of the Second Empire. They were closing the iron grill in front of Brentano's Bookstore, and people were already at dinner behind the trim little bourgeois hedge of Duval's. He had never eaten at a really cheap restaurant in Paris. Five-course dinner, four francs fifty, eighteen cents, wine included. For some odd reason he wished that he had.

As they rolled on to the Left Bank and he felt its sudden provincialism, he thought, "I spoiled this city for myself. I didn't realize it, but the days came along one after another, and then two years were gone, and everything was gone, and I was gone."

He was thirty-five, and good to look at. The Irish mobility of his face was sobered by a deep wrinkle between his eyes. As he rang his brother-in-law's bell in the Rue Palatine, the wrinkle deepened till it pulled down his brows; he felt a cramping sensation in his belly. From behind the maid who opened the door darted a lovely little girl of nine who shrieked "Daddy!" and flew up, struggling like a fish, into his arms. She pulled his head around by one ear and set her cheek against his.

"My old pie," he said.

"Oh, Daddy, Daddy, Daddy, Daddy, Dads, Dads, Dads!"

She drew him into the salon, where the family waited, a boy and a girl his daughter's age, his sister-in-law and her husband. He greeted Marion with his voice pitched carefully to avoid either feigned enthusiasm or dislike, but her response was more frankly tepid, though she minimized her expression of unalterable distrust by directing her regard toward his child. The two men clasped hands in a friendly way and Lincoln Peters rested his for a moment on Charlie's shoulder.

The room was warm and comfortably American. The three children moved intimately about, playing through the yellow oblongs that led to other rooms; the cheer of six o'clock spoke in the eager smacks of the fire and the sounds of French activity in the kitchen. But Charlie did not relax; his heart sat up rigidly in his body and he drew confidence from his daughter, who from time to time came close to him, holding in her arms the doll he had brought.

"Really extremely well," he declared in answer to Lincoln's question. "There's a lot of business there that isn't moving at all, but we're doing even better than ever. In fact, damn well. I'm bringing my sister over from America next month to keep house for me. My income last year was bigger than it was when I had money. You see, the Czechs—"

His boasting was for a specific purpose; but after a moment, seeing a faint restiveness in Lincoln's eye, he changed the subject:

"Those are fine children of yours, well brought up, good manners."

"We think Honoria's a great little girl too."

Marion Peters came back from the kitchen. She was a tall woman with worried eyes, who had once possessed a fresh American loveliness. Charlie had never been sensitive to it and was always surprised when people spoke of how pretty she had been. From the first there had been an instinctive antipathy between them.

"Well, how do you find Honoria?" she asked.

"Wonderful. I was astonished how much she's grown in ten months. All the children are looking well."

"We haven't had a doctor for a year. How do you like being back in Paris?"

"It seems very funny to see so few Americans around."

"I'm delighted," Marion said vehemently. "Now at least you can go into a store without their assuming you're a millionaire. We've suffered like everybody, but on the whole it's a good deal pleasanter."

"But it was nice while it lasted," Charlie said. "We were a sort of royalty, almost infallible, with a sort of magic around us. In the bar this afternoon"—he stumbled, seeing his mistake—"there wasn't a man I knew."

She looked at him keenly. "I should think you'd have had enough of bars."

"I only stayed a minute. I take one drink every afternoon, and no more."

"Don't you want a cocktail before dinner?" Lincoln asked.

"I take only one drink every afternoon, and I've had that."

"I hope you keep to it," said Marion.

Her dislike was evident in the coldness with which she spoke, but Charlie only smiled; he had larger plans. Her very aggressiveness gave him an advantage, and he knew enough to wait. He wanted them to initiate the discussion of what they knew had brought him to Paris.

At dinner he couldn't decide whether Honoria was most like him or her mother. Fortunate if she didn't combine the traits of both that had brought them to disaster. A great wave of protectiveness went over him. He thought he knew what to do for her. He believed in character; he wanted to jump back a whole generation and trust in character again as the eternally valuable element. Everything else wore out.

He left soon after dinner, but not to go home. He was curious to see Paris by night with clearer and more judicious eyes than those of other days. He bought a *strapontin* for the casino and watched Josephine Baker go through her chocolate arabesques.

After an hour he left and strolled toward Montmartre, up the Rue Pigalle into the Place Blanche. The rain had stopped and there were a few people in evening clothes disembarking from taxis in front of cabarets, and cocottes prowling singly or in pairs, and many Negroes. He passed a lighted door from which issued music, and stopped with the sense of familiarity; it was Bricktop's, where he had parted with so many hours and so much money. A few doors farther on he found another ancient rendezvous and incautiously put his head inside. Immediately an eager orchestra burst into sound, a pair of professional dancers leaped to their feet and a maître d'hôtel swooped toward him, crying, "Crowd just arriving, sir!" But he withdrew quickly.

"You have to be damn drunk," he thought.

Zelli's was closed, the bleak and sinister cheap hotels surrounding it were dark; up in the Rue Blanche there was more light and a local, colloquial French crowd. The Poet's Cave had disappeared, but the two great mouths of the Café of Heaven and the Café of Hell still yawned—even devoured, as he watched, the meager contents of a tourist bus—a German, a Japanese, and an American couple who glanced at him with frightened eyes.

So much for the effort and ingenuity of Montmartre. All the catering to vice and waste was on an utterly childish scale, and he suddenly realized the meaning of the word *dissipate*—to dissipate into thin air; to make nothing out of something. In the little hours of the night every move from place to place was an enormous human jump, an increase of paying for the privilege of slower and slower motion.

He remembered thousand-franc notes given to an orchestra for playing a single number, hundred-franc notes tossed to a doorman for calling a cab.

But it hadn't been given for nothing.

It had been given, even the most wildly squandered sum, as an offering to destiny that he might not remember the things most worth remembering, the things that now he would always remember—his child taken from his control, his wife escaped to a grave in Vermont.

In the glare of a brasserie a woman spoke to him. He bought her some eggs and coffee, and then, eluding her encouraging stare, gave her a twenty-franc note and took a taxi to his hotel.

2

He woke upon a fine fall day—football weather. The depression of yesterday was gone and he liked the people on the streets. At noon he sat opposite Honoria at Le Grand Vatel, the only restaurant he could think of not reminiscent of champagne dinners and long luncheons that began at two and ended in a blurred and vague twilight.

"Now, how about vegetables? Oughtn't you to have some vegetables?"

"Well, yes."

"Here's *épinards* and *chou-fleur* and carrots and *haricots*."

"I'd like *chou-fleur*."

"Wouldn't you like to have two vegetables?"

"I usually only have one at lunch."

The waiter was pretending to be inordinately fond of children. "*Qu'elle est mignonne la petite! Elle parle exactement comme une Française.*"

"How about dessert? Shall we wait and see?"

The waiter disappeared. Honoria looked at her father expectantly.

"What are we going to do?"

"First, we're going to that toy store in the Rue Saint-Honoré and buy you anything you like. And then we're going to the vaudeville at the Empire."

She hesitated. "I like it about the vaudeville, but not the toy store."

"Why not?"

"Well, you brought me this doll." She had it with her. "And I've got lots of things. And we're not rich any more, are we?"

"We never were. But today you are to have anything you want."

"All right," she agreed resignedly.

When there had been her mother and a French nurse he had been inclined to be strict; now he extended himself, reached out for a new tolerance; he must be both parents to her and not shut any of her out of communication.

"I want to get to know you," he said gravely. "First let me introduce myself. My name is Charles J. Wales, of Prague."

"Oh, Daddy!" her voice cracked with laughter.

"And who are you, please?" he persisted, and she accepted a role immediately: "Honoria Wales, Rue Palatine, Paris."

"Married or single?"

"No, not married. Single."

He indicated the doll. "But I see you have a child, madame."

Unwilling to disinherit it, she took it to her heart and thought quickly: "Yes, I've been married, but I'm not married now. My husband is dead."

He went on quickly, "And the child's name?"

"Simone. That's after my best friend at school."

"I'm very pleased that you're doing so well at school."

"I'm third this month," she boasted. "Elsie"—that was her cousin—"is only about eighteenth, and Richard is about at the bottom."

"You like Richard and Elsie, don't you?"

"Oh, yes. I like Richard quite well and I like her all right."

Cautiously and casually he asked: "And Aunt Marion and Uncle Lincoln—which do you like best?"

"Oh, Uncle Lincoln, I guess."

He was increasingly aware of her presence. As they came in, a murmur of ". . . adorable" followed them, and now the people at the next table bent all their silences upon her, staring as if she were something no more conscious than a flower.

"Why don't I live with you?" she asked suddenly. "Because Mamma's dead?"

"You must stay here and learn more French. It would have been hard for Daddy to take care of you so well."

"I don't really need much taking care of any more. I do everything for myself."

Going out of the restaurant, a man and a woman unexpectedly hailed him.

"Well, the old Wales!"

"Hello there, Lorraine. . . . Dunc."

Sudden ghosts out of the past: Duncan Schaeffer, a friend from college. Lorraine Quarrles, a lovely, pale blonde of thirty; one of a crowd who had helped them make months into days in the lavish times of three years ago.

"My husband couldn't come this year," she said, in answer to his question. "We're poor as hell. So he gave me two hundred a month and told me I could do my worst on that. . . . This your little girl?"

"What about coming back and sitting down?" Duncan asked.

"Can't do it." He was glad for an excuse. As always, he felt Lorraine's passionate, provocative attraction, but his own rhythm was different now.

"Well, how about dinner?" she asked.

"I'm not free. Give me your address and let me call you."

"Charlie, I believe you're sober," she said judicially. "I honestly believe he's sober, Dunc. Pinch him and see if he's sober."

Charlie indicated Honoria with his head. They both laughed.

"What's your address?" said Duncan skeptically.

He hesitated, unwilling to give the name of his hotel.

"I'm not settled yet. I'd better call you. We're going to see the vaudeville at the Empire."

"There! That's what I want to do," Lorraine said. "I want to see some clowns and acrobats and jugglers. That's just what we'll do, Dunc."

"We've got to do an errand first," said Charlie. "Perhaps we'll see you there."

"All right, you snob. . . . Goodbye, beautiful little girl."

"Goodbye."

Honoria bobbed politely.

Somehow, an unwelcome encounter. They liked him because he was functioning, because he was serious; they wanted to see him, because he was stronger than they were now, because they wanted to draw a certain sustenance from his strength.

At the Empire, Honoria proudly refused to sit upon her father's folded coat. She was already an individual with a code of her own, and Charlie was more and more absorbed by the desire of putting a little of himself into her before she crystallized utterly. It was hopeless to try to know her in so short a time.

Between the acts they came upon Duncan and Lorraine in the lobby where the band was playing.

"Have a drink?"

"All right, but not up at the bar. We'll take a table."

"The perfect father."

Listening abstractedly to Lorraine, Charlie watched Honoria's eyes leave their table, and he followed them wistfully about the room, wondering what they saw. He met her glance and she smiled.

"I liked that lemonade," she said.

What had she said? What had he expected? Going home in a taxi afterward, he pulled her over until her head rested against his chest.

"Darling, do you ever think about your mother?"

"Yes, sometimes," she answered vaguely.

"I don't want you to forget her. Have you got a picture of her?"

"Yes, I think so. Anyhow, Aunt Marion has. Why don't you want me to forget her?"

"She loved you very much."

"I loved her too."

They were silent for a moment.

"Daddy, I want to come and live with you," she said suddenly.

His heart leaped; he had wanted it to come like this.

"Aren't you perfectly happy?"

"Yes, but I love you better than anybody. And you love me better than anybody, don't you, now that Mummy's dead?"

"Of course I do. But you won't always like me best, honey. You'll grow up and meet somebody your own age and go marry him and forget you ever had a daddy."

"Yes, that's true," she agreed tranquilly.

He didn't go in. He was coming back at nine o'clock and he wanted to keep himself fresh and new for the thing he must say then.

"When you're safe inside, just show yourself in that window."

"All right. Goodbye, Dads, Dads, Dads, Dads."

He waited in the dark street until she appeared, all warm and glowing, in the window above and kissed her fingers out into the night.

3

They were waiting. Marion sat behind the coffee service in a dignified black dinner dress that just faintly suggested mourning. Lincoln was walking up and down with the animation of one who had already been talking. They were as anxious as he was to get into the question. He opened it almost immediately:

"I suppose you know what I want to see you about— why I really came to Paris."

Marion played with the black stars on her necklace and frowned.

"I'm awfully anxious to have a home," he continued. "And I'm awfully anxious to have Honoria in it. I appreciate your taking in Honoria for her mother's sake, but things have changed now"—he hesitated and then continued more forcibly—"changed radically with me, and I want to ask you to reconsider the matter. It would be silly for me to deny that about three years ago I was acting badly—"

Marion looked up at him with hard eyes.

"—but all that's over. As I told you, I haven't had more than a drink a day for over a year, and I take that drink deliberately, so that the idea of alcohol won't get too big in my imagination. You see the idea?"

"No," said Marion succinctly.

"It's a sort of stunt I set myself. It keeps the matter in proportion."

"I get you," said Lincoln. "You don't want to admit it's got any attraction for you."

"Something like that. Sometimes I forget and don't take it. But I try to take it. Anyhow, I couldn't afford to drink in my position. The people I represent are more than satisfied with what I've done, and I'm bringing my sister over from Burlington to keep house for me, and I want awfully to have Honoria too. You know that even when her mother and I weren't getting along well we never let anything that happened touch Honoria. I know she's fond of me and I know I'm able to take care of her and—well, there you are. How do you feel about it?"

He knew that now he would have to take a beating. It would last an hour or two hours, and it would be difficult, but if he modulated his inevitable resentment to the chastened attitude of the reformed sinner, he might win his point in the end.

Keep your temper, he told himself. You don't want to be justified. You want Honoria.

Lincoln spoke first: "We've been talking it over ever since we got your letter last month. We're happy to have Honoria here. She's a dear little thing, and we're glad to be able to help her, but of course that isn't the question—"

Marion interrupted suddenly. "How long are you going to stay sober, Charlie?" she asked.

"Permanently, I hope."

"How can anybody count on that?"

"You know I never did drink heavily until I gave up business and came over here with nothing to do. Then Helen and I began to run around with—"

"Please leave Helen out of it. I can't bear to hear you talk about her like that."

He stared at her grimly; he had never been certain how fond of each other the sisters were in life.

"My drinking only lasted about a year and a half—from the time we came over until I—collapsed."

"It was time enough."

"It was time enough," he agreed.

"My duty is entirely to Helen," she said. "I try to think what she would have wanted me to do. Frankly, from the night you did that terrible thing you haven't really existed for me. I can't help that. She was my sister."

"Yes."

"When she was dying she asked me to look out for Honoria. If you hadn't been in a sanitarium then, it might have helped matters."

He had no answer.

"I'll never in my life be able to forget the morning when Helen knocked at my door, soaked to the skin and shivering, and said you'd locked her out."

Charlie gripped the sides of the chair. This was more difficult than he expected; he wanted to launch out into a long expostulation and explanation, but he only said: "The night I locked her out—" and she interrupted, "I don't feel up to going over that again."

After a moment's silence Lincoln said: "We're getting off the subject. You want Marion to set aside her legal guardianship and give you Honoria. I think the main point for her is whether she has confidence in you or not."

"I don't blame Marion," Charlie said slowly, "but I think she can have entire confidence in me. I had a good record up to three years ago. Of course, it's within human possibilities I might go wrong any time. But if we wait much longer I'll lose Honoria's childhood and my chance for a home." He shook his head, "I'll simply lose her, don't you see?"

"Yes, I see," said Lincoln.

"Why didn't you think of all this before?" Marion asked.

"I suppose I did, from time to time, but Helen and I were getting along badly. When I consented to the guardianship, I was flat on my back in a sanitarium and the market had cleaned me out. I knew I'd acted badly, and I thought if it would bring any peace to Helen, I'd agree to anything. But now it's different. I'm functioning, I'm behaving damn well, so far as—"

"Please don't swear at me," Marion said.

He looked at her, startled. With each remark the force of her dislike became more and more apparent. She had built up all her fear of life into one wall and faced it toward him. This trivial reproof was possibly the result of some trouble with the cook several hours before. Charlie became increasingly alarmed at leaving Honoria in this atmosphere of hostility against himself; sooner or later it would come out, in a word here, a shake of the head there, and some of that distrust would be irrevocably implanted in Honoria. But he pulled his temper down out of his face and shut it up inside him; he had won a point, for Lincoln realized the absurdity of Marion's remark and asked her lightly since when she had objected to the word *damn*.

"Another thing," Charlie said: "I'm able to give her certain advantages now. I'm going to take a French governess to Prague with me. I've got a lease on a new apartment—"

He stopped, realizing that he was blundering. They couldn't be expected to accept with equanimity the fact that his income was again twice as large as their own.

"I suppose you can give her more luxuries than we can," said Marion. "When you were throwing away money we were living along watching every ten francs. . . . I suppose you'll start doing it again."

"Oh, no," he said. "I've learned. I worked hard for ten years, you know—until I got lucky in the market, like so many people. Terribly lucky. It didn't seem any use working any more, so I quit."

There was a long silence. All of them felt their nerves straining, and for the first time in a year Charlie wanted a drink. He was sure now that Lincoln Peters wanted him to have his child.

Marion shuddered suddenly; part of her saw that Charlie's feet were planted on the earth now, and her own maternal feeling recognized the naturalness of his desire; but she had lived for a long time with a prejudice—a prejudice founded on a curious disbelief in her sister's happiness, and which, in the shock of one terrible night, had turned to hatred for him. It had all happened at a point in her life where the discouragement of ill health and adverse circumstances made it necessary for her to believe in tangible villainy and a tangible villain.

"I can't help what I think!" she cried out suddenly. "How much you were responsible for Helen's death, I don't know. It's something you'll have to square with your own conscience."

An electric current of agony surged through him; for a moment he was almost on his feet, an unuttered sound echoing in his throat. He hung on to himself for a moment, another moment.

"Hold on there," said Lincoln uncomfortably. "I never thought you were responsible for that."

"Helen died of heart trouble," Charlie said dully.

"Yes, heart trouble." Marion spoke as if the phrase had another meaning for her.

Then, in the flatness that followed her outburst, she saw him plainly and she knew he had somehow arrived at control over the situation. Glancing at her husband, she found no help from him, and as abruptly as if it were a matter of no importance, she threw up the sponge.

"Do what you like!" she cried, springing up from her chair. "She's your child. I'm not the person to stand in your way. I think if it were my child I'd rather see her—" She managed to check herself. "You two decide it. I can't stand this. I'm sick. I'm going to bed."

She hurried from the room; after a moment Lincoln said:

"This has been a hard day for her. You know how strongly she feels—" His voice was almost apologetic: "When a woman gets an idea in her head."

"Of course."

"It's going to be all right. I think she sees now that you—can provide for the child, and so we can't very well stand in your way or Honoria's way."

"Thank you, Lincoln."

"I'd better go along and see how she is."

"I'm going."

He was still trembling when he reached the street, but a walk down the Rue Bonaparte to the *quais* set him up, and as he crossed the Seine, fresh and new by the *quai* lamps, he felt exultant. But back in his room he couldn't sleep. The image of Helen haunted him. Helen whom he had loved so until they had senselessly begun to abuse each other's love, tear it into shreds. On that terrible February night that Marion remembered so vividly, a slow quarrel had gone on for hours. There was a scene at the Florida, and then he attempted to take her home, and then she kissed young Webb at a table; after that there was what she had hysterically said. When he arrived home alone he turned the key in the lock in wild anger. How could he know she would arrive an hour later alone, that there would be a snowstorm in which she wandered about in slippers, too confused to find a taxi? Then the aftermath, her escaping pneumonia by a miracle, and all the attendant horror. They were "reconciled," but that was the beginning of the end, and Marion, who had seen with her own eyes and who imagined it to be one of many scenes from her sister's martyrdom, never forgot.

Going over it again brought Helen nearer, and in the white, soft light that steals upon half sleep near morning he found himself talking to her again. She said that he was perfectly right about Honoria and that she wanted Honoria to be with him. She said she was glad he was being good and doing better. She said a lot of other things—very friendly things—but she was in a swing in a white dress, and swinging faster and faster all the time, so that at the end he could not hear clearly all that she said.

4

He woke up feeling happy. The door of the world was open again. He made plans, vistas, futures for Honoria and himself, but suddenly he grew sad, remembering all the plans he and Helen had made. She had not planned to die. The present was the thing—work to do and someone to love. But not to love too much, for he knew the injury that a father can do to a daughter or a mother to a son by attaching them too closely: afterward, out in the world, the child would seek in the marriage partner the same blind tenderness and, failing probably to find it, turn against love and life.

It was another bright, crisp day. He called Lincoln Peters at the bank where he worked and asked if he could count on taking Honoria when he left for Prague. Lincoln agreed that there was no reason for delay. One thing—the legal guardianship. Marion wanted to retain that a while longer. She was upset by the whole matter, and it would oil things if she felt that the situation was still in her control for another year. Charlie agreed, wanting only the tangible, visible child.

Then the question of a governess. Charles sat in a gloomy agency and talked to a cross Béarnaise and to a buxom Breton peasant, neither of whom he could have endured. There were others whom he would see tomorrow.

He lunched with Lincoln Peters at Griffons, trying to keep down his exultation.

"There's nothing quite like your own child," Lincoln said. "But you understand how Marion feels too."

"She's forgotten how hard I worked for seven years there," Charlie said. "She just remembers one night."

"There's another thing." Lincoln hesitated. "While you and Helen were tearing around Europe throwing money away, we were just getting along. I didn't touch any of the prosperity because I never got ahead enough to carry anything but my insurance. I think Marion felt there was some kind of injustice in it—you not even working toward the end, and getting richer and richer."

"It went just as quick as it came," said Charlie.

"Yes, a lot of it stayed in the hands of chasseurs and saxophone players and maîtres d'hôtel—well, the big party's over now. I just said that to explain Marion's feeling about those crazy years. If you drop in about six o'clock tonight before Marion's too tired, we'll settle the details on the spot."

Back at his hotel, Charlie found a *pneumatique* that had been redirected from the Ritz bar where Charlie had left his address for the purpose of finding a certain man.

> Dear Charlie: You were so strange when we saw you the other day that I wondered if I did something to offend you. If so, I'm not conscious of it. In fact, I have thought about you too much for the last year, and it's always been in the back of my mind that I might see you if I came over here. We *did* have such good times that crazy spring, like the night you and I stole the butcher's tricycle, and the time we tried to call on the president and you had the old derby rim and the wire cane. Everybody seems so old lately, but I don't feel old a bit. Couldn't we get together some time today for old time's sake? I've got a vile hangover for the moment, but will be feeling better this afternoon and will look for you about five in the sweatshop at the Ritz.
>
> Always devotedly,
>
> Lorraine.

His first feeling was one of awe that he had actually, in his mature years, stolen a tricycle and pedaled Lorraine all over the Étoile between the small hours and dawn. In retrospect it was a nightmare. Locking out Helen didn't fit in with any other act of his life, but the tricycle incident did—it was one of many. How many weeks or months of dissipation to arrive at that condition of utter irresponsibility?

He tried to picture how Lorraine had appeared to him then—very attractive; Helen was unhappy about it, though she said nothing. Yesterday, in the restaurant, Lorraine had seemed trite, blurred, worn away. He emphatically did not want to see her, and he was glad Alix had not given away his hotel address. It was a relief to think, instead, of Honoria, to think of Sundays spent with her and of saying good morning to her and of knowing she was there in his house at night, drawing her breath in the darkness.

At five he took a taxi and bought presents for all the Peters—a piquant cloth doll, a box of Roman soldiers, flowers for Marion, big linen handkerchiefs for Lincoln.

He saw, when he arrived in the apartment, that Marion had accepted the inevitable. She greeted him now as though he were a recalcitrant member of the family rather than a menacing outsider. Honoria had been told she was going; Charlie was glad to see that her tact made her conceal her excessive happiness. Only on his lap did she whisper her delight and the question "When?" before she slipped away with the other children.

He and Marion were alone for a minute in the room, and on an impulse he spoke out boldly:

"Family quarrels are bitter things. They don't go according to any rules. They're not like aches or wounds; they're more like splits in the skin that won't heal because there's not enough material. I wish you and I could be on better terms."

"Some things are hard to forget," she answered. "It's a question of confidence." There was no answer to this and presently she asked, "When do you propose to take her?"

"As soon as I can get a governess. I hoped the day after tomorrow."

"That's impossible. I've got to get her things in shape. Not before Saturday."

He yielded. Coming back into the room, Lincoln offered him a drink.

"I'll take my daily whisky," he said.

It was warm here, it was a home, people together by a fire. The children felt very safe and important; the mother and father were serious, watchful. They had things to do for the children more important than his visit here. A spoonful of medicine was, after all, more important than the strained relations between Marion and himself. They were not dull people, but they were very much in the grip of life and circumstances. He wondered if he couldn't do something to get Lincoln out of his rut at the bank.

A long peal at the doorbell; the *bonne à tout faire* passed through and went down the corridor. The door opened upon another long ring, and then voices, and the three in the salon looked up expectantly; Richard moved to bring the corridor within his range of vision, and Marion rose. Then the maid came back along the corridor, closely followed by the voices, which developed under the light into Duncan Schaeffer and Lorraine Quarrles.

They were gay, they were hilarious, they were roaring with laughter. For a moment Charlie was astounded; unable to understand how they ferreted out the Peters' address.

"Ah-h-h!" Duncan wagged his finger roguishly at Charlie. "Ah-h-h!"

They both slid down another cascade of laughter. Anxious and at a loss, Charlie shook hands with them quickly and presented them to Lincoln and Marion. Marion nodded, scarcely speaking. She had drawn back a step toward the fire; her little girl stood beside her, and Marion put an arm about her shoulder.

With growing annoyance at the intrusion, Charlie waited for them to explain themselves. After some concentration Duncan said:

"We came to invite you out to dinner. Lorraine and I insist that all this chichi, cagy business 'bout your address got to stop."

Charlie came closer to them, as if to force them backward down the corridor.

"Sorry, but I can't. Tell me where you'll be and I'll phone you in half an hour."

This made no impression. Lorraine sat down suddenly on the side of a chair, and focusing her eyes on Richard, cried, "Oh, what a nice little boy! Come here, little boy." Richard glanced at his mother, but did not move. With a perceptible shrug of her shoulders, Lorraine turned back to Charlie:

"Come and dine. Sure your cousins won' mine. See you so sel'om. Or solemn."

"I can't," said Charlie sharply. "You two have dinner and I'll phone you."

Her voice became suddenly unpleasant. "All right, we'll go. But I remember once when you hammered on my door at 4 A.M. I was enough of a good sport to give you a drink. Come on, Dunc."

Still in slow motion, with blurred, angry faces, with uncertain feet, they retired along the corridor.

"Good night," Charlie said.

"Good night!" responded Lorraine emphatically.

When he went back into the salon Marion had not moved, only now her son was standing in the circle of her other arm. Lincoln was still swinging Honoria back and forth like a pendulum from side to side.

"What an outrage!" Charlie broke out. "What an absolute outrage!"

Neither of them answered. Charlie dropped into an armchair, picked up his drink, set it down again and said:

"People I haven't seen for two years having the colossal nerve—"

He broke off. Marion had made the sound "Oh!" in one swift, furious breath, turned her body from him with a jerk and left the room.

Lincoln set down Honoria carefully.

"You children go in and start your soup," he said, and when they obeyed, he said to Charlie:

"Marion's not well and she can't stand shocks. That kind of people make her really physically sick."

"I didn't tell them to come here. They wormed your name out of somebody. They deliberately—"

"Well, it's too bad. It doesn't help matters. Excuse me a minute."

Left alone, Charlie sat tense in his chair. In the next room he could hear the children eating, talking in monosyllables, already oblivious to the scene between their elders. He heard a murmur of conversation from a farther room and then the ticking bell of a telephone receiver picked up, and in a panic he moved to the other side of the room and out of earshot.

In a minute Lincoln came back. "Look here, Charlie. I think we'd better call off dinner for tonight. Marion's in bad shape."

"Is she angry with me?"

"Sort of," he said, almost roughly. "She's not strong and—"

"You mean she's changed her mind about Honoria?"

"She's pretty bitter right now. I don't know. You phone me at the bank tomorrow."

"I wish you'd explain to her I never dreamed these people would come here. I'm just as sore as you are."

"I couldn't explain anything to her now."

Charlie got up. He took his coat and hat and started down the corridor. Then he opened the door of the dining room and said in a strange voice, "Good night, children."

Honoria rose and ran around the table to hug him.

"Good night, sweetheart," he said vaguely, and then trying to make his voice more tender, trying to conciliate something, "Good night, dear children."

5

Charlie went directly to the Ritz bar with the furious idea of finding Lorraine and Duncan, but they were not there, and he realized that in any case there was nothing he could do. He had not touched his drink at the Peters', and now he ordered a whisky and soda. Paul came over to say hello.

"It's a great change," he said sadly. "We do about half the business we did. So many fellows I hear about back in the States lost everything, maybe not in the first crash, but then in the second. Your friend George Hardt lost every cent, I hear. Are you back in the States?"

"No, I'm in business in Prague."

"I heard that you lost a lot in the crash."

"I did," and he added grimly, "but I lost everything I wanted in the boom."

"Selling short."

"Something like that."

Again the memory of those days swept over him like a nightmare—the people they had met traveling; then people who couldn't add a row of figures or speak a coherent sentence. The little man Helen had consented to dance with at the ship's party, who had insulted her ten feet from the table; the women and girls carried screaming with drink or drugs out of public places—

—The men who locked their wives out in the snow, because the snow of twenty-nine wasn't real snow. If you didn't want it to be snow, you just paid some money.

He went to the phone and called the Peters' apartment; Lincoln answered.

"I called up because this thing is on my mind. Has Marion said anything definite?"

"Marion's sick," Lincoln answered shortly. "I know this thing isn't altogether your fault, but I can't have her go to pieces about it. I'm afraid we'll have to let it slide for six months; I can't take the chance of working her up to this state again."

"I see."

"I'm sorry, Charlie."

He went back to his table. His whisky glass was empty, but he shook his head when Alix looked at it questioningly. There wasn't much he could do now except send Honoria some things; he would send her a lot of things tomorrow. He thought rather angrily that this was just money—he had given so many people money. . . .

"No, no more," he said to another waiter. "What do I owe you?"

He would come back some day; they couldn't make him pay forever. But he wanted his child, and nothing was much good now, beside that fact. He wasn't young any more, with a lot of nice thoughts and dreams to have by himself. He was absolutely sure Helen wouldn't have wanted him to be so alone.

QUESTIONS

1. Why does Charlie leave his brother-in-law's address for Duncan Schaeffer?

2. Why does Charlie want custody of Honoria?

3. What does Charlie mean when he says that every late-night move was "an enormous human jump, an increase of paying for the privilege of slower and slower motion"? (154)

4. Why does Marion direct all her "fear of life" at Charlie? (162)

5. Why does Charlie think that "locking out Helen [doesn't] fit in with any other act of his life"? (167)

6. Why does Marion become sick when she encounters Duncan and Lorraine?

7. Why is Charlie "absolutely sure Helen wouldn't have wanted him to be so alone"? (173)

FOR FURTHER REFLECTION

1. Is Charlie truly conscious of the repercussions of his former actions? Of his current ones?

2. Is Marion's anger toward Charlie justified?

3. Should Charlie be granted custody of Honoria?

DOROTHY PARKER

Known today as much for her acerbic wit as for her writing, Dorothy
Parker (1893–1967) was a core member of the famous Algonquin
Round Table, that group of actors and writers who, for a time, met
daily for lunch at one of Midtown Manhattan's most celebrated
hotels. A writer of poetry, short stories, criticism, and screenplays,
Parker excelled at verbal sparring with her cohorts during the
group's heyday in the 1920s. Yet despite Parker's gift for the comic
one-liner, she was a deeply serious person with a penetrating sense
of the ridiculous, and she preferred to be known as a satirist. Her
major works include *Collected Poems: Not So Deep As a Well* (1936)
and two collections of stories, *After Such Pleasures* (1932) and
Here Lies (1939). Early in her career, Parker worked for both *Vogue*
and *Vanity Fair* magazines; later, with Lillian Hellmann and Dashiell
Hammett, she helped found the Screen Writers Guild.

The Custard Heart

No living eye, of human being or caged wild beast or dear, domestic animal, had beheld Mrs. Lanier when she was not being wistful. She was dedicated to wistfulness, as lesser artists to words and paint and marble. Mrs. Lanier was not of the lesser; she was of the true. Surely the eternal example of the true artist is Dickens's actor who blacked himself all over to play Othello. It is safe to assume that Mrs. Lanier was wistful in her bathroom, and slumbered soft in wistfulness through the dark and secret night.

If nothing should happen to the portrait of her by Sir James Weir, there she will stand, wistful for the ages. He has shown her at her full length, all in yellows, the delicately heaped curls, the slender, arched feet like elegant bananas, the shining stretch of the evening gown; Mrs. Lanier habitually wore white in the evening, but white is the devil's own hue to paint, and could a man be expected to spend his entire six weeks in the States on the execution of a single commission? Wistfulness rests, immortal, in the eyes dark with sad hope, in the pleading mouth, the droop of the little head on the sweet long neck, bowed as if in submission to the three ropes of Lanier pearls. It is true that, when the portrait was exhibited, one critic expressed in print his puzzlement as to what a woman who owned such pearls had to be wistful about; but that was doubtless because he had sold his saffron-colored soul for a few pennies to the proprietor of a rival gallery. Certainly, no man could touch Sir James on pearls. Each one is as distinct, as individual as is each little soldier's face in a Meissonier battle scene.

For a time, with the sitter's obligation to resemble the portrait, Mrs. Lanier wore yellow of evenings. She had gowns of velvet like poured country cream and satin with the lacquer of buttercups and chiffon that spiraled about her like golden smoke. She wore them, and listened in shy surprise to the resulting comparisons to daffodils, and butterflies in the sunshine, and such; but she knew.

"It just isn't me," she sighed at last, and returned to her lily draperies. Picasso had his blue period, and Mrs. Lanier her yellow one. They both knew when to stop.

In the afternoons, Mrs. Lanier wore black, thin and fragrant, with the great pearls weeping on her breast. What her attire was by morning, only Gwennie, the maid who brought her breakfast tray, could know; but it must, of course, have been exquisite. Mr. Lanier—certainly there was a Mr. Lanier; he had even been seen—stole past her door on his way out to his office, and the servants glided and murmured, so that Mrs. Lanier might be spared as long as possible from the bright new cruelty of the day. Only when the littler, kinder hours had succeeded noon could she bring herself to come forth and face the recurrent sorrows of living.

There was duty to be done, almost daily, and Mrs. Lanier made herself brave for it. She must go in her town car to select new clothes and to have fitted to her perfection those she had ordered before. Such garments as hers did not just occur; like great poetry, they required labor. But she shrank from leaving the shelter of her house, for everywhere without were the unlovely and the sad, to assail her eyes and her heart. Often she stood shrinking for several minutes by the baroque mirror in her hall before she could manage to hold her head high and brave, and go on.

There is no safety for the tender, no matter how straight their route, how innocent their destination. Sometimes, even in front of Mrs. Lanier's dressmaker's or her furrier's or her *lingère's* or her milliner's, there would be a file of thin girls and small, shabby men, who held placards in their cold hands and paced up and down and up and down with slow, measured steps. Their faces would be blue and rough from the wind, and blank with the monotony of their treadmill. They looked so little and poor and strained that Mrs. Lanier's hands would fly to her heart in pity. Her eyes would be luminous with sympathy and her sweet lips would part as if on a whisper of cheer, as she passed through the draggled line into the shop.

Often there would be pencil sellers in her path, a half of a creature set upon a sort of roller skate thrusting himself along the pavement by his hands, or a blind man shuffling after his wavering cane. Mrs. Lanier must stop and sway, her eyes closed, one hand about her throat to support her lovely, stricken head. Then you could actually see her force herself, could see the effort ripple her body, as she opened her eyes and gave these miserable ones, the blind and the seeing alike, a smile of such tenderness, such sorrowful understanding, that it was like the exquisite sad odor of hyacinths on the air. Sometimes, if the man was not too horrible, she could even reach in her purse for a coin and, holding it as lightly as if she had plucked it from a silvery stem, extend her slim arm and drop it in his cup. If he was young and new at his life, he would offer her pencils for the worth of her money; but Mrs. Lanier wanted no returns. In gentlest delicacy she would slip away, leaving him with mean wares intact, not a worker for his livelihood like a million others, but signal and set apart, rare in the fragrance of charity.

So it was, when Mrs. Lanier went out. Everywhere she saw them, the ragged, the wretched, the desperate, and to each she gave her look that spoke with no words.

"Courage," it said. "And you—oh, wish me courage, too!"

Frequently, by the time she returned to her house, Mrs. Lanier would be limp as a freesia. Her maid Gwennie would have to beseech her to lie down, to gain the strength to change her gown for a filmier one and descend to her drawing room, her eyes darkly mournful, but her exquisite breasts pointed high.

In her drawing room, there was sanctuary. Here her heart might heal from the blows of the world, and be whole for its own sorrow. It was a room suspended above life, a place of tender fabrics and pale flowers, with never a paper or a book to report the harrowing or describe it. Below the great sheet of its window swung the river, and the stately scows went by laden with strange stuff in rich tapestry colors; there was no necessity to belong to the sort who must explain that it was garbage. An island with a happy name lay opposite, and on it stood a row of prim, tight buildings, naive as a painting by Rousseau. Sometimes there could be seen on the island the brisk figures of nurses and interns, sporting in the lanes. Possibly there were figures considerably less brisk beyond the barred windows of the buildings, but that was not to be wondered about in the presence of Mrs. Lanier. All those who came to her drawing room came in one cause: to shield her heart from hurt.

Here in her drawing room, in the lovely blue of the late day, Mrs. Lanier sat upon opalescent taffeta and was wistful. And here to her drawing room the young men came and tried to help her bear her life.

There was a pattern to the visits of the young men. They would come in groups of three or four or six, for a while; and then there would be one of them who would stay a little after the rest had gone, who presently would come a little earlier than the others. Then there would be days when Mrs. Lanier would cease to be at home to the other young men, and that one young man would be alone with her in the lovely blue. And then Mrs. Lanier would no longer be at home to that one young man, and Gwennie would have to tell him and tell him, over the telephone, that

Mrs. Lanier was out, that Mrs. Lanier was ill, that Mrs. Lanier could not be disturbed. The groups of young men would come again; that one young man would not be with them. But there would be, among them, a new young man, who presently would stay a little later and come a little earlier, who eventually would plead with Gwennie over the telephone.

Gwennie—her widowed mother had named her Gwendola, and then, as if realizing that no other dream would ever come true, had died—was little and compact and unnoticeable. She had been raised on an upstate farm by an uncle and aunt hard as the soil they fought for their lives. After their deaths, she had no relatives anywhere. She came to New York, because she had heard stories of jobs; her arrival was at the time when Mrs. Lanier's cook needed a kitchen maid. So in her own house, Mrs. Lanier had found her treasure.

Gwennie's hard little farm girl's fingers could set invisible stitches, could employ a flatiron as if it were a wand, could be as summer breezes in the robing of Mrs. Lanier and the tending of her hair. She was as busy as the day was long; and her days frequently extended from daybreak to daybreak. She was never tired, she had no grievance, she was cheerful without being expressive about it. There was nothing in her presence or the sight of her to touch the heart and thus cause discomfort.

Mrs. Lanier would often say that she didn't know what she would do without her little Gwennie; if her little Gwennie should ever leave her, she said, she just couldn't go on. She looked so lorn and fragile as she said it that one scowled upon Gwennie for the potentialities of death or marriage that the girl carried within her. Yet there was no pressing cause for worry, for Gwennie was strong as a pony and had no beau. She had made no friends at all, and seemed not to observe the omission. Her life was for Mrs. Lanier; like all others who were permitted close, Gwennie sought to do what she could to save Mrs. Lanier from pain.

They could all assist in shutting out reminders of the sadness abroad in the world, but Mrs. Lanier's private sorrow was a more difficult matter. There dwelt a yearning so deep, so secret in her heart that it would often be days before she could speak of it, in the twilight, to a new young man.

"If I only had a little baby," she would sigh, "a little, little baby, I think I could be almost happy." And she would fold her delicate arms, and lightly, slowly rock them, as if they cradled that little, little one of her dear dreams. Then, the denied Madonna, she was at her most wistful, and the young man would have lived or died for her, as she bade him.

Mrs. Lanier never mentioned why her wish was unfulfilled; the young man would know her to be too sweet to place blame, too proud to tell. But, so close to her in the pale light, he would understand, and his blood would swirl with fury that such clods as Mr. Lanier remained unkilled. He would beseech Mrs. Lanier, first in halting murmurs, then in rushes of hot words, to let him take her away from the hell of her life and try to make her almost happy. It would be after this that Mrs. Lanier would be out to the young man, would be ill, would be incapable of being disturbed.

Gwennie did not enter the drawing room when there was only one young man there; but when the groups returned she served unobtrusively, drawing a curtain or fetching a fresh glass. All the Lanier servants were unobtrusive, light of step and correctly indistinct of feature. When there must be changes made in the staff, Gwennie and the housekeeper arranged the replacements and did not speak of the matter to Mrs. Lanier, lest she should be stricken by desertions or saddened by tales of woe. Always the new servants resembled the old, alike in that they were unnoticeable. That is, until Kane, the new chauffeur, came.

The old chauffeur had been replaced because he had been the old chauffeur too long. It weighs cruelly heavy on the tender heart when a familiar face grows lined and dry, when familiar shoulders seem daily to droop lower, a familiar nape is hollow between cords. The old chauffeur saw and heard and functioned with no difference; but it was too much for Mrs. Lanier to see what was befalling him. With pain in her voice, she had told Gwennie that she could stand the sight of him no longer. So the old chauffeur had gone, and Kane had come.

Kane was young, and there was nothing depressing about his straight shoulders and his firm, full neck to one sitting behind them in the town car. He stood, a fine triangle in his fitted uniform, holding the door of the car open for Mrs. Lanier and bowed his head as she passed. But when he was not at work, his head was held high and slightly cocked, and there was a little cocked smile on his red mouth.

Often, in the cold weather when Kane waited for her in the car, Mrs. Lanier would humanely bid Gwennie to tell him to come in and wait in the servants' sitting room. Gwennie brought him coffee and looked at him. Twice she did not hear Mrs. Lanier's enameled electric bell.

Gwennie began to observe her evenings off; before, she had disregarded them and stayed to minister to Mrs. Lanier. There was one night when Mrs. Lanier had floated late to her room, after a theater and a long conversation, done in murmurs, in the drawing room. And Gwennie had not been waiting, to take off the white gown, and put away the pearls, and brush the bright hair that curled like the petals of forsythia. Gwennie had not yet returned to the house from her holiday. Mrs. Lanier had had to arouse a parlor maid and obtain unsatisfactory aid from her.

Gwennie had wept, next morning, at the pathos of Mrs. Lanier's eyes; but tears were too distressing for Mrs. Lanier to see, and the girl stopped them. Mrs. Lanier delicately patted her arm, and there had been nothing more of the matter, save that Mrs. Lanier's eyes were darker and wider for this new hurt.

Kane became a positive comfort to Mrs. Lanier. After the sorry sights of the streets, it was good to see Kane standing by the car, solid and straight and young, with nothing in the world the trouble with him. Mrs. Lanier came to smile upon him almost gratefully, yet wistfully, too, as if she would seek of him the secret of not being sad.

And then, one day, Kane did not appear at his appointed time. The car, which should have been waiting to convey Mrs. Lanier to her dressmaker's, was still in the garage, and Kane had not appeared there all day. Mrs. Lanier told Gwennie immediately to telephone the place where he roomed and find out what this meant. The girl had cried out at her, cried out that she had called and called and called, and he was not there and no one there knew where he was. The crying out must have been due to Gwennie's loss of head in her distress at this disruption of Mrs. Lanier's day; or perhaps it was the effect on her voice of an appalling cold she seemed to have contracted, for her eyes were heavy and red and her face pale and swollen.

There was no more of Kane. He had had his wages paid him on the day before he disappeared, and that was the last of him. There was never a word and not another sight of him. At first, Mrs. Lanier could scarcely bring herself to believe that such betrayal could exist. Her heart, soft and sweet as a perfectly made *crème renversée*, quivered in her breast, and in her eyes lay the far light of suffering.

"Oh, how could he do this to me?" she asked piteously of Gwennie. "How could he do this to poor me?"

There was no discussion of the defection of Kane; it was too painful a subject. If a caller heedlessly asked whatever had become of that nice-looking chauffeur, Mrs. Lanier would lay her hand over her closed lids and slowly wince. The caller would be suicidal that he had thus unconsciously added to her sorrows, and would strive his consecrated best to comfort her.

Gwennie's cold lasted for an extraordinarily long time. The weeks went by, and still, every morning, her eyes were red and her face white and puffed. Mrs. Lanier often had to look away from her when she brought the breakfast tray.

She tended Mrs. Lanier as carefully as ever; she gave no attention to her holidays, but stayed to do further service. She had always been quiet, and she became all but silent, and that was additionally soothing. She worked without stopping and seemed to thrive, for, save for the effects of the curious cold, she looked round and healthy.

"See," Mrs. Lanier said in tender raillery, as the girl attended the group in the drawing room, "see how fat my little Gwennie's getting! Isn't that cute?"

The weeks went on, and the pattern of the young men shifted again. There came the day when Mrs. Lanier was not at home to a group; when a new young man was to come and be alone with her, for his first time, in the drawing room. Mrs. Lanier sat before her mirror and lightly touched her throat with perfume, while Gwennie heaped the golden curls.

The exquisite face Mrs. Lanier saw in the mirror drew her closer attention, and she put down the perfume and leaned toward it. She drooped her head a little to the side and watched it closely; she saw the wistful eyes grow yet more wistful, the lips curve to a pleading smile. She folded her arms close to her sweet breast and slowly rocked them, as if they cradled a dream child. She watched the mirrored arms sway gently, caused them to sway a little slower.

"If I only had a little baby," she sighed. She shook her head. Delicately she cleared her throat, and sighed again on a slightly lower note. "If I only had a little, little baby, I think I could be almost happy."

There was a clatter from behind her, and she turned, amazed. Gwennie had dropped the hairbrush to the floor and stood swaying, with her face in her hands.

"Gwennie!" said Mrs. Lanier. "Gwennie!"

The girl took her hands from her face, and it was as if she stood under a green light.

"I'm sorry," she panted. "Sorry. Please excuse me. I'm—oh, I'm going to be sick!"

She ran from the room so violently that the floor shook.

Mrs. Lanier sat looking after Gwennie, her hands at her wounded heart. Slowly she turned back to her mirror, and what she saw there arrested her; the artist knows the masterpiece. Here was the perfection of her career, the sublimation of wistfulness; it was that look of grieved bewilderment that did it. Carefully she kept it upon her face as she rose from the mirror and, with her lovely hands still shielding her heart, went down to the new young man.

QUESTIONS

1. Why is Mrs. Lanier able to give a coin to a beggar only if he is "not too horrible"? (179) Why is she unable to accept a pencil in return for giving money to a young pencil seller?

2. Why is Mrs. Lanier unable to face life? Why does everyone want to shield her from pain?

3. Why does Mrs. Lanier think she "could be almost happy" if she had a little baby? (182)

4. If Mrs. Lanier feels pity and sympathy for the destitute on the street, why does she not feel sympathy for her old chauffeur?

5. Why does Mrs. Lanier entertain a series of young men in her drawing room?

6. Is Kane employed to be a "comfort" to Mrs. Lanier or to Gwennie? (184)

7. What does the author mean when she describes Mrs. Lanier's look of "grieved bewilderment" as the "perfection of her career"? (186)

FOR FURTHER REFLECTION

1. Does the author want us to feel pity or contempt for Mrs. Lanier?

2. Is it more difficult to feel sympathy for the rich than for the poor?

3. Do you agree with the adage that money can't buy happiness?

Greed

W. SOMERSET MAUGHAM

As a young man, W. Somerset Maugham (1874–1965) studied
medicine for six years and held a one-year internship in the slums
of London. He never practiced medicine, but he recommended the
medical profession as a valuable training ground for writers. His
first successful novel, *Of Human Bondage* (1915), is a fictionalized
account of his early years. Cosmopolitan in temperament, Maugham
traveled widely, keenly observing people who were out of their
native milieu. He was not only a prolific writer but also a commer-
cially successful one. Maugham's novels, including *The Moon and
Sixpence* (1919), *Cakes and Ale* (1930), and *The Razor's Edge* (1944),
and numerous short stories have enjoyed great popular appeal.

A Woman of Fifty

My friend Wyman Holt is a professor of English literature in one of the smaller universities of the Middle West, and hearing that I was speaking in a nearby city—nearby as distances go in the vastness of America—he wrote to ask me if I would come and give a talk to his class. He suggested that I should stay with him for a few days so that he could show me something of the surrounding country. I accepted the invitation, but told him that my engagements would prevent me from spending more than a couple of nights with him. He met me at the station, drove me to his house, and after we had had a drink we walked over to the campus. I was somewhat taken aback to find so many people in the hall in which I was to speak, for I had not expected more than twenty at the outside and I was not prepared to give a solemn lecture, but only an informal chat. I was more than a little intimidated to see a number of middle-aged and elderly persons, some of whom I suspected were members of the faculty, and I was afraid they would find what I had to say very superficial. However, there was nothing to do but to start and, after Wyman had introduced me to the audience in a manner that I very well knew I couldn't live up to, that is what I did. I said my say,

192 — W. SOMERSET MAUGHAM

I answered as best I could a number of questions, and then I retired with Wyman into a little room at the back of the stage from which I had spoken.

Several people came in. They said the usual kindly things to me that are said on these occasions, and I made the usual polite replies. I was thirsting for a drink. Then a woman came in and held out her hand to me.

"How very nice it is to see you again," she said. "It's years since we last met."

To the best of my belief I'd never set eyes on her before. I forced a cordial smile to my tired, stiff lips, shook her proffered hand effusively, and wondered who the devil she was. My professor must have seen from my face that I was trying to place her, for he said: "Mrs. Greene is married to a member of our faculty and she gives a course on the Renaissance and Italian literature."

"Really," I said. "Interesting."

I was no wiser than before.

"Has Wyman told you that you're dining with us tomorrow night?"

"I'm very glad," I said.

"It's not a party. Only my husband, his brother, and my sister-in-law. I suppose Florence has changed a lot since then."

"Florence?" I said to myself. "Florence?"

That was evidently where I'd known her. She was a woman of about fifty with gray hair simply done and marcelled without exaggeration. She was a trifle too stout and she was dressed neatly enough, but without distinction, in a dress that I guessed had been bought ready-made at the local branch of a big store. She had rather large eyes of a pale blue and a poor complexion; she wore no rouge and had used a lipstick but sparingly. She seemed a nice creature. There was something maternal in her demeanour, something placid and fulfilled, which I found appealing. I supposed that I had run across her on one of my frequent visits to Florence and because it was perhaps the only time she had been there our meeting made more of an impression on her than on me. I must confess that my acquaintance with the wives of members of a faculty is very limited, but she was just the sort of person I should have expected the wife of a professor to be, and picturing her life, useful but uneventful, on scanty means, with its little social gatherings, its bickerings, its gossip, its busy dullness, I could easily imagine that her trip to Florence must linger with her as a thrilling and unforgettable experience.

On the way back to his house Wyman said to me: "You'll like Jasper Greene. He's clever."

"What's he a professor of?"

"He's not a professor; he's an instructor. A fine scholar. He's her second husband. She was married to an Italian before."

"Oh?' That didn't chime in with my ideas at all. "What was her name?"

"I haven't a notion. I don't believe it was a great success." Wyman chuckled. "That's only a deduction I draw from the fact that she hasn't a single thing in the house to suggest that she ever spent any time in Italy. I should have expected her to have at least a refectory table, an old chest or two, and an embroidered cope hanging on the wall."

I laughed. I knew those rather dreary pieces that people buy when they're in Italy, the gilt wooden candlesticks, the Venetian glass mirrors, and the high-backed, comfortless chairs. They look well enough when you see them in the crowded shops of the dealers in antiques, but when you bring them to another country they're too often a sad disappointment. Even if they're genuine, which they seldom are, they look ill at ease and out of place.

"Laura has money," Wyman went on. "When they married she furnished the house from cellar to attic in Chicago. It's quite a show place; it's a little masterpiece of hideousness and vulgarity. I never go into the living room without marvelling at the unerring taste with which she picked out exactly what you'd expect to find in the bridal suite of a second-class hotel in Atlantic City."

To explain this irony I should state that Wyman's living room was all chromium and glass, rough modern fabrics, with a boldly cubist rug on the floor, and on the walls Picasso prints and drawings by Tchelicheff. However, he gave me a very good dinner. We spent the evening chatting pleasantly about things that mutually interested us and finished it with a couple of bottles of beer. I went to bed in a room of somewhat aggressive modernity. I read for a while and then putting out the light composed myself to sleep.

"Laura?" I said to myself. "Laura what?"

I tried to think back. I thought of all the people I knew in Florence, hoping that by association I might recall when and where I had come in contact with Mrs. Greene. Since I was going to dine with her I wanted to recall something that would prove that I had not forgotten her. People look upon it as a slight if you don't remember them. I suppose we all attach a sort of importance to ourselves, and it is humiliating to realize that we have left no impression at all upon the persons we have associated with. I dozed off, but before I fell into the blessedness of deep sleep, my subconscious, released from the effort of striving at recollection, I suppose, grew active and I was suddenly wide awake, for I remembered who Laura Greene was. It was no wonder that I had forgotten her, for it was twenty-five years since I had seen her, and then only haphazardly during a month I spent in Florence.

It was just after the First World War. She had been engaged to a man who was killed in it and she and her mother had managed to get over to France to see his grave. They were San Francisco people. After doing their sad errand they had come down to Italy and were spending the winter in Florence. At that time there was quite a large colony of English and Americans. I had some American friends, a Colonel Harding and his wife, colonel because he had occupied an important position in the Red Cross, who had a handsome villa in the Via Bolognese, and they asked me to stay with them. I spent most of my mornings sightseeing and met my friends at Doney's in the Via Tornabuoni round about noon to drink a cocktail. Doney's was the gathering place of everybody one knew, Americans, English, and such of the Italians as frequented their society. There you heard all the gossip of the town. There was generally a lunch party either at a restaurant or at one or other of the villas with their fine old gardens a mile or two from the centre of the city. I had been given a card to the Florence Club, and in the afternoon Charley Harding and I used to go there to play bridge or a dangerous game of poker with a pack of thirty-two cards. In the evening there would be a dinner party with more bridge perhaps and often dancing. One met the same people all the time, but the group was large enough, the people sufficiently various, to prevent it from being tedious. Everyone was more or less interested in the arts, as was only right and proper in Florence, so that, idle as life seemed, it was not entirely frivolous.

Laura and her mother, Mrs. Clayton, a widow, lived in one of the better boarding houses. They appeared to be comfortably off. They had come to Florence with letters of introduction and soon made many friends. Laura's story appealed to the sympathies, and people were glad on that account to do what they could for the two women, but they were in themselves nice and quickly liked for themselves. They were hospitable and gave frequent lunches at one or other of the restaurants where one ate macaroni and the inevitable scaloppini, and drank Chianti. Mrs. Clayton was perhaps a little lost in this cosmopolitan society, where matters that were strange to her were seriously or gaily talked about, but Laura took to it as though it were her native element. She engaged an Italian woman to teach her the language and soon was reading the *Inferno* with her; she devoured books on the art of the Renaissance and on Florentine history, and I sometimes came across her,

Baedeker in hand, at the Uffizi or in some church studiously examining works of art.

She was twenty-four or twenty-five then and I was well over forty, so that though we often met, we became cordially acquainted rather than intimate. She was by no means beautiful, but she was comely in rather an unusual way; she had an oval face with bright blue eyes and very dark hair which she wore very simply, parted in the middle, drawn over her ears and tied in a chignon low on the nape of her neck. She had a good skin and a naturally high colour; her features were good without being remarkable, and her teeth were even, small, and white; but her chief asset was her easy grace of movement, and I was not surprised when they told me that she danced "divinely." Her figure was very good, somewhat fuller than was the fashion of the moment; and I think what made her attractive was the odd mingling in her appearance of the Madonna in an altarpiece by one of the later Italian painters and a suggestion of sensuality. It certainly made her very alluring to the Italians who gathered at Doney's in the morning or were occasionally invited to lunch or dinner in the American or English villas. She was evidently accustomed to dealing with amorous young men, for though she was charming, gracious, and friendly with them, she kept them at their distance. She quickly discovered that they were all looking for an American heiress who would restore the family fortunes, and with a demure amusement which I found admirable made them delicately understand that she was far from rich. They sighed a little and turned their attentions at Doney's, which was their happy hunting ground, to more likely objects. They continued to dance with her, and to keep their hand in flirted with her, but their aspirations ceased to be matrimonial.

But there was one young man who persisted. I knew him slightly because he was one of the regular poker players at the club. I played occasionally. It was impossible to win and the disgruntled foreigners used sometimes to say that the Italians ganged up on us, but it may be only that they knew the particular game they played better than we did. Laura's admirer, Tito di San Pietro, was a bold and even reckless player and would often lose sums he could ill afford. (That was not his real name, but I call him that since his own is famous in Florentine history.) He was a good-looking youth, neither short nor tall, with fine black eyes, thick black hair brushed back from his forehead and shining with oil, an olive skin, and features of classical regularity. He was poor and he had some vague occupation, which did not seem to interfere with his amusements, but he was always beautifully dressed. No one quite knew where he lived, in a furnished room perhaps or in the attic of some relation; and all that remained of his ancestors' great possessions was a Cinquecento villa about thirty miles from the city. I never saw it, but I was told that it was of amazing beauty, with a great neglected garden of cypresses and live oaks, overgrown borders of box, terraces, artificial grottoes, and crumbling statues. His widowed father, the count, lived there alone and subsisted on the wine he made from the vines of the small property he still owned and the oil from his olive trees. He seldom came to Florence, so I never met him, but Charley Harding knew him fairly well.

"He's a perfect specimen of the Tuscan nobleman of the old school," he said. "He was in the diplomatic service in his youth and he knows the world. He has beautiful manners and such an air, you almost feel he's doing you a favour when he says how d'you do to you. He's a brilliant talker. Of course he hasn't a penny, he squandered the little he inherited on gambling and women, but he bears his poverty with great dignity. He acts as though money were something beneath his notice."

"What sort of age is he?" I asked.

"Fifty, I should say, but he's still the handsomest man I've ever seen in my life."

"Oh?"

"You describe him, Bessie. When he first came here he made a pass at Bessie. I've never been quite sure how far it went."

"Don't be a fool, Charley," Mrs. Harding laughed.

She gave him the sort of look a woman gives her husband when she has been married to him many years and is quite satisfied with him.

"He's very attractive to women and he knows it," she said. "When he talks to you he gives you the impression that you're the only woman in the world and of course it's flattering. But it's only a game and a woman would have to be a perfect fool to take him seriously. He *is* very handsome. Tall and spare and he holds himself well. He has great dark liquid eyes, like the boy's; his hair is snow white, but very thick still, and the contrast with his bronzed, young face is really breathtaking. He has a ravaged, rather battered look, but at the same time a look of such distinction, it's really quite incredibly romantic."

"He also has his great dark liquid eyes on the main chance," said Charley Harding dryly. "And he'll never let Tito marry a girl who has no more money than Laura."

"She has about five thousand dollars a year of her own," said Bessie. "And she'll get that much more when her mother dies."

"Her mother can live for another thirty years, and five thousand a year won't go far to keep a husband, a father, and two or three children, and restore a ruined villa with practically not a stick of furniture in it."

"I think the boy's desperately in love with her."

"How old is he?" I asked.

"Twenty-six."

A few days after this Charley, on coming back to lunch, since for once we were lunching by ourselves, told me that he had run across Mrs. Clayton in the Via Tornabuoni and she had said that she and Laura were driving out that afternoon with Tito to meet his father and see the villa.

"What d'you suppose that means?" asked Bessie. "My guess is that Tito is taking Laura to be inspected by his old man, and if he approves he's going to ask her to marry him."

"And will he approve?"

"Not on your life."

But Charley was wrong. After the two women had been shown over the house they were taken for a walk round the garden. Without exactly knowing how it had happened Mrs. Clayton found herself alone in an alley with the old count. She spoke no Italian, but he had been an attaché in London and his English was tolerable.

"Your daughter is charming, Mrs. Clayton," he said. "I am not surprised that my Tito has fallen in love with her."

Mrs. Clayton was no fool and it may be that she too had guessed why the young man had asked them to go and see the ancestral villa.

"Young Italians are very impressionable. Laura is sensible enough not to take their attention too seriously."

"I was hoping she was not quite indifferent to the boy."

"I have no reason to believe that she likes him any more than any other of the young men who dance with her," Mrs. Clayton answered somewhat coldly. "I think I should tell you at once that my daughter has a very moderate income and she will have no more till I die."

"I will be frank with you. I have nothing in the world but this house and the few acres that surround it. My son could not afford to marry a penniless girl, but he is not a fortune hunter and he loves your daughter."

The count had not only the grand manner, but a great deal of charm and Mrs. Clayton was not insensible to it. She softened a little.

"All that is neither here nor there. We don't arrange our children's marriages in America. If Tito wants to marry her, let him ask her, and if she's prepared to marry him she'll presumably say so."

"Unless I am greatly mistaken that is just what he is doing now. I hope with all my heart that he will be successful."

They strolled on and presently saw walking towards them the two young people hand in hand. It was not difficult to guess what had passed. Tito kissed Mrs. Clayton's hand and his father on both cheeks.

"Mrs. Clayton, Papa, Laura has consented to be my wife."

The engagement made something of a stir in Florentine society and a number of parties were given for the young couple. It was quite evident that Tito was very much in love, but less so that Laura was. He was good looking, adoring, high spirited, and gay; it was likely enough that she loved him; but she was a girl who did not display emotion and she remained what she had always been, somewhat placid, amiable, serious but friendly, and easy to talk to. I wondered to what extent she had been influenced to accept Tito's offer by his great name, with its historical associations, and the sight of that beautiful house with its lovely view and the romantic garden.

"Anyhow there's no doubt about its being a love match on his side," said Bessie Harding, when we were talking it over. "Mrs. Clayton tells me that neither Tito nor his father has shown any desire to know how much Laura has."

"I'd bet a million dollars that they know to the last cent what she's got and they've calculated exactly how much it comes to in lire," said Harding with a grunt.

"You're a beastly old man, darling," she answered.

He gave another grunt.

Shortly after that I left Florence. The marriage took place from the Hardings' house and a vast crowd came to it, ate their food, and drank their champagne. Tito and his wife took an apartment on the Lungarno and the old count returned to his lonely villa in the hills. I did not go to Florence again for three years and then only for a week. I was staying once more with the Hardings. I asked about my old friends and then remembered Laura and her mother.

"'Mrs. Clayton went back to San Francisco," said Bessie, "and Laura and Tito live at the villa with the count. They're very happy."

"Any babies?"

"No."

"Go on," said Harding.

Bessie gave her husband a look.

"I cannot imagine why I've lived thirty years with a man I dislike so much," she said. "They gave up the apartment on the Lungarno. Laura spent a good deal of money doing things to the villa, there wasn't a bathroom in it, she put in central heating, and she had to buy a lot of furniture to make it habitable, and then Tito lost a small fortune playing poker and poor Laura had to pay up."

"Hadn't he got a job?"

"It didn't amount to anything and it came to an end."

"What Bessie means by that is that he was fired," Harding put in.

"Well, to cut a long story short, they thought it would be more economical to live at the villa and Laura had the idea that it would keep Tito out of mischief. She loves the garden and she's made it lovely. Tito simply worships her and the old count's taken quite a fancy to her. So really it's all turned out very well.'"

"It may interest you to know that Tito was in last Thursday," said Harding. "He played like a madman and I don't know how much he lost."

"Oh, Charley. He promised Laura he'd never play again."

"As if a gambler ever kept a promise like that. It'll be like last time. He'll burst into tears and say he loves her and it's a debt of honour and unless he can get the money he'll blow his brains out. And Laura will pay as she paid before."

"He's weak, poor dear, but that's his only fault. Unlike most Italian husbands he's absolutely faithful to her and he's kindness itself." She looked at Harding with a sort of humorous grimness. "I've yet to find a husband who was perfect."

"You'd better start looking around pretty soon, dear, or it'll be too late," he retorted with a grin.

I left the Hardings and returned to London. Charley Harding and I corresponded in a desultory sort of way, and about a year later I got a letter from him. He told me as usual what he had been doing in the interval, and mentioned that he had been to Montecatini for the baths and had gone with Bessie to visit friends in Rome; he spoke of the various people I knew in Florence, So-and-So had just bought a Bellini and Mrs. Such-and-Such had gone to America to divorce her husband. Then he went on: "I suppose you've heard about the San Pietros. It's shaken us all and we can talk of nothing else. Laura's terribly upset, poor thing, and she's going to have a baby. The police keep on questioning her and that doesn't make it any easier for her. Of course we brought her to stay here. Tito comes up for trial in another month."

I hadn't the faintest notion what all this was about. So I wrote at once to Harding asking him what it meant. He answered with a long letter. What he had to tell me was terrible. I will relate the bare and brutal facts as shortly as I can. I learned them partly from Harding's letter and partly from what he and Bessie told me when two years later I was with them once more.

The count and Laura took to one another at once and Tito was pleased to see how quickly they had formed an affectionate friendship, for he was as devoted to his father as he was in love with his wife. He was glad that the count began to come more often to Florence than he had been used to. They had a spare room in the apartment and on occasion he spent two or three nights with them. He and Laura would go bargain hunting in the antique shops and buy old pieces to put in the villa. He had tact and knowledge, and little by little, the house, with its spacious rooms and marble floors, lost its forlorn air and became a friendly place to live in. Laura had a passion for gardening and she and the count spent long hours together planning and then supervising the workmen who were restoring the gardens to their ancient, rather stately, beauty.

Laura made light of it when Tito's financial difficulties forced them to give up the apartment in Florence; she had had enough of Florentine society by then and was not displeased to live altogether in the grand house that had belonged to his ancestors. Tito liked city life and the prospect dismayed him, but he could not complain since it was his own folly that had made it necessary for them to cut down expenses. They still had the car and he amused himself by taking long drives while his father and Laura were busy, and if they knew that now and then he went into Florence to have a flutter at the club they shut their eyes to it. So a year passed. Then, he hardly knew why, he was seized with a vague misgiving. He couldn't put his finger on anything; he had an uneasy feeling that perhaps Laura didn't care for him so much as she had at first; sometimes it seemed to him that his father was inclined to be impatient with him; they appeared to have a great deal to say to one another, but he got the impression that he was being edged out of their conversation, as though he were a child who was expected to sit still and not interrupt while his elders talked of things over his head; he had a notion that often his presence was unwelcome to them and that they were more at their ease when he was not there. He knew his father, and his reputation, but the suspicion that arose in him was so horrible that he refused to entertain it. And yet sometimes he caught a look passing between them that disconcerted him, there was a tender possessiveness in his father's eyes, a sensual complacency in Laura's, which, if he had seen it in others, would have convinced him that they were lovers. But he couldn't, he wouldn't, believe that there was anything between them. The count couldn't help making love to a woman and it was likely enough that Laura felt his extraordinary fascination, but it was shameful to suppose for a moment that they, these two people he loved, had formed a criminal, almost an incestuous, connexion. He was sure that Laura had no idea that there was anything more in her feeling than the natural affection of a young, happily married woman for her father-in-law. Notwithstanding, he thought it better that she should not remain in everyday contact with his father, and one day he suggested that they should go back to live in Florence. Laura and the count were astonished that he should propose such a thing and would not hear of it. Laura said that, having spent so much money on the villa, she couldn't afford to set up another establishment, and the count that it was absurd to leave it, now that Laura had made it so comfortable, to live in a wretched apartment in the city. An argument started and Tito got rather excited. He took some remark of Laura's to mean that if she lived at the villa it was to keep him out of temptation. This reference to his losses at the poker table angered him.

"You always throw your money in my face," he said passionately. "If I'd wanted to marry money I'd have had the sense to marry someone who had a great deal more than you."

Laura went very pale and glanced at the count.

"You have no right to speak to Laura like that," he said. "You are an ill-mannered oaf."

"I shall speak to my wife exactly as I choose."

"You are mistaken. So long as you are in my house you will treat her with the respect which is her right and your duty."

"When I want lessons in behaviour from you, Father, I will let you know."

"You are very impertinent, Tito. You will kindly leave the room."

He looked very stern and dignified, and Tito, furious and yet slightly intimidated, leapt to his feet and stalked out slamming the door behind him. He took the car and drove in to Florence. He won quite a lot of money that day (lucky at cards, unlucky in love) and to celebrate his winnings got more than a little drunk. He did not go back to the villa till the following morning. Laura was as friendly and placid as ever, but his father was somewhat cool. No reference was made to the scene. But from then on things went from bad to worse. Tito was sullen and moody, the count critical, and on occasion sharp words passed between them. Laura did not interfere, but Tito gained the impression that after a dispute that had been more than acrimonious Laura interceded with his father, for the count thenceforward, refusing to be annoyed, began to treat him with the tolerant patience with which you would treat a wayward child. He convinced himself that they were acting in concert and his suspicions grew formidable. They even increased when Laura in her good-natured way, saying that it must be very dull for him to remain so much in the country, encouraged him to go more often to Florence to see his friends.

He jumped to the conclusion that she said this only to be rid of him. He began to watch them. He would enter suddenly a room in which he knew they were, expecting to catch them in a compromising position, or silently follow them to a secluded part of the garden. They were chatting unconcernedly of trivial things. Laura greeted him with a pleasant smile. He could put his finger on nothing to confirm his torturing suspicions. He started to drink. He grew nervous and irritable. He had no proof, no proof whatever, that there was anything between them, and yet in his bones he was certain that they were grossly, shockingly deceiving him. He brooded till he felt he was going mad. A dark aching fire within him consumed his being. On one of his visits to Florence he bought a pistol. He made up his mind that if he could have proof of what in his heart he was certain of, he would kill them both.

I don't know what brought on the final catastrophe. All that came out at the trial was that, driven beyond endurance, Tito had gone one night to his father's room to have it out with him. His father mocked and laughed at him. They had a furious quarrel and Tito took out his pistol and shot the count dead. Then he collapsed and fell, weeping hysterically, on his father's body; the repeated shots brought Laura and the servants rushing in. He jumped up and grabbed the pistol, to shoot himself he said afterwards, but he hesitated or they were too quick for him, and they snatched it out of his hand. The police were sent for. He spent most of his time in prison weeping; he would not eat and had to be forcibly fed; he told the examining magistrate that he had killed his father because he was his wife's lover. Laura, examined and examined again, swore that there had never been anything between the count and herself but a natural affection. The murder filled the Florentine public with horror. The Italians were convinced of her guilt, but her friends, English and American, felt that she was incapable of the crime of which she was accused. They went about saying that Tito was neurotic and insanely jealous and in his stupid way had mistaken her American freedom of behaviour for a criminal passion. On the face of it Tito's charge was absurd. Carlo di San Pietro was nearly thirty years older than she, an elderly man with white hair; who could suppose that there would have been anything between her and her father-in-law, when her husband was young, handsome, and in love with her?

It was in Harding's presence that she saw the examining magistrate and the lawyers who had been engaged to defend Tito. They had decided to plead insanity. Experts for the defense examined him and decided that he was insane; experts for the prosecution examined him and decided that he was sane. The fact that he had bought a pistol three months before he committed the dreadful crime went to prove that it was premeditated. It was discovered that he was deeply in debt and his creditors were pressing him; the only means he had of settling with them was by selling the villa, and his father's death put him in possession of it. There is no capital punishment in Italy, but murder with premeditation is punished by solitary confinement for life. On the approach of the trial the lawyers came to Laura and told her that the only way in which Tito could be saved from this was for her to admit in court that the count had been her lover. Laura went very pale. Harding protested violently. He said they had no right to ask her to perjure herself and ruin her reputation to save that shiftless, drunken gambler whom she had been so unfortunate as to marry. Laura remained silent for a while.

"Very well," she said at last, "if that's the only way to save him I'll do it."

Harding tried to dissuade her, but she was decided.

"I should never have a moment's peace if I knew that Tito had to spend the rest of his life alone in a prison cell."

And that is what happened. The trial opened. She was called and under oath stated that for more than a year her father-in-law had been her lover. Tito was declared insane and sent to an asylum. Laura wanted to leave Florence at once, but in Italy the preliminaries to a trial are endless and by then she was near her time. The Hardings insisted on her remaining with them till she was confined. She had a child, a boy, but it only lived twenty-four hours. Her plan was to go back to San Francisco and live with her mother till she could find a job, for Tito's extravagance, the money she had spent on the villa, and then the cost of the trial had seriously impoverished her.

It was Harding who told me most of this; but one day when he was at the club and I was having a cup of tea with Bessie and we were again talking over these tragic happenings she said to me:

"You know, Charley hasn't told you the whole story because be doesn't know it. I never told him. Men are funny in some ways; they're much more easily shocked than women."

I raised my eyebrows, but said nothing.

"Just before Laura went away we had a talk. She was very low and I thought she was grieving over the loss of her baby. I wanted to say something to help her. 'You musn't take the baby's death too hardly,' I said. 'As things are, perhaps it's better it died.' 'Why?' she said. 'Think what the poor little thing's future would have been with a murderer for his father.' She looked at me for a moment in that strange quiet way of hers. And then what d'you think she said?"

"I haven't a notion," said I.

"She said: 'What makes you think his father was a murderer?'"

I felt myself grow as red as a turkey cock. I could hardly believe my ears. "Laura, what *do* you mean?" I said. "You were in court," she said. "You heard me say Carlo was my lover."

Bessie Harding stared at me as she must have stared at Laura.

"What did you say then?" I asked.

"What was there for me to say? I said nothing. I wasn't so much horrified, I was bewildered. Laura looked at me and, believe it or not, I'm convinced there was a twinkle in her eyes. I felt a perfect fool."

"Poor Bessie," I smiled.

Poor Bessie, I repeated to myself now as I thought of this strange story. She and Charley were long since dead and by their death I had lost good friends. I went to sleep then, and next day Wyman Holt took me for a long drive.

We were to dine with the Greenes at seven and we reached their house on the dot. Now that I had remembered who Laura was I was filled with an immense curiosity to see her again. Wyman had exaggerated nothing. The living room into which we went was the quintessence of commonplace. It was comfortable enough, but there was not a trace of personality in it. It might have been furnished en bloc by a mail-order house. It had the bleakness of a government office. I was introduced first to my host Jasper Greene and then to his brother Emery and to his brother's wife Fanny. Jasper Greene was a large, plump man with a moon face and a shock of black, coarse, unkempt hair. He wore large cellulose-rimmed spectacles. I was staggered by his youth. He could not have been much over thirty and was therefore nearly twenty years younger than Laura. His brother, Emery, a composer and teacher in a New York school of music, might have been seven or eight and twenty. His wife, a pretty little thing, was an actress for the moment out of a job. Jasper Green mixed us some very adequate cocktails but for a trifle too much vermouth, and we sat down to dinner. The conversation was gay and even boisterous. Jasper and his brother were loud voiced and all three of them, Jasper, Emery, and Emery's wife, were loquacious talkers. They chaffed one another, they joked and laughed; they discussed art, literature, music, and the theatre. Wyman and I joined in when we had a chance, which was not often; Laura did not try to. She sat at the head of the table, serene, with an amused, indulgent smile on her lips as she listened to their scatterbrained nonsense; it was not stupid nonsense, mind you, it was intelligent and modern, but it was nonsense all the same. There was something maternal in her attitude, and I was reminded oddly of a sleek dachshund lying quietly in the sun while she looks lazily, and yet watchfully, at her litter of puppies romping round her. I wondered whether it crossed her mind that all this chatter about art didn't amount to much when compared with those incidents of blood and passion that she remembered. But did she remember? It had all happened a long time ago and perhaps it seemed no more than a bad dream. Perhaps these commonplace surroundings were part of her deliberate effort to forget, and to be among these young people was restful to her spirit. Perhaps Jasper's clever stupidity was a comfort. After that searing tragedy it might be that she wanted nothing but the security of the humdrum.

Possibly because Wyman was an authority on the Elizabethan drama the conversation at one moment touched on that. I had already discovered that Jasper Greene was prepared to lay down the law on subjects all and sundry, and now he delivered himself as follows: "Our theatre has gone all to pot because the dramatists of our day are afraid to deal with the violent emotions which are the proper subject matter of tragedy," he boomed. "In the sixteenth century they had a wealth of melodramatic and bloody themes to suit their purpose and so they produced great plays. But where can our playwrights look for themes? Our Anglo-Saxon blood is too phlegmatic, too supine, to provide them with material they can make anything of, and so they are condemned to occupy themselves with the trivialities of social intercourse."

I wondered what Laura thought of this, but I took care not to catch her eye. She could have told them a story of illicit love, jealousy, and parricide which would have been meat to one of Shakespeare's successors, but had he treated it, I suppose he would have felt bound to finish it with at least one more corpse strewn about the stage. The end of her story, as I knew it now, was unexpected certainly, but sadly prosaic and a trifle grotesque. Real life more often ends things with a whimper than with a bang. I wondered too why she had gone out of her way to renew our old acquaintance. Of course she had no reason to suppose that I knew as much as I did; perhaps with a true instinct she was confident that I would not give her away; perhaps she didn't care if I did. I stole a glance at her now and then while she was quietly listening to the excited babbling of the three young people, but her friendly, pleasant face told me nothing. If I hadn't known otherwise I would have sworn that no untoward circumstance had ever troubled the course of her uneventful life.

The evening came to an end and this is the end of my story, but for the fun of it I am going to relate a small incident that happened when Wyman and I got back to his house. We decided to have a bottle of beer before going to bed and went into the kitchen to fetch it. The clock in the hall struck eleven and at that moment the phone rang. Wyman went to answer it and when he came back was quietly chortling to himself.

"What's the joke?" I asked.

"It was one of my students. They're not supposed to call members of the faculty after ten-thirty, but he was all hot and bothered. He asked me how evil had come into the world."

"And did you tell him?"

"I told him that St. Thomas Aquinas had got hot and bothered too about that very question and he'd better worry it out for himself. I said that when he found the solution he was to call me, no matter what time it was. Two o'clock in the morning if he liked."

"I think you're pretty safe not to be disturbed for many a long night," I said.

"I won't conceal from you that I have formed pretty much the same impression myself," he grinned.

QUESTIONS

1. Why does Laura make a point of reminding the narrator that they had met years earlier in Florence?

2. Why does the count encourage the marriage of Laura and Tito, contrary to Harding's opinion that the count would never let his son "marry a girl who has no more money than Laura"? (198)

3. What does Laura hope to gain by marrying Tito, as she knows his reputation for gambling and losing large sums of money?

4. Why didn't Bessie Harding previously tell her husband the whole story about Laura? Why does she choose to reveal everything she knows years later?

5. Why does Laura reveal herself to Bessie Harding by asking, "What makes you think his father was a murderer"? (208)

6. Why does the narrator say, "The end of her story, as I knew it now, was unexpected certainly, but sadly prosaic and a trifle grotesque"? (210)

7. Why does the narrator add to his story, "for the fun of it," the incident about Wyman's student inquiring about "how evil had come into the world"? (210–11)

FOR FURTHER REFLECTION

1. What is the significance of the title, "A Woman of Fifty"?

2. What is the cause of the tragedy that occurs between Laura, Tito, and the count?

3. Is the narrator correct in thinking that Laura surrounded herself with commonplace things because "she wanted nothing but the security of the humdrum"?

ROSE TREMAIN

Born in London, Rose Tremain (1943–) was educated at the Sorbonne in Paris, where she earned a diploma in literature before returning to the United Kingdom to study at the University of East Anglia. Her first book, *The Fight for Freedom for Women*, was published in 1973, followed by *Stalin*, an illustrated biography (1975), and her first novel, *Sadler's Birthday* (1976). In 1983 Tremain was named one of twenty best young British novelists by *Granta* magazine. Although she resists such a designation, Tremain often has been categorized as a writer of historical fiction, mainly on the strength of her celebrated novels *Restoration: A Novel of Seventeenth-Century England* (1989) and *Music and Silence* (1999). In 2007 she received the title Commander of the Order of the British Empire. "My Wife Is a White Russian" first appeared in *The Colonel's Daughter and Other Stories* (1984).

My Wife Is a White Russian

I'm a financier. I have financial assets, worldwide. I'm in nickel and pig iron and gold and diamonds. I like the sound of all these words. They have an edge, I think. The glitter of saying them sometimes gives me an erection.

I'm saying them now, in this French restaurant, where the tablecloths and the table napkins are blue linen, where they serve seafood on platters of seaweed and crushed ice. It's noisy at lunchtime. It's May and the sun shines in London, through the open restaurant windows. Opposite me, the two young Australians blink as they wait (so damned courteous, and she has freckles like a child) for me to stutter out my hard-word list, to manipulate tongue and memory so that the sound inside me forms just behind my lips and explodes with extraordinary force above my oysters: "Diamonds!"

But then I feel a soft, perfumed dabbing at my face. I turn away from the Australians and there she is. My wife. She is smiling as she wipes me. Her gold bracelets rattle. She is smiling at me. Her lips are astonishing, the colour of claret. I've been wanting to ask her for some time, "Why are your lips this terrible dark colour these days? Is it a lipstick you put on?"

Still smiling at me, she's talking to the Australians with her odd accent: "He's able to enjoy the pleasures of life once more, thank God. For a long time afterwards, I couldn't take him out. Terrible. We couldn't do one single thing, you know. But now—he enjoys his wine again."

The dabbing stops. To the nurse I tried to say when I felt a movement begin: "Teach me how to wipe my arse. I cannot let my wife do this because she doesn't love me. If she loved me, she probably wouldn't mind wiping my arse and I wouldn't mind her wiping my arse. But she doesn't love me."

The Australian man is talking now. I let my hand go up and take hold of my big-bowled wine glass into which the waiter has poured the expensive Chablis my wife likes to drink when she eats fish. Slowly, I guide the glass across the deadweight distance between the table and my mouth. I say "deadweight" because the spaces between all my limbs and the surfaces of tangible things have become mighty. To walk is to wade in waist-high water. And to lift this wine glass . . . "Help me," I want to say to her, "just this once. Just this once." Just this once.

"Heck," says the Australian man, "we honestly thought he'd made a pretty positive recovery." His wife, with blue eyes the colour of the napkins, is watching my struggles with the glass. She licks her fine line of a mouth, sensing I suppose, my longing to taste the wine. The nurse used to stand behind me, guiding the feeding cup in my hand. I never explained to her that the weight of gravity had mysteriously increased. Yet often, as I drank from the feeding cup, I used to imagine myself prancing on the moon.

"Oh, this is a very positive recovery," says my wife. "There's very little he can't do now. He enjoys the ballet, you know, and the opera. People at Covent Garden and the better kind of place are very considerate. We don't go to the cinema because there you have a very inconsiderate type of person. Don't you agree? So riffraffy? Don't you agree?"

The Australian wife hasn't listened to a word. The Australian wife puts out a lean freckled arm and I watch it come towards me, astounded as usual these days by the speed with which other people can move parts of their bodies. But the arm, six inches from my hand holding the glass, suddenly stops. "Don't help him!" snaps my wife. The napkin-blue eyes are lowered. The arm is folded away.

Heads turn in the restaurant. I suppose her voice has carried its inevitable echo round the room where we sit: "Don't help him! Don't help him!" But now that I have an audience, the glass begins to jolt, the wine splashing up and down the sides of the bowl. I smile. My smile widens as I watch the Chablis begin to slop onto the starched blue cloth. WASTE. She of all people understands the exquisite luxury of waste. Yet she snatches the glass out of my hand and sets it down by her own. She snaps her fingers and a young beanpole of a waiter arrives. He spreads out a fresh blue napkin where I have spilled my wine. My wife smiles her claret smile. She sucks an oyster into her dark mouth.

The Australian man is, I was told, the manager of the Toomin Valley Nickel Consortium. The wife is, as far as I know, just a wife. I own four-fifths of the Toomin Valley Nickel Consortium. The Australian man is here to discuss expansion, supposedly with me, unaware until he met me this lunchtime that, despite the pleasing cadences of the words, I'm unable to say "Toomin Valley Nickel Consortium." I can say "nickel." My tongue lashes around in my throat to form the click that comes in the middle of the word. Then out it spills: *Nickel!* In my mind, oddly enough, the word "nickel" is the exact grayish-white colour of an oyster. But "consortium" is too difficult for me. I know my limitations.

My wife is talking again: "I've always loved the ballet, you see. This is my only happy memory of Russia—the wonderful classical ballet. A little magic. Don't you think? I would never want to be without this kind of magic, would you? Do you have the first-rate ballet companies in Australia? You do? Well, that's good. *Giselle,* of course. That's the best one. Don't you think? The dead girl. Don't you think? Wonderful."

We met on a pavement. I believe it was in the Avenue Matignon, but it could have been in the Avenue Montaigne. I often get these muddled. It was in Paris, anyway. Early summer, as it is now. Chestnut candle blooms blown along the gutters. I waited to get into the taxi she was leaving. But I didn't get into it. I followed her. In a bar, she told me she was very poor; her father drove the taxi I had almost hired. She spoke no English then, only French with a heavy Russian accent. I was just starting to be a financier at that time, but already I was quite rich, rich by her standards—she who had been used to life in postwar Russia. My hotel room was rather grand. She said in her odd French: "I'll fuck for money."

I gave her fifty francs. I suppose it wasn't much, not as much as she'd hoped for, a poor rate of exchange for the white, white body that rode astride me, head thrown back, breasts bouncing. She sat at the dressing table in the hotel room. She smoked my American cigarettes. More than anything, I wanted to brush her gold hair, brush it smooth and hold it against my face. But I didn't ask her if I could do this. I believe I was afraid she would say, "You can do it for money."

The thin waiter is clearing away our oyster platters. I've eaten only three of my oysters, yet I let my plate go. She lets it go. She pretends not to notice how slow I've been with the oysters. And my glass of wine still stands by hers, untasted. Yet she's drinking quite fast. I hear her order a second bottle.

The Australian man says: "First-rate choice, if I may say. We like Chably."

I raise my left arm and touch her elbow, nodding at the wine. Without looking at me, she puts my glass down in front of me. The Australian wife stares at it. Neither she nor I dare to touch it.

My wife is explaining to the Australians what they are about to eat, as if they were children: "I think you will like the turbot very much. *Turbot poché hollandaise.* They cook it very well. And the hollandaise sauce—you know this, of course? Very difficult to achieve, the lightness of this sauce. But here they do it very well. And the scallops in saffron. Again, a very light sauce. Excellent texture. Just a little cream added. And fresh scallops, naturally. We never go to any restaurant where the products are frozen. So I think you will like these dishes very much . . ."

We have separate rooms. Long before my illness, when I began to look (yet hardly to feel) old, she demanded her privacy. This was how she put it: She wanted to be private. The bedroom we used to share and which is now hers is very large. The walls are silk.

She said: "There's no sense in being rich and cooped up together in one room."

Obediently, I moved out. She wouldn't let me have the guest room, which is also big. I have what we call "the little room," which I always used to think of as a child's room.

I expect in her "privacy" that she is smiling: "The child's room is completely right for him. He's a helpless baby." Yet she's not a private person. She likes to go out four or five nights a week, returning at two or three in the morning, sometimes with friends, and they sit and drink brandy. Sometimes, they play music. Elton John. She has a lover (I don't know his name) who sends her lilies.

I'm trying to remember the Toomin Valley. I believe it's an immense desert of a place, inhabited by no one and nothing except the mining machinery and the nickel consortium employees, whose clusters of houses I ordered to be whitewashed to hide the cheap gray building blocks. The windows of the houses are small, to keep out the sun. In the backyards are spindly eucalyptus trees, blown by the scorching winds. I want to ask the Australian wife, Did you have freckles before you went to live in the Toomin Valley, and does some wandering prima ballerina dance *Giselle* on the gritty escarpment above the mine?

My scallops arrive, saffron yellow and orange in the blue and white dish—the colours of a childhood summer. The flesh of a scallop is firm yet soft, the texture of a woman's thigh (when she is young, of course, before the skin hardens and the flesh bags out). A forkful of scallop is immeasurably easier to lift than the glass of wine, and the Australian wife (why don't I know either of their names?) smiles at me approvingly as I lift the succulent parcel of food to my mouth and chew it without dribbling. My wife, too, is watching, ready with the little scented handkerchief, yet talking as she eats, talking of Australia as the second bottle of Chablis arrives and she tastes it hurriedly with a curt nod to the thin waiter. I exist only in the corner of her eye, at its inmost edge, where the vulnerable triangle of red flesh is startling.

"Of course, I've often tried to tell Hubert" (she pronounces my name "Eieu-bert," trying and failing with what she recognizes as the upper-class *h*), "that it's very unfair to expect people like you to live in some out-of-the-way place. I was brought up in a village, you see, and I know that an out-of-the-way village is so dead. No culture. The same in Toomin, no? Absolutely no culture at all. Everybody dead."

The Australian wife looks—seemingly for the first time —straight at my wife. "We're outdoor people."

I remember now. A river used to flow through the Toomin Valley. Torrential in the rainy season, they said. It dried up in the early forties. One or two sparse willows remain, gray testimony to the long-ago existence of water-rich soil. I imagine the young Australian couple, brown as chestnuts, swimming in the Toomin River, resting on its gentle banks with their fingers touching, a little loving nest of bone. There is no river. Yet when they look at each other—almost furtively under my vacant gaze—I recognize the look. The look says: "These moments with strangers are nothing. Into our private moments together—only there—is crammed all that we ask of life."

"Yes, we're outdoor folk." The Australian man is smiling. "You can play tennis most of the year round at Toomin. I'm president of the tennis club. And we have our own pool now."

I don't remember these things: tennis court and swimming pools.

"Well, of course, you have the climate for these things." My wife is signalling our waiter to bring her Perrier water. "And it's something to do, isn't it? Perhaps when the new expansions of the company are made, a concert hall could be built for you, or a theatre."

"A theatre!" The Australian wife's mouth opens to reveal perfect, freshly peeled teeth and a laugh escapes. She blushes.

My wife's dark lips are puckered into a sneer.

But the Australian man is laughing too—a rich laugh you might easily remember on the other side of the world—and slapping his thigh. "A theatre! What about that, ay!"

She wanted, she said, as she smoked my American cigarettes, to see *Don Giovanni*. Since leaving Russia with her French mother and her Russian father, no one had ever taken her to the opera. She had seen the posters advertising *Don Giovanni* and had asked her father to buy her a ticket.

He had shouted at her: "Remember whose child you are! Do you imagine taxi drivers can afford seats at the opera?"

"Take me to see *Don Giovanni*," she said to me, "and I will fuck for nothing."

I've never really appreciated the opera. The don was fat. It was difficult to imagine so many women wanting to lie with this fat man. Yet afterwards, she leant over to me and put her head on my shoulder and wept. Nothing, she told me, had ever moved her so much—nothing in her life had ever touched the core of her being—as this had done, this production of *Don Giovanni*.

"If only," she said, "I had money as you have money, then I would go to hear music all the time and see the classical ballet and learn from these what is life."

The scallops are good. She never learned what is life. I feel emboldened by the food. I put my hand to my glass, heavier than ever now because the waiter has filled it up. The sun shines on my wine and on my hand, blotched (splattered, it seems) with the oddly repulsive stains of old age. For a second, I see my hand and the wine glass as a still life. But then I lift the glass. The Australian wife lowers her eyes. My wife, for a moment, is silent. I drink. I smile at the Australian wife because I know she wants to applaud.

I'm talking. The words are like stones weighing down my lower jaw. *Nickel*. I'm trying to tell the Australian man that I dream about the nickel mine. In my dreams, the Australian miners drag wooden carts loaded with three-penny bits. I run my hands through the coins as through a sack of wheat, and the touch of them is pleasurable and perfect. I also want to say to the Australian man: "I hope you're happy in your work. When I was in control, I visited all my mines and all my subsidiaries at least once a year. Even in South Africa, I made sure a living wage was paid.

I said to the men underground, 'I hope you're happy in your work.'"

But now I have a manager, a head manager to manage all the other managers, including this one from the Toomin Valley. I am trundled out in my chair to meet them when they come here to discuss redundancy or expansion. My wife and I give them lunch in a restaurant. They remind me that I still have an empire to rule, if I were capable, if indeed my life had been different since the night of *Don Giovanni*.

When I stopped paying her to sleep with me, her father came to see me. He held his cap in his hands. "We're hoping for a marriage," he said. And what more could I have given—what less—to the body I had begun to need? The white and gold of her, I thought, will ornament my life.

Yet now I never touch her. The white and the gold of her lies only in the lilies they send, the unknown lovers she finds in the night, while I lie in the child's room and dream of the nickel mines. My heart is scorched dry, like the dry hills of the Toomin Valley. I am punished for my need of her while her life stalks my silence; the white of her, the gold of her, the white of Dior, the gold of Cartier. Why did she never love me? In my dreams, too, the answer comes from deep underground: It's the hardness of my words.

QUESTIONS

1. Why does the wife repeatedly ask the Australian couple what they think and whether they agree?

2. Why does the wife shout, "Don't help him!" when the Australian wife moves the glass? (217)

3. What does Hubert mean when he says, "I exist only in the corner of her eye, at its inmost edge, where the vulnerable triangle of red flesh is startling"? (220)

4. What does the narrator mean by this observation: "The look says: 'These moments with strangers are nothing. Into our private moments together—only there—is crammed all that we ask of life' "? (221)

5. Why is Hubert the only character with a name?

6. Why does Hubert's wife say, "I would go to hear music all the time and see the classical ballet and learn from these what is life"? (222)

7. What is the meaning of "White Russian" in the title?

FOR FURTHER REFLECTION

1. Can money buy happiness?

2. Why does Hubert let his wife have her way so easily?

3. Is the wife's greed acceptable because she grew up poor?

Gluttony

ITALO CALVINO

Italo Calvino (1923–1985), one of the most prominent twentieth-century Italian novelists and short story writers, came of age during World War II fighting fascism as a participant in the Italian resistance movement. After the war, he wrote several works in a traditional, realist manner, but he soon developed his own distinctive style that incorporated literary elements of fable and fantasy. In novels such as *The Cloven Viscount* (1952), *The Baron in the Trees* (1957), and *The Nonexistent Knight* (1959), Calvino's fantastic plots serve the deeper purpose of exploring perennial questions of how humans should live their lives. His later works, such as *Invisible Cities* (1972) and *If on a Winter's Night a Traveler* (1979), make use of complex narrative structures to investigate the nature of reality and causality.

Theft in a Pastry Shop

When Dritto got to the place where they were to meet, the others had already been waiting some time. There were two of them, Baby and Uora-Uora. The street was so silent that the ticking of the clocks in the houses could be heard. With two jobs to do, they'd have to hurry to get through them by dawn.

"Come on," said Dritto.

"Where to?" they asked.

But Dritto was never one to explain about any job he was going to do.

"Come on now," he replied. And he walked along in silence, through streets empty as dry rivers, with the moon following them along the tramlines, Dritto ahead, gazing around with those restless yellow eyes of his, his nostrils moving as if they were smelling something peculiar.

Baby was called that because he had a big head like a newborn baby and a stumpy body; also perhaps because of his short hair and pretty little face with its small black mustache. All muscle, he moved so softly he might have been a cat; there was no one like him at climbing up walls and squeezing through openings, and Dritto always had good reason to take him along.

"Will it be a good job, Dritto?" asked Baby.

"If we bring it off," answered Dritto—a reply that didn't mean much.

Meanwhile, by a devious route that only he knew, he had led them around a corner into a yard. The other two soon realized that they were going to work on the back of a shop, and Uora-Uora pushed ahead in case he was left as lookout. It always fell to Uora-Uora to be lookout man; he longed to break into houses, search around, and fill his pockets like the others, but he always found himself standing guard on cold streets, in danger from police patrols, his teeth chattering in the cold, and chain-smoking to calm his nerves. Uora-Uora was an emaciated Sicilian, with a sad mulatto face and wrists jutting out of his sleeves. When on a job he always dressed up in his best, God knows why, complete with hat, tie, and raincoat, and if forced to run for it, he'd snatch up the ends of his raincoat as if spreading wings.

"You're lookout, Uora-Uora," said Dritto, dilating his nostrils. Uora-Uora took off quietly; he knew Dritto and the danger signal of those dilating nostrils, which would move quicker and quicker until they suddenly stopped and he whipped out a revolver.

"There," Dritto said to Baby. He pointed to a little window high off the ground, a piece of cardboard in place of a broken pane.

"You climb up, get in, and open for me," he said. "Be sure not to put on the lights: They'll be seen from outside."

Baby pulled himself up on the smooth wall like a monkey, pushed in the cardboard without a sound, and stuck his head through. It was then that he became aware of the smell; he took a deep breath and up through his nostrils wafted an aroma of freshly baked cakes. It gave him a feeling of shy excitement, of remote tenderness, rather than of actual greed.

Oh, what a lot of cakes there must be in here, he thought. It was years since he had eaten a proper piece of cake, not since before the war perhaps. He decided to search around till he found them. He jumped down into the darkness, kicked against a telephone, got a broomstick up his trouser leg, and then hit the ground. The smell of cakes was stronger than ever but he couldn't tell where it was coming from.

Yes, there must be a lot of cakes in here, thought Baby.

He reached out a hand, trying to feel his way in the dark, so he could reach the door and open it for Dritto. Quickly he recoiled in horror; he must be face-to-face with some animal, some soft slimy sea thing, perhaps. He stood there with his hand in the air, a hand that had suddenly become damp and sticky, as if covered with leprosy. Between the fingers had sprouted something round and soft, an excrescence, maybe a tumor. He strained his eyes in the dark but could see nothing, not even when he put his hand under his nose. But he could smell, even though he could not see; and he burst out laughing. He realized he had touched a tart and was holding a blob of cream and a crystallized cherry.

At once he began licking the hand, and groping around with the other at the same time. It touched something solid but soft, with a thin covering of fine sugar—a doughnut! Still groping, he popped the whole of it into his mouth and gave a little cry of pleasure on discovering it had jam inside. This really was the most wonderful place; whatever way he stretched out his hand in the dark, it found new kinds of cakes.

Suddenly he became aware of an impatient knocking on a door nearby; it was Dritto waiting to be let in. As Baby moved toward the sound, his hands bumped first into a meringue and then into an almond cake. He opened the door and Dritto's flashlight lit up his little face, its mustache already white with cream.

"It's full of cakes here!" exclaimed Baby, as if the other did not know.

"There isn't time for cakes," said Dritto, pushing him aside. "We've got to hurry." And he went ahead, twisting the beam of his flashlight around in the dark. Everywhere

it touched it lit up rows of shelves, and on the shelves rows
of trays, and on the trays rows of cakes of every conceiv-
able shape and color, tarts filled with cream that glittered
like candle wax, piles of sugar-coated buns, and castles of
almond cakes.

It was then that a terrible worry came over Baby, the
worry of not having time to eat all he wanted, of being
forced to make his escape before he had sampled all the different kinds of cakes, of having all this land of milk and
honey at his disposal for only a few minutes in his whole
life. And the more cakes he discovered, the more his anxiety
increased, so that every new corner and every fresh view of
the shop that was lit up by Dritto's flashlight seemed to be
about to shut him off.

He flung himself at the shelves, choking himself with
cakes, cramming two or three inside his mouth at a time,
without even tasting them; he seemed to be battling with
the cakes, as if they were threatening enemies, strange monsters besieging him, a crisp and sticky siege that he must
break through by the force of his jaw. The slit halves of the
big sugared buns seemed to be opening yellow throats and
eyes at him, the cream horns to be blossoming like flowers
of carnivorous plants; for a horrible moment Baby had the
feeling that it was he who was being devoured by the cakes.

Dritto pulled him by the arm. "The till," he said. 'We've
got to open the till."

At the same time, as he passed, he stuffed a piece of mul-
ticolored spongecake into his mouth, a cherry off a tart and
then a brioche—hurriedly, as if anxious not to be distracted
from the job at hand. He had switched off his flashlight.

"From outside they could see us clearly," he said.

They had now reached the front of the pastry shop,
with its showcases and marble countertops. Through the
grilled shutters the lights from the streets entered in streaks;
outside they could see strange shadows on the trees and
houses.

Now the moment had come to force the till.

"Hold this," said Dritto, handing the flashlight to Baby with the beam pointing downward so that it could not be seen from outside.

But Baby was holding the flashlight with one hand and groping around with the other. He seized an entire plum cake and, while Dritto was busy at the lock with his tools, began chewing it as if it were a loaf of bread. But he soon tired of it and left it half eaten on the marble slab.

"Get away from there! Look what a filthy mess you're making," hissed Dritto through clenched teeth; in spite of his trade he had a strange respect for tidy work. Then he couldn't resist the temptation, either, and stuffed two cakes, the kind that were half sponge and half chocolate, into his mouth, though without interrupting his work.

Baby, meanwhile, in order to have both hands free, had constructed a kind of lampshade from tray cloths and pieces of nougat. He then espied some large cakes with "Happy Birthday" written on them. He circled them, studying the plan of attack; first he reviewed them with a finger and licked off a bit of chocolate cream, then he buried his face inside and began biting them from the middle, one by one.

But he still felt a kind of frenzy, which he did not know how to satisfy; he could not discover any way of enjoying everything completely. Now he was crouching on all fours over a table laden with tarts; he would have liked to lie down in those tarts, cover himself with them, never have to leave them. But five or ten minutes from now it would be all over; for the rest of his life pastry shops would be out of bounds to him again, forever, like when he was a child squashing his nose against the windowpane. If only, at least, he could stay there three or four hours . . .

"Dritto," he exclaimed, "suppose we hide here till dawn, who'll see us?"

"Don't be a fool," said Dritto, who had now succeeded in forcing the till and was searching around among the notes. "We've got to get out of here before the cops show up."

Just at that moment they heard a rap on the window. In the dim moonlight Uora-Uora could be seen knocking on the blind and making signs to them. The two in the shop gave a jump, but Uora-Uora motioned for them to keep calm and for Baby to come out and take his place, so that he could come in. The other two shook their fists and made faces at him and gestured for him to get away from the front of the shop if he didn't want his brains blown out.

Dritto, however, had found only a few thousand lire in the till, and was cursing and blaming Baby for not trying to help him. But Baby seemed beside himself; he was biting into doughnuts, picking at raisins, licking syrups, plastering himself all over and leaving sticky marks on the showcases and counters. He found that he no longer had any desire for cakes—in fact a feeling of nausea was beginning to creep up from the pit of his stomach—but he refused to take it seriously, he simply could not give up yet. And the doughnuts began to turn into soggy pieces of spongecake, the tarts to flypaper, the cakes to asphalt. Now he saw only the corpses of cakes lying putrefying on their marble slabs, or felt them disintegrating like turgid glue inside his stomach.

Dritto, meanwhile, was cursing and swearing at the lock on another till, forgetful of cakes and hunger. Suddenly, from the back of the shop appeared Uora-Uora, swearing in his Sicilian dialect, which was quite unintelligible to either of them.

"The cops?" they asked, already pale.

"Change of guard! Change of guard!" Uora-Uora was croaking in his dialect, trying hard to explain how unjust it was to leave him starving out in the cold while they gorged themselves with cakes inside.

"Go back and keep watch, go and keep watch!" shouted Baby angrily, the nausea from having eaten too much making him feel savage and selfish.

Dritto knew that it was only fair to Uora-Uora to make the change, but he also knew that Baby would not be convinced so easily, and without someone on guard they couldn't stay. So he pulled out his revolver and pointed it at Uora-Uora.

"Back to your post right now, Uora-Uora," he said.

Desperately, Uora-Uora thought of getting some supplies before leaving, and gathered in his big hands a small pile of little almond cakes with nuts.

"And suppose they catch you with your hands full of cakes, you fool, what'll you tell them?" Dritto swore at him. "Leave them all there and get out."

Uora-Uora burst into tears. Baby felt he hated him. He picked up a cake with "Happy Birthday" written on it and flung it in Uora-Uora's face. Uora-Uora could easily have avoided it, but instead he extended his face to get the full force, then burst out laughing, for his face, hat, and tie were all covered in cream cake. Off he went, licking himself right up to his nose and cheeks.

At last Dritto succeeded in forcing the till and was stuffing into his pocket all the notes he could find, cursing because they stuck to his jammy fingers.

"Come on, Baby, time to go," he said.

But Baby could not leave just like that; this was a feast to be talked over for years to come with his cronies and with Tuscan Mary. Tuscan Mary was Baby's girl friend; she had long smooth legs and a face and body that were almost horselike. Baby liked her because he could curl himself up and wind around her like a cat.

Uora-Uora's second entrance interrupted the course of these thoughts. Dritto quickly pulled out his revolver, but Uora-Uora shouted, "The cops!" and rushed off, flapping the ends of his raincoat. Dritto gathered up the last few notes and was at the door in a couple of leaps, with Baby behind.

Baby was still thinking of Tuscan Mary, and it was then that he remembered he might have taken some cakes for her; he never gave her presents and she might make a scene about it. He went back, snatched up some cream rolls, thrust them under his shirt, then, quickly realizing that he had chosen the most fragile ones, looked around for some more solid things and stuffed those into his bosom, too. At that moment he saw the shadows of policemen moving on the window, waving their arms and pointing at something at the end of the street; one of them aimed a revolver in that direction and fired.

Baby squatted down behind a counter. The shot did not seem to have hit its target; now they were making angry gestures and peering inside the shop. Shortly afterward he heard them finding the little door open, and then coming in. Now the shop was teeming with armed policemen. Baby remained crouching there, but meanwhile he found some candied fruit within arm's reach and chewed at slivers of citron and bergamot to calm his nerves.

The police had now discovered the theft and also found the remains of half-eaten cakes on the shelves. And so, distractedly, they, too, began to nibble little cakes that were lying about—taking care, though, to leave the traces of the thieves. After a few moments, becoming more enthusiastic in their search for evidence, they were all eating away heartily.

Baby was chewing, but the others were chewing even more loudly and drowned out the sound. All of a sudden he felt a thick liquid oozing up from between his skin and his shirt, and a mounting nausea from his stomach. He was so dizzy with candied fruit that it was some time before he realized that the way to the door was free. Later the police described how they had seen a monkey, its nose plastered with cream, swing across the shop, overturning trays and tarts; and how, by the time that they had recovered from their amazement and cleared the tarts from under their feet, he had escaped.

When Baby got to Tuscan Mary's and opened his shirt, he found his whole chest covered with a strange sticky paste. And they stayed till morning, he and she, lying on the bed, licking and picking at each other till they had finished the last crumb of cake and blob of cream.

QUESTIONS

1. Why was it never Dritto's way "to explain about any job he was going to do"? (229)

2. Why is Uora-Uora always made to be the lookout?

3. What accounts for Baby's first response to the smell of freshly baked cakes as "a feeling of shy excitement, of remote tenderness, rather than of actual greed"? (230)

4. Why does Baby eventually have the feeling that "it was he who was being devoured by the cakes"? (232)

5. Why does Calvino use animal similes to describe Baby and Tuscan Mary ("horselike," "like a cat")? (235)

6. Why aren't Dritto and the policemen able to resist eating the pastries, even though doing so jeopardizes their work?

7. What is the significance of the story's shift of scene from the pastry shop to Tuscan Mary's bedroom? What does it mean that Baby and Tuscan Mary lick each other clean?

FOR FURTHER REFLECTION

1. Is Baby's eventual inability to "discover any way of enjoying everything completely" a characteristic of gluttony?

2. Is gluttony an indiscriminate desire to consume food, regardless of whether the experience of eating it is enjoyable?

3. Does Baby's feeling "savage and selfish" as a result of his overconsumption of pastries suggest the dangers of gluttony?

ALISON LURIE

Alison Lurie (1926–) is a novelist and professor emerita of literature at Cornell University. Beginning with her first novel, *Love and
Friendship* (1962), her characters have been drawn primarily from
her experience of academia, and she has turned an ironic eye on
the articulate, well-educated, professional middle class to create a
comedy of manners. Sometimes compared to Jane Austen, Lurie
is known for her ability to deftly portray the foibles of a tightly cir-
cumscribed sector of society while maintaining genuine compassion
for her characters. A recurrent theme in her work is the attempt to
offset well-balanced but stultifying lives through sexual adventure
and adultery. Lurie's novels include *Imaginary Friends* (1967), *The
War Between the Tates* (1974), and *Foreign Affairs* (1984), for which
she was awarded the Pulitzer Prize for fiction.

Fat People

I never ran into any spooks in sheets, no headless horsemen, haunted mansions, nothing like that. But there was something weird once—

It was a while ago, when Scott went to India on that research grant. The first thing that happened was I began noticing fat people. I saw them snatching the shrimps and stuffed eggs at parties; I saw them strolling along Cayuga Street with the swaying sailor's gait of the obese, and pawing through the queen-size housecoats in JCPenney. They were buying tubs of popcorn at the flicks, ahead of me in line at the post office and the bank, and pumping self-serve gas into their pickup trucks when I went to the garage.

I didn't pay much attention at first; I figured that since I was dieting I was more aware of people who should be doing the same. My idea was to lose fifteen pounds while Scott was away—twenty if possible, because of what he'd said just before he left.

We were at the county airport on a cold weepy day in March, waiting for Scott's plane and trying to keep up a conversation, repeating things we'd already said. I'd seen Scott off on trips before; but this time he'd be gone over three months. He was saying he wished I were coming, and promising to wire from Delhi and write twice a week, and telling me he loved me and reminding me again to check the oil on the Honda. I said I would, and was there anything else I should do while he was away?

Then the flight was announced and we grabbed each other. But we were both wearing heavy down jackets, and it didn't feel real. It was like two bundles of clothes embracing, I said, all choked up. And Scott said, "Well, there is one thing we could both do while I'm gone, Ellie; we could lose a few pounds." He was kissing my face and I was trying not to break down and howl.

Then Scott was through the X-ray scanner into the boarding lounge, and then he was crossing the wet tarmac with his carry-on bag, getting smaller and smaller, and climbing the steps. It wasn't till I'd gone back to the main waiting room and was standing inside the teary steamed-up window watching his plane shrink and blur into fog that I really registered his last remark.

I drove back to Pine Grove Apartments and dragged off my fat coat and looked at myself in the mirror on the back of the closet door. I knew I was a big girl, at the top of the range for my height, but it had never bothered me before. And as far as I knew it hadn't bothered Scott, who was hefty himself. Maybe when he suggested we lose a few pounds he was just kidding. But it was the last thing I'd hear him say for three months. Or possibly forever, I thought, because India was so far away and full of riots and diseases, and maybe in one of the villages he was going to they wouldn't want to change their thousand-year-old agricultural methods, and they would murder Scott with long wavy decorated knives or serve him curry with thousand-year-old undetectable poisons in it.

I knew it was bad luck to think that way; Scott had said so himself. I looked back at the mirror again, turning sideways. Usually I was pleased by what I saw there, but now I noticed that when I didn't breathe in, my tummy stuck out as far as my breasts.

Maybe I had put on some extra pounds that winter, I thought. Well, it should be pretty easy to take them off. It could be a project, something to do while Scott was gone. I wouldn't write him about it, I'd save it for a surprise when he got back. "Wow, Ellie," he would say, "you look great."

Only it turned out not to be as easy as all that. After two weeks, I weighed exactly the same. One problem was that all our friends kept asking me over and serving meals it would have been a shame to refuse, not to mention rude. And when I didn't have anywhere to go in the evening, I started wandering around the apartment and usually ended up wandering into the kitchen and opening the fridge, just for something to do.

It was about then that I began to notice how many fat people there were in town. All sorts and all ages: overweight country-club types easing themselves out of overweight cars; street people shoving rusted grocery carts jammed with bottles and bundles. Fat old men like off-duty Santa Clauses waddling through the shopping mall, fat teenagers with acne, and babies so plump they could hardly get their thumbs into their mouths.

Of course I'd seen types like this before occasionally, but now they seemed to be everywhere. At first I put it down to coincidence, plus having the subject on my mind. It didn't bother me; in a way it was reassuring. When some bulgy high school senior came for an interview at the college, and tried to fit their rear end onto the chair by my desk, I would think as I smiled nicely and asked the standard questions, Well, at least I don't look like that.

My folks knew I was trying to lose weight, and wanted to help, but they only made it worse. Every time I went over to the house for Sunday dinner Dad would ask first thing if I'd heard from Scott. It got to be over three weeks, and I still had to say, "No, nothing since the telegram," and remind them that we'd been warned about how bad the mails were.

Then we'd sit down to the table and Mom would pass my plate, and there'd be this measly thin slice of chicken on it, and a bushel of cooked greens, as if I was in some kind of concentration camp for fatties. The salads all started to have sour low-cal dressing, and there was never anything but fruit for dessert: watery melon, or oranges cut up with a few shreds of dry coconut on top, like little undernourished white worms.

All through the meal Mom and Dad wouldn't mention Scott again, so as not to upset me. There was nothing in the dining room to remind anybody of Scott either, and of course there wasn't any place set for him at the table. It was as if he'd disappeared or maybe had never even existed. By the time dinner was over, I'd be so low in my mind I'd have to stop on the way home for a pint of chocolate marshmallow.

I'd hang up my coat and turn on the television and measure out exactly half a cup of ice cream, 105 calories, less than a bagel. I'd put the rest in the freezer and feel virtuous. But when the next commercial came on I'd open the freezer and have a few more spoonfuls. And then the whole process would repeat, like a commercial, until the carton was scraped clean down to the wax.

It got to be four weeks since Scott had left, and I still didn't weigh any less, even when I shifted my feet on the scale to make the needle wobble downward. I'd never tried to lose weight before; I'd always thought it was ridiculous the way some people went into agonies over diets. I'd even been kind of shocked when one of my married friends made more fuss about taking a second slice of peach pie than she did about taking a lover. Displaced guilt, I used to think.

Now I was as hysterical about food as any of them. I brooded all afternoon over a fudge brownie I hadn't had for lunch; and if I broke down and ordered one I made up excuses for hours afterward. I didn't promise Scott I'd lose weight, I would tell myself, or, It's not fair asking someone to give up both food and love at the same time.

I started to read all the articles on losing weight that I used to skip before, and I took books out of the library. Over the next couple of weeks I tried one crazy diet after another: no-carbohydrate, no-fat, grapefruit and corn-flakes, chipped beef and bananas and skim milk. Only I couldn't stick with any of them. Things went wrong at night when I started thinking about how I'd written nine letters to Scott and hadn't got one back. I'd lie in bed asking myself where the hell was he, what was he doing now? And pretty soon I'd feel hungry, starving.

Another thing I kept asking myself, especially when I chewed through some dried-out salad or shook Sweet'N Low into my coffee, was what Scott, assuming he was still alive, was eating over there on the other side of the world. If he wasn't on a diet, what was the point? I would think, watching my hand reach out for the blue-cheese dressing or the half-and-half. He hadn't meant it seriously, I'd tell myself.

But suppose he had meant it? Suppose Scott was becoming slimmer and trimmer every day; what would he think if he knew I hadn't lost a pound in nearly five weeks?

Trying to do it on my own wasn't working. I needed support, and I thought I knew where to find it. There was a young woman in the admissions office called Dale. She was only a couple of years older than me, maybe twenty-six, but in two months she'd just about reorganized our files, and she obviously had her life under control. She was a brunette, with a narrow neat little figure and a narrow neat little poodle face; you got the feeling her hair wouldn't dare get itself mussed up, and she'd never weigh one ounce more than she chose to.

I figured that Dale would have ideas about my problem, because she was always talking about interesting new diets. And whenever some really heavy person came in she'd make a yapping noise under her breath and remark later how awful it was for people to let themselves go physically. "Heaven knows how that hippopotamus is going to fulfill

his athletic requirement," she would say, or "That girl's
mother ought to be in a circus; she hardly looked human."
And I'd think, Do I look human to Dale?

So one day when we were alone in the washroom I let
on that I was trying to lose some weight. Dale lit up like a
fluorescent tube. "Yes, I think that's a good idea, Ellie," she
said, looking from herself to me, poodle to hippo, in the
mirror over the basins. "And I'd like to help you, okay?"

"Okay, thanks," I said. I didn't have any idea what I
was getting into.

On our way back to the office, Dale explained to me
that being overweight was a career handicap. It was a known
fact that heavy people didn't get ahead as fast in business.
Besides, fat was low class: the Duchess of Windsor had said
you could never be too rich or too thin. When I told her
there wasn't much danger of my ever being either one, Dale
didn't laugh. She printed her Duchess of Windsor line out
in computer-graphic caps, and fastened it on the side of my
filing cabinet with two pineapple magnets.

The next thing Dale did was persuade me to see a
doctor to make sure I was healthy, the way they tell you
to do in the diet books. Then she started organizing my
life. She got me enrolled in an aerobics class, and set up a
schedule for me to jog every day after work, regardless of
the weather. Then she invited herself over to my apartment
and cleaned out the cupboards and icebox. Bags of pretzels
and Fritos, butter and cream cheese and cold cuts, a loaf of
cinnamon-raisin bread, most of a pound of Jones bacon—
Dale packed everything up, and we hauled it down to the
local soup kitchen. I kind of panicked when I saw all that
lovely food disappearing, but I was hopeful too.

The next day Dale brought in a calorie counter and
planned my meals for a week in advance. She kept a chart,
and every day she'd ask how much I'd weighed that morning and write it down.

Only the scale still stuck at the same number. If there
was nothing in the apartment, there was always plenty in

the grocery. I'd go in for celery and cottage cheese and RyKrisp, but when I was pushing the cart down the last aisle it was as if the packages of cookies on the shelves were crying out to me, especially the chocolate-covered grahams and the Mallomars. I could almost hear them squeaking inside their cellophane wrappers, in these little high sugary voices: "Ellie, Ellie! Here we are, Ellie!"

When I confessed to falling off my diet, Dale didn't lose her cool. "Never mind, Ellie, that's all right," she said. "I know what we'll do. From now on, don't you go near a supermarket alone. I'll shop with you twice a week on the way home."

So the next day she did. But as soon as she got a little ahead of me in the bakery section, I began drifting toward a tray of apricot croissants. Dale looked round and shook her poodle curls and said, "Naughty, naughty"—which kind of made me feel crazy, because I hadn't done anything naughty yet—and then she grabbed my arm and pulled me along fast.

There'd been several fat people in the A&P that day, the way there always were lately. When we were in line at the checkout with a load of groceries only a rabbit could love, I noticed one of them, a really heavy blonde girl about my own age, leaving the next register. Her cart was full, and a couple of plump bakery boxes, a carton of potato chips, and a giant bottle of Coke were bulging out of the brown-paper bags. As she came past the fat girl picked up a package of Hershey bars and tore it open, and half smiled in my direction as if she were saying, "Come on, Ellie, have one."

I looked round at Dale, figuring she would make some negative comment, but she didn't. Maybe she hadn't seen the fat girl yet. The funny thing was, when I looked back I didn't see her either; she must have been in a big rush to get home. And she was going to have a really good time when she got there, too, I thought.

Another week dragged by full of carrots and diet soda and frozen Weight Watchers dinners, and no news from Scott. My diet wasn't making much progress either. I'd take a couple of pounds off, but then I'd go out to dinner or a party and put three or four back on. Instead of losing I was gaining.

I was still seeing fat people too, more and more of them. I tried to convince myself it was just because they weren't disguised inside winter clothes any longer. The only problem was, the people I was seeing weren't just heavy, they were gross.

The first time I knew for sure that something strange was going on was one day when I was in the shopping plaza downtown, sitting on the edge of a planter full of sticky purple petunias and listening to a band concert instead of eating lunch, which had been Dale's idea naturally. I was feeling kind of dizzy and sick, and when I touched my head it seemed to vibrate, as if it wasn't attached to my body too well.

Then I happened to glance across the plaza, and through the window of the Home Bakery I saw two middle-aged women, both of them bulging out of flowered blouses and slacks as if they'd been blown up too full. I couldn't make out their faces well because of the way the light shimmered and slid on the shop window; but I could see that one of them was looking straight at me and pointing to a tray of strawberry tarts: big ones with thick ruby glaze and scallops of whipped cream. It was as if she was saying, "Come and get it, Ellie."

Without even intending to I stood up and started to push through the crowd. But when I reached the bakery there weren't any fat women, and I hadn't seen them leave either. There'd been a moment when I was blocked by a twin stroller; but it still didn't make sense, unless maybe the fat women hadn't really been there. Suddenly I started feeling sick to my stomach. I didn't want a strawberry tart anymore; I just wanted to go somewhere and lie down, only I was due back in the admissions office.

When I got there, I said to Dale, making my voice casual, "You know something funny, I keep seeing all these really fat people around lately."

"There are a lot of them around, Ellie," Dale said. "Americans are terribly overweight."

"But I'm seeing more. I mean, lots more than I ever did before. I mean, do you think that's weird?"

"You're just noticing them more," Dale said, stapling forms together bang-bang. "Most people block out unpleasant sights of that sort. They don't see the disgusting rubbish in the streets, or the way the walls are peeling right in this office." She pointed with her head to a corner above the swing doors, where the cream-colored paint was swollen into bubbles and flaking away; I hadn't noticed it before. Somehow that made me feel better.

"I guess you could be right," I said. I knew that Dale was getting impatient with me. She'd stopped keeping my weight chart, and when we went shopping now she read the labels on things aloud in a cross way, as if she suspected I was cheating on my diet and had a package of shortbread or a box of raisins hidden away at home, which was sometimes true.

It was around that time that eating and sex started to get mixed up in my mind. Sometimes at night I still woke up hot and tense and longing for Scott; but more often I got excited about food. I read articles on cooking and restaurants in a greedy lingering way, and had fantasies about veal paprika with sour cream and baby onions, or lemon meringue pie. Once after I'd suddenly gone up to a pushcart and bought a giant hot dog with ketchup and relish I heard myself saying half aloud, "I just had to have it." And that reminded me of the way men talked in tough-guy thrillers. "I had to have her," they always said, and they would speak of some woman as if she was a rich dessert and call her a dish or a cupcake and describe parts of her as melons or buns. Scott isn't really a macho type, but he's always liked thrillers; he says they relax him on trips. And when he got on the plane that awful day he'd had one with him.

He'd been gone over six weeks by then, and no news since the telegram from Delhi. Either something really terrible had happened to him or he deliberately wasn't writing. Maybe while I was cheating on my diet, Scott was cheating on me, I thought. Maybe he'd found some Indian cupcake to relax him. As soon as I had that idea I tried to shove it out of my head, but it kept oozing back.

Then one sunny afternoon early in June I came home from work and opened the mailbox, and there among the bills and circulars was a postcard from Scott. There wasn't any apology for not writing, just a couple of lines about a beautiful temple he'd visited, and a scrawled "love and kisses." On the other side was a picture of a sexy over-decorated Indian woman and a person or god with the head of an elephant, both of them wearing smug smiles.

As I looked at that postcard something kind of exploded inside me. For weeks I'd been telling myself and everyone, "If only I knew Scott was all right, I'd feel fine." Now I knew he was all right, but what I felt was a big rush of suspicion and fury.

Pictures from the coffee-table books on India Scott had borrowed from the library crowded into my mind. I saw sleek prune-eyed exotic beauties draped in shiny silk and jewels, looking at me with hard sly expressions; and plump nearly naked blue gods with bedroom eyes; and close-ups of temple sculptures in pockmarked stone showing one thousand and one positions for sexual intercourse. The idea came to me that at that exact moment Scott was making out in one thousand different positions with some woman who had an elephant's head or was completely blue. I knew that was crazy, but still he had to be doing something he didn't want to tell me about and was ashamed of, or he would have written.

I didn't go on upstairs to the apartment. Instead I got back into the car, not knowing where I was going till the Honda parked of its own volition in front of a gourmet shop and café that I hadn't been near for weeks. There were five other customers there, which wasn't unusual at that time of day. The unusual thing was, all of them were fat; and not just overweight: humongously huge. All of them looked at me in a friendly way when I came in, as if maybe they knew me and had something to tell me.

For a moment I couldn't move. I just stood there stuck to the indoor-outdoor carpeting and wondered if I was going out of my mind. Five out of five; it wasn't reasonable, but there they were, or anyhow I was seeing them.

The fat people knew about Scott, I thought. They'd known all along. That was what they'd been trying to say to me when they smiled and held up cones or candy bars: "Come on, honey, why should you deny yourself? You can bet your life Scott isn't."

A huge guy with a grizzly-bear beard left the counter, giving me a big smile, and I placed my order. A pound of assorted butter cookies, a loaf of cinnamon bread, and a date-walnut coffee ring with white sugar icing. As soon as I got into the car I tore open the box and broke off a piece of the coffee ring, and it was fantastic: the sweet flaky yellow pastry, and the sugar-glazed walnuts; a lot better than sex with Scott, I told myself.

For the next four days I pigged out. I finished the cookies and coffee ring that same evening, and on Friday afternoon I sneaked over to the grocery without telling Dale and bought everything I'd dreamed about for weeks: bacon and sausages and sliced Virginia ham, butter and sour cream and baking potatoes, pretzels and barbecue potato chips and frozen french fries. And that was just the beginning.

When I went in to work Monday morning with a box of assorted jelly doughnuts, I let Dale know I was off my diet for good. Dale tried to shove me back on. It didn't really matter about the weekend binge, she yipped. If I skipped lunch all week and cut way down on dinner and jogged two miles a day I'd be back on track.

"I don't want to be on track," I told her. "Eight weeks Scott has been gone, and all I've had from him is one disgusting postcard."

Dale looked pained and started talking about self-respect and self-image, but I wasn't having any. "Leave me alone, please," I said. "I know what I'm doing."

Two days and a lot of pork chops and baked potatoes and chicken salad and chocolate-almond bark and cherry pie later, I walked into my building, steadied a bag of high-calorie groceries against my hip, and opened the mailbox.

Jesus, I practically dropped the bag. The galvanized-metal slot was crammed with fat white and flimsy blue airmail letters from India. Most of them looked as if they'd been opened and read and crumpled up and walked on, and they were covered with stamps and cancellations.

An hour later, sitting on my sofa surrounded by two months' worth of Scott's letters, I faced facts. He was dieting: his second letter said so, mentioning that he didn't want to look overfed when he walked through a village full of hungry people. All right. I had three weeks, which meant—I went into the bathroom and dragged out the scale from the bottom of the cupboard where I'd shoved it on Friday—Which meant, oh God, I'd have to lose over two pounds a week just to get back to where I was when Scott left.

It was an awful three weeks. I had cereal and skim milk and fruit for breakfast and lunch, to get through work, but otherwise I didn't eat anything much. Pretty soon I was blurred and headachy most of the time, in spite of all the vitamins and minerals I was scarfing down, and too tired to exercise. And I was still behind schedule on losing weight.

What made it worse was the fat people. I was seeing them again everywhere, only now they didn't look happy or friendly. "You're making a big mistake, Ellie," they seemed to be telling me at first. Then they began to get angry and disgusted. "Sure, he wrote you, stupid," their expressions said. "That doesn't prove he's not helping himself to some Indian dish right this minute."

I quit going out after work; I didn't have the energy. Mostly I just stayed home drinking diet soda and rereading Scott's letters, kind of to prove to myself that he existed, I guess, because there hadn't been any more. Then I'd watch a little television and go to bed early, hoping to forget about food for awhile. But for the first time in my life I was having insomnia, jolting awake in the small hours and lying there starving.

The day Scott was due back, I woke up about 4 A.M. and couldn't doze off again even with Valium. For what seemed like hours I thrashed around in bed. Finally I got up and opened a can of diet soda and switched on the TV. Only now, on all the channels that were still broadcasting, everybody was overweight: the third-string newscasters, the punk MTV singers, the comics in an old black-and-white film. On the weather channel I could tell that the girl was hiding thighs like hams under the pleated skirt she kept swishing around as she pointed out the tornado areas. Then the picture changed and a soft plump guy smiled from between chipmunk cheeks and told me that airports were fogged in all over Europe and Scott would never get home.

I turned off the television, dragged on some jeans and a T-shirt, and went out. It was a warm June night full of noises: other tenants' air conditioners and fans, traffic out on the highway; and planes overhead. There was a hard wind blowing, which made me feel kind of dizzy and slapped about, and it was that uneasy time just before dawn when you start to see shapes but can't make out colors. The sky was a pale sick lemon, but everything else was lumps of blurred gray.

Pine Grove Apartments is surrounded on three sides by an access road, and I'd just turned the corner and was starting toward the dead end. That was when I saw them, way down by the trees. There was a huge sexless person with long stringy hair waving its arms and walking slowly toward me out of the woods, and behind it came more angry fat gray people, and then more and more.

I wanted to run, but I knew somehow that if I turned around the fat people would rush after me the way kids do when you play giant steps, and they would catch me and, God, I didn't know what. So I just backed up slowly step by step toward the corner of the building, breathing in shallow gasps.

They kept coming out of the woods in the half light, more and more, maybe ten or twenty or fifty, I didn't know. I thought I recognized the women from the bakery, and the big guy with the beard. And then I realized I could hear them too, kind of mumbling and wailing. I couldn't take it anymore. I turned and raced for home, stumbling over the potholes in the drive.

Well, somehow I made it to the apartment, and slammed the door and double locked it and put on the chain, and leaned up against the wall panting and gulping. For what seemed like hours I stood there, listening to the sounds of the fat people coming after me, crowding up the stairs, all gray and blubbery, and roaring and sobbing and sliding and thumping against the walls and door.

Then the noises started to change. Gradually they turned into the wind in the concrete stairwell and the air conditioner downstairs and the six-thirty plane to New York flying over the complex and a dog barking somewhere. It was light out now, nearly seven o'clock. I unbolted my door, keeping the chain on, and eased it open a slow inch. The hall was empty.

I still felt completely exhausted and crazy, but I got myself dressed somehow and choked down some coffee and left for work. On the way I took a detour in the Honda round the corner of the building. At first I was afraid to look, even though I was safe inside the locked car. At the edge of the woods where the mob of fat people had been there was nothing but some big old spirea bushes blowing and tossing about.

That evening Scott came home, ten pounds overweight. A couple of days later, when he was talking about his trip, he said that Indian food was great, especially the sweets, but the women were hard to talk to and not all that good looking.

"A lot of Indians are heavy too, you know," he told me.

"Really?" I asked. I wondered if Scott had had some spooky experience like mine, which I still hadn't mentioned: I didn't want him to think I was going to crack up whenever he left town.

"It's a sign of prosperity, actually. You notice them especially in the cities, much more than in this country. I mean, you don't see many fat people around here, for instance, do you?"

"No," I agreed, cutting us both another slice of pineapple upside-down cake. "Not lately, anyhow."

QUESTIONS

1. Why does Ellie call "noticing fat people" "weird" and compare it to supernatural events, such as "spooks in sheets . . . headless horsemen, haunted mansions"? (239) Why hadn't she noticed many fat people before?

2. When Scott suggests that they lose a little weight, why does this make such an impact on Ellie?

3. Does Ellie think she is gluttonous? Does she think the fat people she starts to notice are gluttonous?

4. What does Ellie mean when she says, "If [Scott] wasn't on a diet, what was the point?" (243)

5. Why does Ellie stop taking Dale's advice and support?

6. Why does Ellie begin to imagine that Scott has been unfaithful to her?

7. What does Ellie mean by saying the overweight people outside the café "looked at me in a friendly way when I came in, as if maybe they knew me and had something to tell me"? (249)

FOR FURTHER REFLECTION

1. Is Ellie overweight? Are her nightmares and waking visions a sign that she recognizes her problem or an indication of mental illness?

2. Ellie says, "It was around that time that eating and sex started to get mixed up in my mind." Why does she start confusing the two? Why might others confuse the two?

3. If Ellie is indeed overweight and looking for help, is Dale's attempt to help her a virtuous response?

Lust

ALDOUS HUXLEY

His ambition for a career in medicine was cut short by an eye disease that, at the age of sixteen, left him partially blind, so Aldous Huxley (1894–1963) went on to become a writer. He is best known for his novel *Brave New World* (1932), one of the darkest dystopias ever envisioned. He was born into an eminent family; his father, Thomas Huxley, a famous university professor and champion for the embattled theory of evolution, became known as "Darwin's bulldog." Huxley followed in his father's footsteps, interested in fusing the scientific quest with a passion for literary beauty. He described his novel *Point Counter Point* (1928) as the "musicalization of fiction." Later, Huxley transferred his natural skepticism and curiosity to explorations of mystical experience. His important later works include *The Doors of Perception* (1954), which describes his experimentation with the hallucinogenic drug mescaline. Huxley's purpose was explained by his equally renowned brother, Julian, as the desire "to achieve self-transcendence while yet remaining a committed social being."

Nuns at Luncheon

"hat have I been doing since you saw me last?" Miss Penny repeated my question in her loud, emphatic voice. "Well, when did you see me last?"

"It must have been June," I computed.

"Was that after I'd been proposed to by the Russian general?"

"Yes; I remember hearing about the Russian general."

Miss Penny threw back her head and laughed. Her long earrings swung and rattled—corpses hanging in chains: an agreeably literary simile. And her laughter was like brass, but that had been said before.

"That was an uproarious incident. It's sad you should have heard of it. I love my Russian general story. '*Vos yeux me rendent fou.*'" She laughed again.

Vos yeux—she had eyes like a hare's, flush with her head and very bright with a superficial and expressionless brightness. What a formidable woman. I felt sorry for the Russian general.

"'*Sans coeur et sans entrailles,*'" she went on, quoting the poor devil's words. "Such a delightful motto, don't you think? Like '*Sans peur et sans reproche.*' But let me think;

what have I been doing since then?" Thoughtfully she bit into the crust of her bread with long, sharp, white teeth.

"Two mixed grills," I said parenthetically to the waiter.

"But of course," exclaimed Miss Penny suddenly. "I haven't seen you since my German trip. All sorts of adventures. My appendicitis; my nun."

"Your nun?"

"My marvellous nun. I must tell you all about her."

"Do." Miss Penny's anecdotes were always curious. I looked forward to an entertaining luncheon.

"You knew I'd been in Germany this autumn?"

"Well, I didn't, as a matter of fact. But still—"

"I was just wandering round." Miss Penny described a circle in the air with her gaudily jewelled hand. She always twinkled with massive and improbable jewellery. "Wandering round, living on three pounds a week, partly amusing myself, partly collecting materials for a few little articles. 'What It Feels Like to Be a Conquered Nation'—sob stuff for the Liberal press, you know—and 'How the Hun Is Trying to Wriggle Out of the Indemnity,' for the other fellows. One has to make the best of all possible worlds, don't you find? But we mustn't talk shop. Well, I was wandering round, and very pleasant I found it. Berlin, Dresden, Leipzig. Then down to Munich and all over the place. One fine day I got to Grauburg. You know Grauburg? It's one of those picture-book German towns with a castle on a hill, hanging beer gardens, a Gothic church, an old university, a river, a pretty bridge, and forests all round. Charming. But I hadn't much opportunity to appreciate the beauties of the place. The day after I arrived there—bang!—I went down with appendicitis, screaming, I may add."

"But how appalling!"

"They whisked me off to hospital, and cut me open before you could say 'knife.' Excellent surgeon, highly efficient Sisters of Charity to nurse me—I couldn't have been in better hands. But it was a bore being tied there by the leg for four weeks—a great bore. Still, the thing had its compensations. There was my nun, for example. Ah, here's the food, thank heaven!"

The mixed grill proved to be excellent. Miss Penny's description of the nun came to me in scraps and snatches. A round, pink, pretty face in a winged coif; blue eyes and regular features; teeth altogether too perfect—false, in fact; but the general effect extremely pleasing. A youthful Teutonic twenty-eight.

"She wasn't my nurse," Miss Penny explained. "But I used to see her quite often when she came in to have a look at the *tolle Engländerin*. Her name was Sister Agatha. During the war, they told me, she had converted any number of wounded soldiers to the true faith—which wasn't surprising, considering how pretty she was."

"Did she try and convert you?" I asked.

"She wasn't such a fool," Miss Penny laughed, and rattled the miniature gallows of her ears.

I amused myself for a moment with the thought of Miss Penny's conversion—Miss Penny confronting a vast assembly of fathers of the church, rattling her earrings at their discourses on the Trinity, laughing her appalling laugh at the doctrine of the Immaculate Conception, meeting the stern look of the Grand Inquisitor with a flash of her bright, emotionless hare's eyes. What was the secret of the woman's formidableness?

But I was missing the story. What had happened? Ah, yes, the gist of it was that Sister Agatha had appeared one morning, after two or three days' absence, dressed, not as a nun, but in the overalls of a hospital charwoman, with a handkerchief instead of a winged coif on her shaven head.

"Dead," said Miss Penny; "she looked as though she were dead. A walking corpse, that's what she was. It was a shocking sight. I shouldn't have thought it possible for anyone to change so much in so short a time. She walked painfully, as though she had been ill for months, and she had great burnt rings round her eyes and deep lines in her face. And the general expression of unhappiness—that was something quite appalling."

She leaned out into the gangway between the two rows of tables, and caught the passing waiter by the end of one of his coattails. The little Italian looked round with an expression of surprise that deepened into terror on his face.

"Half a pint of Guinness," ordered Miss Penny. "And, after this, bring me some jam roll."

"No jam roll today, madam."

"Damn!" said Miss Penny. "Bring me what you like, then."

She let go of the waiter's tail, and resumed her narrative.

"Where was I? Yes, I remember. She came into my room, I was telling you, with a bucket of water and a brush, dressed like a charwoman. Naturally I was rather surprised. 'What on earth are you doing, Sister Agatha?' I asked. No answer. She just shook her head, and began to scrub the floor. When she'd finished, she left the room without so much as looking at me again. 'What's happened to Sister Agatha?' I asked my nurse when she next came in. 'Can't say.' 'Won't say,' I said. No answer. It took me nearly a week to find out what really had happened. Nobody dared tell me; it was *strengst verboten*, as they used to say in the good old days. But I wormed it out in the long run. My nurse, the doctor, the charwomen—I got something out of all of them. I always get what I want in the end." Miss Penny laughed like a horse.

"I'm sure you do," I said politely.

"Much obliged," acknowledged Miss Penny. "But to proceed. My information came to me in fragmentary whispers. 'Sister Agatha ran away with a man.' Dear me! 'One of the patients.' You don't say so. 'A criminal out of the jail.' The plot thickens. 'He ran away from her.' It seems to grow thinner again. 'They brought her back here; she's been disgraced. There's been a funeral service for her in the chapel—coffin and all. She had to be present at it—her own funeral. She isn't a nun any more. She has to do charwoman's work now, the roughest in the hospital. She's not allowed to speak to anybody, and nobody's allowed to speak to her. She's regarded as dead.'" Miss Penny paused to signal to the harassed little Italian. "My small Guinness," she called out.

"Coming, coming," and the foreign voice cried "Guinness" down the lift, and from below another voice echoed, "Guinness."

"I filled in the details bit by bit. There was our hero, to begin with; I had to bring him into the picture, which was rather difficult, as I had never seen him. But I got a photograph of him. The police circulated one when he got away; I don't suppose they ever caught him." Miss Penny opened her bag. "Here it is," she said. "I always carry it about with me; it's become a superstition. For years, I remember, I used to carry a little bit of heather tied up with string. Beautiful, isn't it? There's a sort of Renaissance look about it, don't you think? He was half Italian, you know."

Italian. Ah, that explained it. I had been wondering how Bavaria could have produced this thin-faced creature with the big dark eyes, the finely modelled nose and chin, and the fleshy lips so royally and sensually curved.

"He's certainly very superb," I said, handing back the picture.

Miss Penny put it carefully away in her bag. "Isn't he?" she said. "Quite marvellous. But his character and his mind were even better. I see him as one of those innocent, child-like monsters of iniquity who are simply unaware of the existence of right and wrong. And he had genius—the real Italian genius for engineering, for dominating and exploiting nature. A true son of the Roman aqueduct builders he was, and a brother of the electrical engineers. Only Kuno—that was his name—didn't work in water; he worked in women. He knew how to harness the natural energy of passion; he made devotion drive his mills. The commercial exploitation of love power, that was his specialty. I sometimes wonder," Miss Penny added in a different tone, "whether I shall ever be exploited, when I get a little more middle aged and celibate, by one of these young engineers of the passions. It would be humiliating, particularly as I've done so little exploiting from my side."

She frowned and was silent for a moment. No, decidedly, Miss Penny was not beautiful; you could not even honestly say that she had charm or was attractive. That high Scotch colouring, those hare's eyes, the voice, the terrifying laugh, and the size of her, the general formidableness of the woman. No, no, no.

"You said he had been in prison," I said. The silence, with all its implications, was becoming embarrassing.

Miss Penny sighed, looked up, and nodded. "He was fool enough," she said, "to leave the straight and certain road of female exploitation for the dangerous courses of burglary. We all have our occasional accesses of folly. They gave him a heavy sentence, but he succeeded in getting pneumonia, I think it was, a week after entering jail. He was transferred to the hospital. Sister Agatha, with her known talent for saving souls, was given him as his particular attendant. But it was he, I'm afraid, who did the converting."

Miss Penny finished off the last mouthful of the ginger pudding which the waiter had brought in lieu of jam roll.

"I suppose you don't smoke cheroots," I said, as I opened my cigar case.

"Well, as a matter of fact, I do," Miss Penny replied. She looked sharply round the restaurant. "I must just see if there are any of those horrible little gossip paragraphers here today. One doesn't want to figure in the social and personal column tomorrow morning: 'A fact which is not so generally known as it ought to be, is that Miss Penny, the well-known woman journalist, always ends her luncheon with a six-inch Burma cheroot. I saw her yesterday in a restaurant—not a hundred miles from Carmelite Street—smoking like a house on fire.' You know the touch. But the coast seems to be clear, thank goodness."

She took a cheroot from the case, lit it at my proffered match, and went on talking.

"Yes, it was young Kuno who did the converting. Sister Agatha was converted back into the worldly Melpomene Fugger she had been before she became the bride of holiness."

"Melpomene Fugger?"

"That was her name. I had her history from my old doctor. He had seen all Grauburg, living and dying and propagating, for generations. Melpomene Fugger—why, he had brought little Melpel into the world, little Melpchen. Her father was Professor Fugger, the great Professor Fugger, the *berühmter Geolog.* Oh yes, of course, I know the name. So well . . . He was the man who wrote the standard work on Lemuria—you know, the hypothetical continent where the lemurs come from. I showed due respect. Liberal-minded he was, a disciple of Herder, a world burgher, as they beautifully call it over there. Anglophile, too, and always ate porridge for breakfast— up till August 1914. Then, on the radiant morning of the fifth, he renounced it forever, solemnly and with tears in his eyes. The national food of a people who had betrayed culture and civilization—how could he go on eating it? It would stick in his throat. In future he would have a lightly boiled egg. He sounded, I thought, altogether charming. And his daughter, Melpomene—she sounded charming, too; and such thick, yellow pigtails when she was young! Her mother was dead, and a sister of the great professor's ruled the house with an iron rod. Aunt Bertha was her name. Well, Melpomene grew up, very plump and appetizing. When she was seventeen, something very odious and disagreeable happened to her. Even the doctor didn't know exactly what it was; but he wouldn't have been surprised if it had had something to do with the then professor of Latin, an old friend of the family's, who combined, it seems, great erudition with a horrid fondness for very young ladies."

Miss Penny knocked half an inch of cigar ash into her empty glass.

"If I wrote short stories," she went on reflectively "(but it's too much bother), I should make this anecdote into a sort of potted life history, beginning with a scene immediately after this disagreeable event in Melpomene's life. I see the scene so clearly. Poor little Melpel is leaning over the bastions of Grauburg Castle, weeping into the June night and the mulberry trees in the gardens thirty feet below. She is besieged by the memory of what happened this dreadful afternoon. Professor Engelmann, her father's old friend, with the magnificent red Assyrian beard . . . Too awful—too awful! But then, as I was saying, short stories are really too much bother; or perhaps I'm too stupid to write them. I bequeath it to you. You know how to tick these things off."

"You're generous."

"Not at all," said Miss Penny. "My terms are a 10 per cent commission on the American sale. Incidentally there won't be an American sale. Poor Melpchen's history is not for the chaste public of those states. But let me hear what you propose to do with Melpomene now you've got her on the castle bastions."

"That's simple," I said. "I know all about German university towns and castles on hills. I shall make her look into the June night, as you suggest; into the violet night with its points of golden flame. There will be the black silhouette of the castle, with its sharp roofs and hooded turrets, behind her. From the hanging beer gardens in the town below the voices of the students, singing in perfect four-part harmony, will float up through the dark blue spaces. 'Röslein, Röslein, Röslein rot' and 'Das Ringlein sprang in zwei'—the heart-rendingly sweet old songs will make her cry all the more. Her tears will patter like rain among the leaves of the mulberry trees in the garden below. Does that seem to you adequate?"

"Very nice," said Miss Penny. "But how are you going to bring the sex problem and all its horrors into your landscape?"

"Well, let me think." I called to memory those distant foreign summers when I was completing my education. "I know. I shall suddenly bring a swarm of moving candles and Chinese lanterns under the mulberry trees. You imagine the rich lights and shadows, the jewel-bright leafage, the faces and moving limbs of men and women, seen for an instant and gone again. They are students and girls of the town come out to dance, this windless, blue June night, under the mulberry trees. And now they begin, thumping round and round in a ring, to the music of their own singing:

> *Wir können spielen*
> *Vio-vio-vio-lin,*
> *Wir können spielen*
> *Vi-o-lin.*

Now the rhythm changes, quickens:

> *Und wir können tanzen Bumstarara,*
> *Bumstarara, Bumstarara,*
> *Und wir können tanzen Bumstarara,*
> *Bumstarara-rara.*

The dance becomes a rush, an elephantine prancing on the dry lawn under the mulberry trees. And from the bastion Melpomene looks down and perceives, suddenly and apocalyptically, that everything in the world is sex, sex, sex. Men and women, male and female—always the same, and all, in the light of the horror of the afternoon, disgusting. That's how I should do it, Miss Penny."

"And very nice, too. But I wish you could find a place to bring in my conversation with the doctor. I shall never forget the way he cleared his throat and coughed before embarking on the delicate subject. 'You may know, ahem, gracious miss,' he began—'you may know that religious phenomena are often, ahem, closely connected with sexual causes.' I replied that I had heard rumours which might justify me in believing this to be true among Roman Catholics, but that in the Church of England—and I for one was a practitioner of *Anglicanismus*—it was very different. That might be, said the doctor; he had had no opportunity in the course of his long medical career of personally studying *Anglicanismus*. But he could vouch for the fact that among his patients, here in Grauburg, *mysticismus* was very often mixed up with the *Geschlechtsleben*. Melpomene was a case in point. After that hateful afternoon she had become extremely religious; the professor of Latin had diverted her emotions out of their normal channels. She rebelled against the placid *Agnosticismus* of her father, and at night, in secret, when Aunt Bertha's dragon eyes were closed, she would read such forbidden books as *The Life of St. Theresa*, *The Little Flowers of St. Francis*, *The Imitation of Christ*, and the horribly enthralling *Book of Martyrs*. Aunt Bertha confiscated these works whenever she came upon them; she considered them more pernicious than the novels of Marcel Prévost. The character of a good potential housewife might be completely undermined by reading of this kind. It was rather a relief for Melpomene when Aunt Bertha shuffled off, in the summer of 1911, this mortal coil. She was one of those indispensables of whom one makes the discovery, when they are gone, that one can get on quite as well without them. Poor Aunt Bertha!"

"One can imagine Melpomene trying to believe she was sorry, and horribly ashamed to find that she was really, in secret, almost glad." The suggestion seemed to me ingenious, but Miss Penny accepted it as obvious.

"Precisely," she said; "and the emotion would only further confirm and give new force to the tendencies which her aunt's death left her free to indulge as much as she liked. Remorse, contrition—they would lead to the idea of doing penance. And for one who was now wallowing in the martyrology, penance was the mortification of the flesh. She used to kneel for hours, at night, in the cold; she ate too little, and when her teeth ached, which they often did—for she had a set, the doctor told me, which had given trouble from the very first—she would not go and see the dentist, but lay awake at night, savouring to the full her excruciations, and feeling triumphantly that they must, in some strange way, be pleasing to the mysterious powers. She went on like that for two or three years, till she was poisoned through and through. In the end she went down with gastric ulcer. It was three months before she came out of hospital, well for the first time in a long space of years, and with a brand new set of imperishable teeth, all gold and ivory. And in mind, too, she was changed—for the better, I suppose. The nuns who nursed her had made her see that in mortifying herself she had acted supererogatively and through spiritual pride; instead of doing right, she had sinned. The only road to salvation, they told her, lay in discipline, in the orderliness of established religion, in obedience to authority. Secretly, so as not to distress her poor father, whose *Agnosticismus* was extremely dogmatic, for all its unobtrusiveness, Melpomene became a Roman Catholic. She was twenty-two. Only a few months later came the war and Professor Fugger's eternal renunciation of porridge. He did not long survive the making of that patriotic gesture. In the autumn of 1914 he caught a fatal influenza. Melpomene was alone in the world. In the spring of 1915 there was a new and very conscientious Sister of Charity at work among the wounded in the hospital of Grauburg. Here," explained Miss Penny, jabbing the air with her forefinger, "you put a line of asterisks or dots to signify a six years' gulf in the narrative. And you begin again right in the middle of a dialogue between Sister Agatha and the newly convalescent Kuno."

"What's their dialogue to be about?" I asked.

"Oh, that's easy enough," said Miss Penny. "Almost anything would do. What about this, for example? You explain that the fever has just abated; for the first time for days the young man is fully conscious. He feels himself to be well, reborn, as it were, in a new world—a world so bright and novel and jolly that he can't help laughing at the sight of it. He looks about him; the flies on the ceiling strike him as being extremely comic. How do they manage to walk upside down? They have suckers on their feet, says Sister Agatha, and wonders if her natural history is quite sound. Suckers on their feet—ha, ha! What an uproarious notion! Suckers on their feet—that's good that's damned good! You can say charming, pathetic, positively tender things about the irrelevant mirth of convalescents—the more so in this particular case, where the mirth is expressed by a young man who is to be taken back to jail as soon as he can stand firmly on his legs. Ha, ha! Laugh on, unhappy boy! It is the quacking of the Fates, the Parcae, the Norns!"

Miss Penny gave an exaggerated imitation of her own brassy laughter. At the sound of it the few lunchers who still lingered at the other tables looked up, startled.

"You can write pages about destiny and its ironic quacking. It's tremendously impressive, and there's money in every line."

"You may be sure I shall."

"Good! Then I can get on with my story. The days pass and the first hilarity of convalescence fades away. The young man remembers and grows sullen; his strength comes back to him, and with it a sense of despair. His mind broods incessantly on the hateful future. As for the consolations of religion, he won't listen to them. Sister Agatha perseveres—oh, with what anxious solicitude!—in the attempt to make him understand and believe and be comforted. It is all so tremendously important, and in this case, somehow, more important than in any other. And now you see the *Geschlechtsleben* working yeastily and obscurely, and once again the quacking of the Norns is audible. By the way," said Miss Penny, changing her tone and leaning confidentially across the table, "I wish you'd tell me something. Do you really—honestly, I mean—do you seriously believe in literature?"

"Believe in literature?"

"I was thinking," Miss Penny explained, "of ironic fate and the quacking of the Norns and all that."

" 'M yes."

"And then there's this psychology and introspection business; and construction and good narrative and word pictures and *le mot juste* and verbal magic and striking metaphors."

I remembered that I had compared Miss Penny's tinkling earrings to skeletons hanging in chains.

"And then, finally, and to begin with—alpha and omega—there's ourselves: two professionals gloating, with an absolute lack of sympathy, over a seduced nun, and speculating on the best method of turning her misfortunes into cash. It's, all very curious, isn't it?—when one begins to think about it dispassionately."

"Very curious," I agreed. "But, then, so is everything else if you look at it like that."

"No, no," said Miss Penny. "Nothing's so curious as our business. But I shall never get to the end of my story if I get started on first principles."

Miss Penny continued her narrative. I was still thinking of literature. Do you believe in it? Seriously? Ah! Luckily the question was quite meaningless. The story came to me rather vaguely, but it seemed that the young man was getting better; in a few more days, the doctor had said, he would be well—well enough to go back to jail. No, no. The question was meaningless. I would think about it no more. I concentrated my attention again.

"Sister Agatha," I heard Miss Penny saying, "prayed, exhorted, indoctrinated. Whenever she had half a minute to spare from her other duties she would come running into the young man's room. 'I wonder if you fully realize the importance of prayer?' she would ask, and, before he had time to answer, she would give him a breathless account of the uses and virtues of regular and patient supplication. Or else it was: 'May I tell you about St. Theresa?' or 'St. Stephen, the first martyr—you know about him, don't you?' Kuno simply wouldn't listen at first. It seemed so fantastically irrelevant, such an absurd interruption to his thoughts, his serious, despairing thoughts about the future. Prison was real, imminent, and this woman buzzed about him with her ridiculous fairy tales. Then, suddenly, one day he began to listen, he showed signs of contrition and conversion. Sister Agatha announced her triumph to the other nuns, and there was rejoicing over the one lost sheep. Melpomene had never felt so happy in her life, and Kuno, looking at her radiant face, must have wondered how he could have been such a fool as not to see from the first what was now so obvious. The woman had lost her head about him. And he had only four days now—four days in which to tap the tumultuous love power, to canalize it, to set it working for his escape. Why hadn't he started a week ago? He could have made certain of it then. But now? There was no knowing. Four days was a horribly short time."

"How did he do it?" I asked, for Miss Penny had paused.

"That's for you to say," she replied, and shook her earrings at me. "I don't know. Nobody knows, I imagine, except the two parties concerned and perhaps Sister Agatha's confessor. But one can reconstruct the crime, as they say. How would you have done it? You're a man, you ought to be familiar with the processes of amorous engineering."

"You flatter me," I answered. "Do you seriously suppose—" I extended my arms. Miss Penny laughed like a horse. "No. But, seriously, it's a problem. The case is a very special one. The person, a nun; the place, a hospital; the opportunities, few. There could be no favourable circumstance—no moonlight, no distant music; and any form of direct attack would be sure to fail. That audacious confidence which is your amorist's best weapon would be useless here."

"Obviously," said Miss Penny. "But there are surely other methods. There is the approach through pity and the maternal instincts. And there's the approach through higher things, through the soul. Kuno must have worked on those lines, don't you think? One can imagine him letting himself be converted, praying with her, and at the same time appealing for her sympathy and even threatening—with a great air of seriousness—to kill himself rather than go back to jail. You can write that up easily and convincingly enough. But it's the sort of thing that bores me so frightfully to do. That's why I can never bring myself to write fiction. What is the point of it all? And the way you literary men think yourselves so important—particularly if you write tragedies. It's all very queer, very queer indeed."

I made no comment. Miss Penny changed her tone and went on with the narrative.

"Well," she said, "whatever the means employed, the engineering process was perfectly successful. Love was made to find out a way. On the afternoon before Kuno was to go back to prison, two Sisters of Charity walked out of the hospital gates, crossed the square in front of it, glided down the narrow streets towards the river, boarded a tram at the bridge, and did not descend till the car had reached its terminus in the farther suburbs. They began to walk briskly along the high road out into the country. 'Look!' said one of them, when they were clear of the houses; and with the gesture of a conjurer produced from nowhere a red leather purse. 'Where did it come from?' asked the other, opening her eyes. Memories of Elisha and the ravens, of the widow's cruse, of the loaves and fishes, must have floated through the radiant fog in poor Melpomene's mind. 'The old lady I was sitting next to in the tram left her bag open. Nothing could have been simpler.' 'Kuno! You don't mean to say you stole it?' Kuno swore horribly. He had opened the purse. 'Only sixty marks. Who'd have thought that an old camel, all dressed up in silk and furs, would only have sixty marks in her purse? And I must have a thousand at least to get away.' It's easy to reconstruct the rest of the conversation down to the inevitable, 'For God's sake, shut up,' with which Kuno put an end to Melpomene's dismayed moralizing. They trudge on in silence. Kuno thinks desperately. Only sixty marks; he can do nothing with that. If only he had something to sell, a piece of jewellery, some gold or silver—anything, anything. He knows such a good place for selling things. Is he to be caught again for lack of a few marks? Melpomene is also thinking. Evil must often be done that good may follow. After all, had not she herself stolen Sister Mary of the Purification's clothes when she was asleep after night duty? Had not she run away from the convent, broken her vows? And yet how convinced she was that she was doing rightly! The mysterious powers emphatically approved; she felt sure of it. And now there was the red purse. But what was a red purse in comparison with a saved soul—and, after all, what was she doing but saving Kuno's soul?" Miss Penny, who had adopted the voice and gestures of a debater asking rhetorical questions, brought her hand with a slap on to the table. "Lord, what a bore this sort of stuff is!" she exclaimed. "Let's get to the end of this dingy anecdote as quickly as possible. By this time, you must imagine, the shades of night were falling fast—the chill November twilight, and so on; but I leave the natural descriptions to you. Kuno gets into the ditch at the roadside and takes off his robes. One imagines that he would feel himself safer in trousers, more capable of acting with decision in a crisis. They tramp on for miles. Late in the evening they leave the high road and strike up through the fields towards the forest. At the fringe of the wood they find one of those wheeled huts where the shepherds sleep in the lambing season."

"The real Maison du Berger."

"Precisely," said Miss Penny, and she began to recite:

> Si ton coeur gémissant du poids de notre vie
> Si traîne et se débat comme un aigle blessé. . . .

"How does it go on? I used to adore it all so much when I was a girl:

Le seuil est parfumé, l'alcôve est large et sombre,
Et là parmi les fleurs, nous trouverons dans l'ombre,
Pour nos cheveux unis un lit silencieux.

I could go on like this indefinitely."

"Do," I said.

"No, no. No, no. I'm determined to finish this wretched story. Kuno broke the padlock of the door. They entered. What happened in that little hut?" Miss Penny leaned forward at me. Her large hare's eyes glittered, the long earrings swung and faintly tinkled. "Imagine the emotions of a virgin of thirty, and a nun at that, in the terrifying presence of desire. Imagine the easy, familiar brutalities of the young man. Oh, there's pages to be made out of this—the absolutely impenetrable darkness, the smell of straw, the voices, the strangled crying, the movements! And one likes to fancy that the emotions pulsing about in that confined space made palpable vibrations like a deep sound that shakes the air. Why, it's ready-made literature, this scene. In the morning," Miss Penny went on, after a pause, "two woodcutters on their way to work noticed that the door of the hut was ajar. They approached the hut cautiously, their axes raised and ready for a blow if there should be need of it. Peeping in, they saw a woman in a black dress lying face downwards in the straw. Dead? No; she moved, she moaned. 'What's the matter?' A blubbered face, smeared with streaks of tear-clotted gray dust, is lifted towards them. 'What's the matter?' 'He's gone!' What a queer, indistinct utterance. The woodcutters regard one another. What does she say? She's a foreigner, perhaps. 'What's the matter?' they repeat once more. The woman bursts out violently crying. 'Gone, gone! He's gone,' she sobs out in her vague, inarticulate way. 'Oh, gone. That's what she says. Who's gone?' 'He's left me.' 'What?' 'Left me . . .' 'What the devil . . . ? Speak a little more distinctly.' 'I can't,' she wails; 'he's taken my teeth.' 'Your what?' 'My teeth!'—and the shrill voice breaks into a scream, and she falls back sobbing into the straw. The woodcutters look significantly at one another. They nod. One of them applies a thick yellow-nailed forefinger to his forehead."

Miss Penny looked at her watch.

"Good heavens!" she said, "it's nearly half-past three. I must fly. Don't forget about the funeral service," she added, as she put on her coat. "The tapers, the black coffin in the middle of the aisle, the nuns in their white-winged coifs, the gloomy chanting, and the poor cowering creature without any teeth, her face all caved in like an old woman's, wondering whether she wasn't really and in fact dead—wondering whether she wasn't already in hell. Goodbye."

QUESTIONS

1. Why does Miss Penny tell the story of the disgraced nun over lunch?

2. Why does Miss Penny always carry Kuno's photograph in her purse?

3. After displaying Kuno's photograph, why does Miss Penny tell the narrator that she wonders whether she will "ever be exploited"? (263)

4. Why does Miss Penny repeatedly say that stories are too much of a bother and a bore to write, and then proceed to tell the narrator how she would write the nun's story?

5. Why does Miss Penny want to know how the narrator will bring "the sex problem and all its horrors" into the story instead of telling him how? (266)

6. Why does Miss Penny want her conversation with the doctor about the connection between religious phenomena and sex brought into the story?

7. Why does Miss Penny interrupt her story with the question, "Do you really—honestly, I mean—do you seriously believe in literature?" (270) Why does the narrator regard the question as meaningless?

FOR FURTHER REFLECTION

1. Do you agree with the narrator that Miss Penny's question about believing in literature is meaningless?

2. What does Miss Penny mean when she says the last scene is "ready-made literature"? Is she right?

3. Why are religious experience and sex seen by some to be connected? Why is the narrator willing to believe that, while that may be true of Catholicism, it is not true of Anglicanism?

PAM HOUSTON

Pam Houston (1962–) writes about women in the wilderness of the American West while incorporating her own taste for adventure: She has been a river and hunting guide, a ski instructor, and a horse trainer, among other things. "Cowboys Are My Weakness" is the title story from her best-selling first collection, published in 1992. Houston grew up in Bethlehem, Pennsylvania, in a family environment marked by alcoholism and violence, which she draws on both in her second book of short stories, *Waltzing the Cat* (1998), and in her collection of essays *A Little More About Me* (1999). She received her bachelor's degree in 1983 from Denison University and later attended graduate school at the University of Utah. Houston published her first novel, *Sight Hound*, in 2005. She directs the creative writing program at the University of California, Davis.

Cowboys Are My Weakness

I have a picture in my mind of a tiny ranch on the edge of a stand of pine trees with some horses in the yard. There's a woman standing in the doorway in cutoffs and a blue chambray work shirt and she's just kissed her tall, bearded, and soft-spoken husband goodbye. There's laundry hanging outside and the morning sun is filtering through the tree branches like spider webs. It's the morning after a full moon, and behind the house the deer have eaten everything that was left in the garden.

If I were a painter, I'd paint that picture just to see if the girl in the doorway would turn out to be me. I've been out West ten years now, long enough to call it my home, long enough to know I'll be here forever, but I still don't know where that ranch is. And even though I've had plenty of men here, some of them tall and nearly all of them bearded, I still haven't met the man who has just walked out of the painting, who has just started his pickup truck, whose tire marks I can still see in the sandy soil of the drive.

The West isn't a place that gives itself up easily. Newcomers have to sink into it slowly, to descend through its layers, and I'm still descending. Like most easterners, I started out in the transitional zones, the big cities and the ski towns that outsiders have set up for their own comfort, the places so often referred to as "the best of both worlds." But I was bound to work my way back, through the land, into the small towns and beyond them. That's half the reason I wound up on a ranch near Grass Range, Montana; the other half is Homer.

I've always had this thing about cowboys, maybe because I was born in New Jersey. But a real cowboy is hard to find these days, even in the West. I thought I'd found one on several occasions, I even at one time thought Homer was a cowboy, and though I loved him like crazy for a while and in some ways always will, somewhere along the line I had to face the fact that even though Homer looked like a cowboy, he was just a capitalist with a Texas accent who owned a horse.

Homer's a wildlife specialist in charge of a whitetail deer management project on the ranch. He goes there every year to observe the deer from the start of the mating season in late October until its peak in mid-November. It's the time when the deer are most visible, when the bucks get so lusty they lose their normal caution, when the does run around in the middle of the day with their white tails in the air. When Homer talked me into coming with him, he said I'd love the ranch, and I did. It was sixty miles from the nearest paved road. All of the buildings were whitewashed and plain. One of them had been ordered from a 1916 Sears catalog. The ranch hands still rode horses, and when the late-afternoon light swept the grain fields across from headquarters, I would watch them move the cattle in rows that looked like waves. There was a peace about the ranch that was uncanny and might have been complete if not for the eight or nine hungry barn cats that crawled up your legs if you even smelled like food, and the exotic chickens of almost every color that fought all day in their pens.

Homer has gone to the ranch every year for the last six, and he has a long history of stirring up trouble there. The ranch hands watch him sit on the hillside and hate him for the money he makes. He's slept with more than one or two of their wives and girlfriends. There was even some talk that he was the reason the ranch owner got divorced.

When he asked me to come with him I knew it would be me or somebody else and I'd heard good things about Montana so I went. There was a time when I was sure Homer was the man who belonged in my painting and I would have sold my soul to be his wife, or even his only girlfriend. I'd come close, in the spring, to losing my mind because of it, but I had finally learned that Homer would always be separate, even from himself, and by the time we got to Montana I was almost immune to him.

Homer and I live in Fort Collins, Colorado, most of the year, in houses that are exactly one mile apart. He's out of town as often as not, keeping track of fifteen whitetail deer herds all across the West. I go with him when he lets me, which is lately more and more. The herds Homer studies are isolated by geography, given plenty of food in bad winters, and protected from hunters and wolves. Homer is working on reproduction and genetics, trying to create, in the wild, superbucks bigger and tougher than elk. The Montana herd has been his most successful, so he spends the long mating season there. Under his care the bucks have shown incredible increases in antler mass, in body weight, and in fertility.

The other scientists at the university that sponsors Homer respect him, not only for his success with the deer, but for his commitment to observation, for his relentless dedication to his hours in the field. They also think he is eccentric and a bit overzealous.

At first I thought he just liked to be outdoors, but when we got to the ranch his obsession with the deer made him even more like a stranger. He was gone every day from way before sunrise till long after dark. He would dress all in camouflage, even his gloves and socks, and sit on the hillsides above where the deer fed and watch, making notes a few times an hour, changing position every hour or two. If I went with him I wasn't allowed to move except when he did, and I was never allowed to talk. I'd try to save things up for later that I thought of during the day, but by the time we got back to our cabin they seemed unimportant and Homer liked to eat his dinner in front of the TV. By the time we got the dishes done it was way past Homer's bedtime. We were making love less and less, and when we did, it was always from behind.

The ranch owner's name was David, and he wasn't what you'd think a Montana ranch owner would be. He was a poet, and a vegetarian. He listened to Andreas Vollenweider and drank hot beverages with names like Suma and Morning Rain. He wouldn't let the ranch hands use pesticides or chemicals; he wouldn't hire them if they smoked cigarettes. He undergrazed the ranch by about 50 percent, so the organic grain was belly high to a horse almost everywhere.

David had an idea about re-creating on his forty thousand acres the Great Plains that only the Indians and the first settlers had seen. He wasn't making a lot of money ranching, but he was producing the fattest, healthiest, most organic Black Angus cattle in North America. He was sensitive, thoughtful, and kind. He was the kind of man I always knew I should fall in love with, but never did.

Homer and David ate exactly one dinner a week together, which I always volunteered to cook. Homer was always polite and full of incidental conversation and much too quick to laugh. David was quiet and sullen and so restrained that he was hard to recognize.

The irreconcilable differences between Homer and me had been revealing themselves one at a time since late summer. In early November I asked him what he wanted to do on Thanksgiving, and he said he'd like most of all to stay on the ranch and watch the does in heat.

Homer was only contracted to work on the ranch until the Sunday before Thanksgiving. When he asked me to come with him he told me we would leave the ranch in plenty of time to have the holidays at home.

I was the only child in a family that never did a lot of celebrating because my parents couldn't plan ahead. They were sun worshipers, and we spent every Thanksgiving in a plane on the way to Puerto Rico, every Christmas in a car on Highway 95, heading for Florida. What I remember most from those days is Casey Kasem's Christmas shows, the long-distance dedications, "I'll be home for Christmas" from Bobby D. in Spokane to Linda S. in Decatur. We never had hotel reservations and the places we wound up in had no phones and plastic mattress covers and triple locks on the doors. Once we spent Christmas night parked under a fluorescent streetlight, sleeping in the car.

I've spent most of the holidays in my adult life making up for those road trips. I spend lots of money on hand-painted ornaments. I always cook a roast ten pounds bigger than anything we could possibly eat.

Homer thinks my enthusiasm about holidays is childish and self-serving. To prove it to me, last Christmas morning he set the alarm for six-thirty and went back to his house to stain a door. This year I wanted Thanksgiving in my own house. I wanted to cook a turkey we'd be eating for weeks.

I said, "Homer, you've been watching the deer for five weeks now. What else do you think they're gonna do?"

"You don't know anything about it," he said. "Thanksgiving is the premium time. Thanksgiving," he shook one finger in the air, "is the height of the rut."

David and I drank tea together, and every day took walks up into the canyon behind ranch headquarters. He talked about his ex-wife, Carmen, about the red flowers that covered the canyon walls in June, about imaging away nuclear weapons. He told me about the woman Homer was sleeping with on the ranch the year before, when I was back in Colorado counting days till he got home. She was the woman who took care of the chickens, and David said that when Homer left the ranch she wrote a hundred love songs and made David listen while she sang them all.

"She sent them on a tape to Homer," David said, "and when he didn't call or write, she went a little nuts. I finally told her to leave the ranch. I'm not a doctor, and we're a long way from anywhere out here."

From the top of the canyon we could see Homer's form blending with the trees on the ridge above the garden, where the deer ate organic potatoes by the hundreds of pounds.

"I understand if he wasn't interested anymore," David said. "But I can't believe even he could ignore a gesture that huge."

We watched Homer crawl along the ridge from tree to tree. I could barely distinguish his movements from what the wind did to the tall grass. None of the deer below him even turned their heads.

"What is it about him?" David said, and I knew he was looking for an explanation about Carmen, but I'd never even met her and I didn't want to talk about myself.

"Homer's always wearing camouflage," I said. "Even when he's not."

The wind went suddenly still and we could hear, from headquarters, the sounds of cats fighting, a hen's frantic scream, and then, again, the cats.

David put his arm around me. "We're such good people," he said. "Why aren't we happy?"

One day when I got back from my walk with David, Homer was in the cabin in the middle of the day. He had on normal clothes and I could tell he'd shaved and showered. He took me into the bedroom and climbed on top of me frontwards, the way he did when we first met and I didn't even know what he did for a living.

Afterwards he said, "We didn't need a condom, did we?" I counted the days forward and backward and forward again. Homer always kept track of birth control and groceries and gas mileage and all the other things I couldn't keep my mind on. Still, it appeared to be exactly ten days before my next period.

"Yes," I said. "I think we did."

Homer has never done an uncalculated thing in his life, and for a moment I let myself entertain the possibility that his mistake meant that somewhere inside he wanted to have a baby with me, that he really wanted a family and love and security and the things I thought everybody wanted before I met Homer. On the other hand, I knew that one of the ways I had gotten in trouble with Homer, and with other men before him, was by inventing thoughts for them that they'd never had.

"Well," he said. "In that case we better get back to Colorado before they change the abortion laws."

Sometimes the most significant moments of your life reveal themselves to you even as they are happening, and I knew in that moment that I would never love Homer the same way again. It wasn't so much that not six months before, when I had asked Homer what we'd do if I got pregnant, he said we'd get married and have a family. It wasn't even that I was sure I wanted a baby. It wasn't even that I thought there was going to be a baby to want.

It all went back to the girl in the log cabin, and how the soft-spoken man would react if she thought she was going to have a baby. It would be winter now, and snowing outside the windows warm with yellow light. He might dance with the sheepdog on the living room floor, he might sing the theme song from *Father Knows Best*, he might go out and do a swan dive into the snow.

I've been to a lot of school and read a lot of thick books, but at my very core there's a made-for-TV-movie mentality I don't think I'll ever shake. And although there's a lot of doubt in my mind about whether or not an ending as simple and happy as I want is possible anymore in the world, it was clear to me that afternoon that it wasn't possible with Homer.

Five o'clock the next morning was the first time I saw the real cowboy. He was sitting in the cookhouse eating cereal and I couldn't make myself sleep next to Homer so I'd been up all night wandering around.

He was tall and thin and bearded. His hat was white and ratty and you could tell by looking at his stampede strap that it had been made around a campfire after lots of Jack Daniel's. I'd had my fingers in my hair for twelve hours and my face was breaking out from too much stress and too little sleep and I felt like such a grease ball that I didn't say hello. I poured myself some orange juice, drank it, rinsed the glass, and put it in the dish drainer. I took one more look at the cowboy, and walked back out the door, and went to find Homer in the field.

Homer's truck was parked by a culvert on the South Fork road, which meant he was walking the brush line below the cliffs that used to be the Blackfeet buffalo jumps. It was a boneyard down there, the place where hundreds of buffalo, chased by the Indians, had jumped five hundred feet to their death, and the soil was extremely fertile. The grass was thicker and sweeter there than anywhere on the ranch, and Homer said the deer sucked calcium out of the buffalo bones. I saw Homer crouched at the edge of a meadow I couldn't get to without being seen, so I went back and fell asleep in the bed of his truck.

It was hunting season, and later that morning Homer and I found a deer by the side of the road that had been poached but not taken. The poacher must have seen head-lights or heard a truck engine and gotten scared.

I lifted the back end of the animal into the truck while Homer picked up the antlers. It was a young buck, two and a half at the oldest, but it would have been a monster in a few years, and I knew Homer was taking the loss pretty hard.

We took it down to the performance center, where they weigh the organic calves. Homer attached a meat hook to its antlers and hauled it into the air above the pickup.

"Try and keep it from swinging," he said. And I did my best, considering I wasn't quite tall enough to get a good hold, and its blood was bubbling out of the bullet hole and dripping down on me.

That's when the tall cowboy, the one from that morning, walked out of the holding pen behind me, took a long slow look at me trying to steady the back end of the dead deer, and settled himself against the fence across the driveway. I stepped back from the deer and pushed the hair out of my eyes. He raised one finger to call me over. I walked slow and didn't look back at Homer.

"Nice buck," he said. "Did you shoot it?"

"It's a baby," I said. "I don't shoot animals. A poacher got it last night."

"Who was the poacher?" he said, and tipped his hat just past my shoulder toward Homer.

"You're wrong," I said. "You can say a lot of things about him, but he wouldn't poach a deer."

"My name's Montrose T. Coty," he said. "Everyone calls me Monte."

I shook his hand. "Everyone calls you Homer's girl-friend," he said, "but I bet that's not your name."

"You're right," I said, "it's not."

I turned to look at Homer. He was taking measurements off the hanging deer: antler length, body length, width at its girth.

"Tonight's the Stock Growers' Ball in Grass Range," Monte said. "I thought you might want to go with me."

Homer was looking into the deer's hardened eyeballs. He had its mouth open, and was pulling on its tongue.

"I have to cook dinner for Homer and David," I said. "I'm sorry. It sounds like fun."

In the car on the way back to the cabin, Homer said, "What was that all about?"

I said, "Nothing," and then I said, "Monte asked me to the Stock Growers' Ball."

"The Stock Growers' Ball?" he said. "Sounds like a great time. What do stock growers do at a ball?" he said. "Do they dance?"

I almost laughed with him until I remembered how much I loved to dance. I'd been with Homer chasing white-tail so long that I'd forgotten that dancing, like holidays, was something I loved. And I started to wonder just then what else being with Homer had made me forget. Hadn't I, at one time, spent whole days listening to music? Wasn't there a time when I wanted, more than anything, to buy a sailboat? And didn't I love to be able to go outdoors and walk anywhere I wanted, and to make, if I wanted, all kinds of noise?

I wanted to blame Homer, but I realized then it was more my fault than his. Because even though I'd never let the woman in the chambray work shirt out of my mind, I'd let her, in the last few years, become someone different, and she wasn't living, anymore, in my painting. The painting she was living in, I saw, belonged to somebody else.

"So what did you tell him?" Homer said.

"I told him I'd see if you'd cook dinner," I said.

I tried to talk to Homer before I left. First I told him that it wasn't a real date, that I didn't even know Monte, and really I was only going because I didn't know if I'd ever have another chance to go to a Stock Growers' Ball. When he didn't answer at all I worked up to saying that maybe it was a good idea for me to start seeing other people. That maybe we'd had two different ideas all along and we needed to find two other people who would better meet our needs. I told him that if he had any opinions I wished he'd express them to me, and he thought for a few minutes and then he said, "Well, I guess we have Jimmy Carter to thank for all the trouble in Panama."

I spent the rest of the day getting ready for the Stock Growers' Ball. All I'd brought with me was some of Homer's camouflage and blue jeans, so I wound up borrowing a skirt that David's ex-wife had left behind, some of the chicken woman's dress shoes that looked ridiculous and made my feet huge, and a vest that David's grandfather had been shot at in by the Plains Indians.

Monte had to go into town early to pick up ranch supplies, so I rode in with his friends Buck and Dawn, who spent the whole drive telling me what a great guy Monte was, how he quit the rodeo circuit to make a decent living for himself and his wife, how she'd left without saying goodbye not six months before.

They told me that he'd made two thousand dollars in one afternoon doing a Wrangler commercial. That he'd been in a laundromat on his day off and the director had seen him through the window, had gone in and said, "Hey, cowboy, you got an hour? You want to make two thousand bucks?"

"Ole Monte," Buck said. "He's the real thing."

After an hour and a half of washboard road we pulled into the dance hall just on our edge of town. I had debated about wearing the cowboy hat I'd bought especially for my trip to Montana, and was thankful I'd decided against it. It was clear, once inside, that only the men wore hats, and only dress hats at that. The women wore high heels and stockings and in almost every case hair curled away from their faces in great airy rolls.

We found Monte at a table in the corner, and the first thing he did was give me a corsage, a pink one, mostly roses that couldn't have clashed more with my rust-colored blouse. Dawn pinned it on me, and I blushed, I suppose, over my first corsage in ten years, and a little old woman in spike heels leaned over and said, "Somebody loves you!" just loud enough for Monte and Buck and Dawn to hear.

During dinner they showed a movie about a cattle drive. After dinner a young enthusiastic couple danced and sang for over an hour about cattle and ranch life and the Big Sky, a phrase that since I'd been in Montana had seemed perpetually on the tip of everybody's tongue.

After dinner the dancing started, and Monte asked me if I knew how to do the Montana two-step. He was more than a foot taller than me, and his hat added another several inches to that. When we stood on the dance floor my eyes came right to the place where his silk scarf disappeared into the shirt buttons on his chest. His big hands were strangely light on me and my feet went the right direction even though my mind couldn't remember the two-step's simple form.

"That's it," he said into the part in my hair. "Don't think. Just let yourself move with me."

And we were moving together, in turns that got tighter and tighter each time we circled the dance floor. The songs got faster and so did our motion until there wasn't time for anything but the picking up and putting down of feet, for the swirling colors of Carmen's ugly skirt, for breath and sweat and rhythm.

I was farther west than I'd ever imagined, and in the strange, nearly flawless synchronization on the dance floor I knew I could be a Montana ranch woman, and I knew I could make Monte my man. It had taken me ten years, and an incredible sequence of accidents, but that night I thought I'd finally gotten where I'd set out to go.

The band played till two and we danced till three to the jukebox. Then there was nothing left to do but get in the car and begin the two-hour drive home.

First we talked about our horses. It was the logical choice, the only thing we really had in common, but it only lasted twenty minutes.

I tried to get his opinion on music and sailing, but just like a cowboy, he was too polite for me to tell anything for sure.

Then we talked about the hole in my vest that the Indians shot, which I was counting on, and half the reason I wore it.

The rest of the time we just looked at the stars.

I had spent a good portion of the night worrying about what I was going to say when Monte asked me to go to bed with him. When he pulled up between our two cabins he looked at me sideways and said, "I'd love to give you a great big kiss, but I've got a mouthful of chew."

I could hear Homer snoring before I got past the kitchen.

Partly because I didn't like the way Monte and Homer eyed each other, but mostly because I couldn't bear to spend Thanksgiving watching does in heat, I loaded my gear in my truck and got ready to go back to Colorado.

On the morning I left, Homer told me that he had decided that I was the woman he wanted to spend the rest of his life with after all, and that he planned to go to town and buy a ring just as soon as the rut ended.

He was sweet on my last morning on the ranch, generous and attentive in a way I'd never seen. He packed me a sack lunch of chicken salad he mixed himself, and he went out to my car and dusted off the inch of snow that had fallen in our first brush with winter, overnight. He told me to call when I got to Fort Collins, he even said to call collect, but I suppose one of life's big tricks is to give us precisely the thing we want, two weeks after we've stopped wanting it, and I couldn't take Homer seriously, even when I tried.

When I went to say goodbye to David he hugged me hard, said I was welcome back on the ranch anytime. He said he enjoyed my company and appreciated my insight. Then he said he liked my perfume and I wondered where my taste in men had come from; I wondered whoever taught me to be so stupid about men.

I knew Monte was out riding the range, so I left a note on his car thanking him again for the dancing and saying I'd be back one day and we could dance again. I put my hat on, that Monte had never gotten to see, and rolled out of headquarters. It was the middle of the day, but I saw seven bucks in the first five miles, a couple of them giants, and when I slowed down they just stood and stared at the truck. It was the height of the rut and Homer said that's how they'd be, love crazed and fearless as bears.

About a mile before the edge of ranch property, I saw something that looked like a lone antelope running across the skyline, but antelope are almost never alone, so I stopped the car to watch. As the figure came closer I saw it was a horse, a big chestnut, and it was carrying a rider at a full gallop, and it was coming right for the car.

I knew it could have been anyone of fifty cowboys employed on the ranch, and yet I've learned to expect more from life than that, and so in my heart I knew it was Monte. I got out of the car and waited, pleased that he'd see my hat most of all, wondering what he'd say when I said I was leaving.

He didn't get off his horse, which was sweating and shaking so hard I thought it might die while we talked.

"You on your way?" he said.

I smiled and nodded. His chaps were sweat soaked, his leather gloves worn white.

"Will you write me a letter?" he said.

"Sure," I said.

"Think you'll be back this way?" he asked.

"If I come back," I said, "will you take me dancing?"

"Damn right," he said, and a smile that seemed like the smile I'd been waiting for my whole life spread wide across his face.

"Then it'll be sooner than later," I said.

He winked and touched the horse's flank with his spurs and it hopped a little on the takeoff and then there was just dirt flying while the high grass swallowed the horse's legs. I leaned against the door of my pickup truck watching my new cowboy riding off toward where the sun was already low in the sky and the grass shimmering like nothing I'd ever seen in the mountains. And for a minute I thought we were living inside my painting, but he was riding away too fast to tell. And I wondered then why I had always imagined my cowboy's truck as it was leaving. I wondered why I hadn't turned the truck around and painted my cowboy coming home.

There's a story—that isn't true—that I tell about myself when I first meet someone, about riding a mechanical bull in a bar. In the story, I stay on through the first eight levels of difficulty, getting thrown on level nine only after dislocating my thumb and winning my boyfriend, who was betting on me, a big pile of money. It was something I said in a bar one night, and I liked the way it sounded so much I kept telling it. I've been telling it for so many years now, and in such scrupulous detail, that it has become a memory and it's hard for me to remember that it isn't true. I can smell the smoke and beer-soaked carpets, I can hear the cheers of all the men. I can see the bar lights blur and spin, and I can feel the cold iron buck between my thighs, the painted saddle slam against my tailbone, the surprise and pain when my thumb extends too far and I let go. It's a good story, a story that holds my listeners' attention, and although I consider myself almost pathologically honest, I have somehow allowed myself this one small lie.

And watching Monte ride off through the long grains, I thought about the way we invent ourselves through our stories, and in a similar way, how the stories we tell put walls around our lives. And I think that may be true about cowboys. That there really isn't much truth in my saying cowboys are my weakness; maybe, after all this time, it's just something I've learned how to say.

I felt the hoofbeats in the ground long after Monte's white shirt and ratty hat melded with the sun. When I couldn't even pretend to feel them anymore, I got in the car and headed for the hard road.

I listened to country music the whole way to Cody, Wyoming. The men in the songs were all either brutal or inexpressive and always sorry later. The women were victims, every one. I started to think about coming back to the ranch to visit Monte, about another night dancing, about another night wanting the impossible love of a country song, and I thought:

This is not my happy ending.

This is not my story.

QUESTIONS

1. What does the narrator mean when she says, "The West isn't a place that gives itself up easily"? (279)

2. Why does the narrator describe in detail Homer's job as a wildlife specialist?

3. Why does the narrator describe the manner in which she and Homer make love?

4. Why does the narrator call Monte "the real cowboy"? (286)

5. The narrator says, "You can say a lot of things about [Homer], but he wouldn't poach a deer." (287) What does this reveal about Homer and the narrator's view of him?

6. When the narrator says goodbye to David, why does she question where her taste in men comes from?

7. Why does the narrator conclude with the words, "This is not my story"? (294)

FOR FURTHER REFLECTION

1. To what extent do the characters in this story engage in fantasy? Is it necessary for people to engage in some degree of fantasy in their daily lives?

2. Is the narrator right to consider herself "almost pathologically honest"?

3. The narrator says that all of the women depicted in country songs "were victims, every one." Is the narrator a victim, and if so, in what way?

ACKNOWLEDGMENTS

All possible care has been taken to trace ownership and secure permission for each selection in this anthology. The Great Books Foundation wishes to thank the following authors, publishers, and representatives for permission to reprint copyrighted material:

La Grande Bretèche, from FRENCH SHORT STORIES by Honoré de Balzac, edited and translated by K. Rebillon Lambley. Copyright © 1933 by Oxford University Press. Reprinted by permission of Oxford University Press.

The Old Gentleman, from TRANSPARENCY by Frances Hwang. Copyright © 2007 by Frances Hwang. Reprinted by permission of Little, Brown and Company.

Krakatau, from BATTLING AGAINST CASTRO by Jim Shepard. Copyright © 1996 by Jim Shepard. Reprinted by permission of SLL/Sterling Lord Literistic.

Weekend, by Fay Weldon. Copyright © 1978 by Fay Weldon. Reprinted by permission of Capel and Land, Ltd.

Torch Song, from THE STORIES OF JOHN CHEEVER by John Cheever. Copyright © 1978 by John Cheever. Reprinted by permission of Alfred A. Knopf, a division of Random House, Inc.

My First Two Women, from SIX FEET OF THE COUNTRY: FIFTEEN SHORT STORIES BY NADINE GORDIMER, by Nadine Gordimer. Copyright © 1956 by Nadine Gordimer, renewed 1984 by Nadine Gordimer. Reprinted by permission of Russell and Volkening as agents for the author.

Babylon Revisited, from THE STORIES OF F. SCOTT FITZGERALD by F. Scott Fitzgerald, edited by Matthew J. Bruccoli. Copyright © 1931 by The Curtis Publishing Company, renewed 1959 by Frances Scott Fitzgerald Lanahan. Reprinted by permission of Scribner, a division of Simon and Schuster, Inc.

The Custard Heart from DOROTHY PARKER: COMPLETE STORIES by Dorothy Parker. Copyright © 1924–29, 1931–34, 1937–39, 1941, 1943, 1955, 1958, 1995 by The National Association for the Advancement of Colored People. Reprinted by permission of Penguin, a division of Penguin Group (USA) Inc.

A Woman of Fifty, from W. SOMERSET MAUGHAM: COLLECTED SHORT STORIES, VOLUME 4 by Somerset Maugham. Published by Penguin by arrangement with Doubleday, 1978. Copyright © W. Somerset Maugham. Reprinted by permission of the Trustees of the Estate of W. S. Maugham.

My Wife Is a White Russian, from THE COLONEL'S DAUGHTER by Rose Tremain. Copyright © 1983, 1984 by Rose Tremain, published by Vintage. Reprinted by permission of Sheil Land Associates Ltd.

Theft in a Pastry Shop, from DIFFICULT LOVES by Italo Calvino. Copyright © 1949 by Giulio Einaudi editore, Torino, renewed 1958. English translation copyright © 1984 by Houghton Mifflin Harcourt Publishing Company. Reprinted by permission of Houghton Mifflin Harcourt Publishing Company.

Fat People, by Alison Lurie. Copyright © 1989 by Alison Lurie. First published in *Vogue*. Reprinted by permission of Melanie Jackson Agency, LLC.

Nuns at Luncheon, from MORTAL COILS by Aldous Huxley. Copyright © 1922, 1949 by Aldous Leonard Huxley. Reprinted by permission of Georges Borchardt, Inc., for the Aldous and Laura Huxley Literary Trust, Mark Trevenen Huxley, and Teresa Huxley.

Cowboys Are My Weakness, from COWBOYS ARE MY WEAKNESS by Pam Houston. Copyright © 1992 by Pam Houston. Reprinted by permission of W. W. Norton and Company.